The Beast in the Pines
by S. W. Lynch

serotoninpress.com

First Edition, June 2025
Copyright © 2025 by S.W. Lynch

Published in the U.S.A. by Serotonin Press, Philadelphia, PA.
All characters and situations in this novel are a work of fiction and any resemblance or similarity to real people or events are merely a coincidence and not intentional.

Edited by Dr. Ian Duncan.
Cover art and design by Nora Kelly.

…The darkness drops again; but now I know
That twenty centuries of stony sleep
Were vexed to nightmare by a rocking cradle,
And what rough beast, its hour come round at last,
Slouches towards Bethlehem to be born?

From "the Second Coming," by W.B. Yeats

Chapter One

Atlantic Ocean gusts converged with the Gulf Stream over the town of Woodville, New Jersey, forming spirals in the sky. Cody grew anxious as tendrils extended out of violet-colored clouds. His jaw tightened, and without the ability to control himself, he began grinding his teeth. He looked up at the ominous horizon, his tousled dirty blond hair blowing as he moved against the headwind, and quickened his pace, wanting to get home as soon as possible, but knowing he had to make a stop on his way back from work. The thick flannel shirt and baggy blue jeans he wore were not enough protection to prevent him from shivering as he arrived at his mother's job to drop off his paycheck to her. A black and white cop car sat in the middle of the parking lot. He grasped the crinkled piece of paper in his hand as he walked by the police cruiser.

Cody's mom worked as a waitress at the Woodville Diner, which was established in 1953, right in the center of town, on the corner of River and Main Streets. By the late

80's, downtown businesses were boarded up. Most of the population left in the ensuing years. Buildings decayed. This diner was no exception, although it was still open, and a garish, floppy banner hung over the doorway, celebrating the restaurant's fifty-year anniversary.

He opened the door to an eerie silence. People sat uneasily at their tables. His mother stooped over cleaning up broken dishes and spilled coffee off of the floor. Her name tag hung lopsidedly from her periwinkle uniform blouse. The name tag read, "ANNA." Customers looked unnerved, as if a whirlwind had just swept through the restaurant. A police officer stared at Cody's mother from behind her while pretending to write an incident report on a miniature yellow legal pad.

Cody's muscles tensed as he recognized the cop. The man was the father of his childhood bully, Michael Ciliberti. He hoped not to be noticed by him. Someone dropped a fork and Cody's mom jumped at the clanging. She had cut herself on jagged ceramic and clung onto a darkened dish towel that was wrapped around her hand. The officer wore glasses and had a crew cut. He held her for a moment, whispering in her ear as he sneered down at her, and she turned around to pull away. She saw her son and approached him.

"Mom, what happened?"

"Oh, nothing sweetheart, just a little incident."

"Doesn't look like nothing."

She turned her head to gaze back with her mousey face at the officer who was still staring at her with a smirk. Her brunette ponytail swung, silver streaks of hair glinting in the fluorescent light. The disheveled, grease covered line cook was demonstrative in trying to explain what had happened, asking the cop what was to be done, with the policeman not paying attention to him. People passed by them quietly, leaving their food on the tables without paying their bills.

His mother frowned, "well, all right, there was this awful man who came in here, sitting over at the bar there, drinking a cup of coffee and reading a book, when out of nowhere he just goes crazy."

"How so?"

"I came over to ask if he'd like some more coffee and he starts saying these terrible things."

"Like what?"

"Don't you mind what the man said."

"Come on mom, tell me what he said."

"Cody, no, it's improper."

He waved the paycheck in the air playfully, "go ahead and tell me ma', or I ain't paying rent this month."

"Don't threaten me young man. How many times do I have to tell you that you're not paying rent? You're just helping out while your father is injured."

"I'm jokin' mom. But seriously, tell me."

"Well, fine," she lowered her voice, "he started harassing other customers, speaking like he was an old-timey preacher or something, using thees and thous, talkin' all fire and brimstone, talkin' 'bout the end of the world and how he has this refuge in the Pine Barrens. He kept calling out to the children, telling them to come sit on his lap; it was… it was lewd. Once I asked him if he wanted a refill and motioned for him to quiet down, well, he just threw a fit even more, started tossing things around, saying he was gonna' come back with a shotgun and herd the sheep, all sorts of wild stuff."

"Sounds like this guy's fun at parties."

"It's not a joke Cody, the man was frightening. Downright terrifying he was. A big brute, about six and a half feet tall at least, completely bald, and with these awful, dark eyes."

"Aw, I'm sorry mom, really, that must have been scary."

"He… he called me the whore of Babylon."

"Jesus Christ," Cody had to hold in his laughter at the absurdity even though he was angry that someone insulted his mother.

"Don't take the Lord's name in vain."

"Sorry mom, Geez Louise, I meant."

The cop shook his head. Johnny the cook yelled something unclear, then pointed at the remaining customers and told them to get out of the restaurant. Cody's mom turned back to look at him.

"And now Johnny has gone and made everyone leave without paying their bills. I'm going to lose all my tips," she sighed.

"Damn, that sucks."

"Cody, don't curse."

"Okay. Well, what happened to the guy?"

"He stormed out right before the police showed up."

"Figures."

"I've got to get back to work and finish cleaning up. Hopefully we reopen after this and some folks come in for dinner. I can't afford to have the shift be a wash. I'll be home later."

"Okay, I'm gonna' run outta' here before the rain starts."

"All right. Oh, and Cody! There's some TV dinners in the freezer that you can microwave for you and your father."

After he gave her the check, Cody's mom walked into the back of the diner and the pudgy cook followed her, pulling at her apron to stop her and yell at her in the kitchen. The cop approached Cody with his hand unnecessarily resting on his gun holster. He put the notepad in his pocket with his other hand, stopped in front of Cody, and crossed his arms.

"Well if it isn't little Cody! What are you up to bucko?"

Cody stiffened, "nothing, just dropping something off for my mom."

"You better get home before the storm starts. Need a ride? Wouldn't be the first time you sat in the back of a cop car!" Officer Ciliberti nudged Cody's arm as he chuckled. Cody snickered insincerely.

"No, I'm fine."

"You still working at that old pharmacy?"

"Yeah."

"Why don't you get a real job or go off to college?"

"Why doesn't your son?"

The officer smirked, "Michael is getting ready for the police academy. He wanted to enlist in the Marines, but I think he's better off waiting a few years and going to college so he can do ROTC."

"Really? Wow, there's a college that accepted him?" Cody tried to sound sincere halfway through blurting out the elongated wow like he was on a rollercoaster, but the sarcasm still showed.

"He hasn't applied yet. Like I said, he's going to the police academy. What are you going to do with your life?"

"I was thinking of enlisting in the Army myself."

Officer Ciliberti bellowed with laughter, "you won't make it kid, you're too short! Just stick to your little clerk job."

"Yeah, sure."

The police officer slapped him on the shoulder then left, so that it was just Cody standing alone in the front of the restaurant with half-eaten food spread out on the tables. "You're too short!" Cody mimicked the cop while scrunching up his face. There was a side plate of untouched bacon, still warm, grease slicked, and crispy, on a table nearby that he eyed, then snatched a strip and munched on, the saltiness crackling his tongue. He kept mocking Officer Ciliberti to the empty room as he chewed on more bacon. "Stick to your little clerk job!" He rolled his eyes as he sidled up to the counter where his mother had been cleaning, noticing the black, hard-covered book that the strange, scary man had left behind. It looked like a bible. The cover was blank except for the title, which read The Jersey Devil.

He picked the book up and held it in the air, "The Jersey Devil… huh," he said, tucked it under his arm, and walked out of the diner without giving it a second thought.

An early October frost fingered the branches and gutters throughout Woodville, New Jersey. Trees shook in anticipation of the coming storm. The Indian summer of October had vanished. There was no autumn in between summer and winter that year. Piles of fallen leaves had already begun appearing throughout Woodville, although instead of bright shades of orange, yellow, and red, the leaves were a dull gray and brown.

On his walk home he thought about how he felt stuck in a dead-end job while living with his parents. The wind picked up as it started to drizzle. Many of his classmates had left home after graduating the previous spring from George Washington High School. Not him. Most everyone who lived in town had left in the past decade, ever since the soda syrup factory scaled down, one of the few sources of jobs left in the area. He was surrounded by looming husks that used to house beacons of industry.

He passed an abandoned glass factory, and then an empty soda and juice company that had gone out of business years before. Concrete corpses haunted the skyline, blocking gentle breezes from the Delaware Bay. Wind cut through ruined structures with a bitter sharpness. After walking a few blocks he passed one story, whitewashed ranchers, and a few crumbling Victorian houses.

Cody had a habit of gazing at the cracks that marked the sidewalks and streets. He was tired of having to look up at everything and everyone. Even at nineteen years old, he still did not stand much higher than five feet tall. He had tried everything from stretching to testosterone pills he had stolen from the pharmacy he worked at in the hopes that they would give him a late growth spurt. He blamed it on his dad, who was also short in stature, and resented him greatly for it.

As he passed the rusting water tower that bore the town's name in huge block letters, he picked up a rock and threw it at one of the metal beams, the clanging lost in the sound of the wind. He scanned the towering structure as he quickened his pace. The rain grew heavier. Cody was almost home.

He opened the front door to find his father sitting on the couch reading a book. His dad said hello and kept on reading as Cody dropped the book that he had found on the coffee table and went to the kitchen to open the freezer and microwave the frozen dinners. There was a draft coming in through the poorly insulated window, and Cody sat down shivering while his hands were hot from the microwaved food that he placed on TV dinner trays in front of him and his father. He sunk into the olive and sage colored plaid couch next to the quiet man. Random parts of the microwaved food were still cold, but Cody did not feel like getting back up to finish heating his dinner, so he chewed through the coldness and savored whatever was lukewarm. Cody's father looked up from his book at the window as the sound of the rain grew louder.

"It's getting bad out there, huh?"

"Yup," Cody replied.

"What's that?"

"Nothing. Just an old book I found."

Cody picked the book up and tucked it between his thigh and the arm of the couch. His dad raised his eyebrows and went back to reading.

Cody's father was a shell of his old self. He was in his late forties, and the past few years had put a heavy strain on him. His wrinkled face was covered in red splotches from his stress related eczema. His forehead reached back to his neck from balding — the salt and pepper hairs left on the sides of his head stood like little coiled wires. His gut protruded from under his stained off-white undershirt; he had only gained so much weight recently, since he lost his job from the injury at his workplace. A temp drove a forklift into him and broke his leg. The union lawyer stopped returning his father's calls. There was trouble in the soda factory the whole year leading up to the incident. Rumors spread that the bosses were inclined to move the factory down south where there would be no unions. The union itself was no longer of any help, and acted like it was stepping on eggshells to avoid a factory closure.

His dad leaned to scratch under his leg cast, then put down his book, The History of the Decline and Fall of the Roman Empire Volume 3, and turned on the TV, so that they could listen together to the local newscaster's familiar voice as he sounded off the enemy body count. His father could remember watching TV reports on the Vietnam War as a child with his own father, who was a Korean War veteran. He had related this to Cody when the Iraq War began that past spring. According to the flashy news segment title, the terrorists were losing the war on terror. An electric guitar blared distorted power chords over the television during the report on the war. His father once told him the war was really about oil. Cody still wanted to enlist and fight.

The segment briefly summarized the latest news regarding the Iraq War and up next were local interest stories. There had been sightings of the Jersey Devil throughout the state in recent months and the mustachioed anchor chuckled as he mocked the mythical creature.

A reporter wearing a red dress interviewed a man in camouflage with missing teeth, "can you describe to us what you saw?"

"I seen a flying kangaroo in my own backyard pick up a chicken and tear it apart. The beast was all black and made an awful sound."

She turned back to the camera. "That's right, we've had multiple reports in the Pine Barrens of the Jersey Devil stealing small pets and farm animals with its claws and carrying them off in broad daylight. Back to you Jim."

The news anchors laughed. "Thanks Jessica, now, we all know that the Jersey Devil is a myth, but this next story is seriously scary. Peter?"

"Absolutely Jim, there's been an update to the missing children crisis in South Jersey, several children have vanished recently in the Delaware Valley, with no leads as to their whereabouts. Another child has gone missing, his name is Bobby Marshall. He's 8 years old with blue eyes and brown hair. He was last seen wearing a green jacket and jeans at a grocery store in Cherry Hill when he went missing. If you have seen Bobby, or any of the other children we've featured on the missing children report, please call the hotline below."

"It's so sad Peter."

"I know Jim, a terrible ongoing tragedy."

Cody wondered whether the Jersey Devil sightings had a connection to the missing children. He glanced at the book that he had found at his mother's job and was tucked next to him on the couch. When the report was over, the camera moved to another man in a suit who was standing to the side while holding a football.

"Today in sports: can the Eagles turn it around this weekend against the Giants after losing a heartbreaker to the Cowboys last Sunday? We'll be back with more after this commercial break."

Cody's cell phone vibrated in his pocket. He took it out and saw that his sister Emma had texted him, "Hi lil bro how r u? Worried bout u hmu soon plz…" but he was out of text messages for the month and could not afford to buy any more. Besides, three out of the nine buttons on his phone were sticky, so that he was not able to use certain letters with the T9 predictive text. He had to remind himself to call her later because he did not feel like talking to her in front of his dad. Cody and his sister spoke less and less since she moved to California for college a few years before. He sighed as he looked toward the window facing west where the sun had set behind storm clouds.

Dust froze over the home's old windowpanes. A layer of sediment became attached to the glass that was carried aloft by the wind blowing from the Pine Barrens, a forest to the north of town formed amid inland sand dunes where the Jersey Devil was said to lurk. Rain never washed the dirt away. The wind rattled the glass from three different directions. Cody was not able to see clearly out of the windows save blurry lights from passing cars on the desolate highway that abutted their front yard.

He stewed in his thoughts on the edge of the couch where the metal springs poked out so close to his nearby yet distant father, eating the remaining bits of the TV dinner while watching the evening news. His thoughts turned to the war again, imagining shooting other humans.

"Maybe the President will call an emergency draft tomorrow and I'll be sent away by the end of the month. What do you think about that, dad?" Cody held on to his grin longer than normal while leering at his old man.

"Son, that's not the way these things work. Anyway, you're too short," his tone of voice was stern.

"I'm tall enough, and how does starting a war work anyway?" Cody asked, sincerely, his voice energetic and youthfully raspy from all of the cigarettes and weed he would smoke. His father vaguely pointed at a bookshelf nearby, indicating that his son should find out for himself. David, Cody's dad, was a history buff who had several bookcases in the living room. His son held no interest in history unless it was regarding war.

After a long silence, Cody's father suddenly spoke up, "Congress is supposed to declare war, technically, although they haven't since World War Two. The Selective Service will hold a draft lottery. It'll take months. It's not going to happen though. Hasn't happened since Vietnam. Besides, President Bush announced that it was mission accomplished anyway. He flew onto that aircraft carrier and everything. This war will end soon enough. There's just a few insurgents causing trouble because Iran's stoking the flames." Cody rubbed his chin. He wanted to ask more questions but could not think of anything good to say.

"You really think that?" Cody asked but received no answer.

His father changed the channel from local news to a twenty-four-hour cable news network. The corner of the screen said it was 7:13 PM ET, October 15th. The images on their small television at first were just pieces of paper, memorandums from the Chairman of the Joint Chiefs of Staff, then it showed a press conference with a bald general speaking at a podium. Cody thought it was odd for a general in a press conference to look as nervous as he did while he talked about the search for Weapons of Mass Destruction. What he kept calling WMD's had to have existed, somewhere, and there was proof, and these pieces of paper with words that could not actually be seen by the viewer were the evidence of that proof. The general wore drab green gilded with many medals pinned to his chest. He looked shiny himself. His skin seemed ready to evaporate. He cleared his throat. He said the military was leaving all of the options on the table. That they not only were searching for the WMD's, but also still on the hunt for Saddam Hussein.

"I wish they showed more of like actual gun battles instead of the same old press conferences and the aftermath of bombings. I bet it's more exciting."

"War is not exciting, son, it's horrifying. You don't know what war is really like, no matter how much you watch the news or the movies and talk about it. I'll have no more of this war talk. That's the end of it," and that was the end of it.

Cody's dad dropped the TV remote plastic against the wooden TV dinner tray, the batteries falling out of the back of it and rolling off onto the carpet, then groaned and shifted on the couch next to him after giving this lecture, like the effort drained him, trying again to move his broken leg because of an itch under his cast. He leaned over to scratch it and knocked over his glass of water, spilling it onto the rug by the remote that was cloven in two. Cody thought about picking up the glass and bringing it to the kitchen, but instead just leaned over to put the remote back together, placing the batteries back in carefully, positive to positive and negative to negative, then immediately plopped down on the couch. He was eager not to miss any of the cable news half hour special report about the war.

The next segment portrayed a soldier of Cody's age being interviewed by a journalist. The soldier had a thick brown mustache and baby blue eyes. His helmet hung loose on his head. The middle-aged reporter asked questions of the soldier who was dressed in worn out tan fatigues. Cody's dad chewed on mushy microwaved TV dinner corn while staring into the television set with a furrowed brow.

"How old are you son?" The reporter's voice had a bit of a twang.

"Well, I done turned nineteen a few weeks back, but didn't think nothin' of it, completely forgot to be honest, because shit, I mean stuff went crazy," the kid soldier had a thick southern drawl. He was chewing gum loudly with his mouth open.

"And by 'went crazy' you mean the insurgency?"

"Yeah, I suppose so. Been a hell of a week here in Baghdad. We got shipped here to the city from the countryside last week to put the Shia militia down on the streets. This week it's some Sunnis all riled up. Lots of what they callin' protests, but I ain't see no protests. It's a bunch of mobs. Can't really tell the difference between the two to be honest, the Sunni and the Shiite I mean."

"Just this week there've been a number of attacks on checkpoints in the Green Zone, which is a heavily fortified area in Baghdad where the international coalition forces are based. How much fighting have you seen?"

"Not much. The ones on the streets scream and holler at us. Can't do nothin' 'bout that. Well, for now," he grinned, "we're mainly worried about IED's, really."

"Now, can you tell the viewers at home what an IED is?"

"Yeah, sure. It stands for improvised explosive device. They're basically homemade bombs filled with a bunch of sharp stuff to cause maximum damage." Cody's dad suddenly turned towards him to look him in the eye.

"Go to your room, son."

"What, why?"

"Because you've been watching too much about war. Go to your room to pray."

"What the hell are you talking about? You're the one who put on the news, and you've never asked me to go to my room and pray before. That's fucking dumb."

"Don't speak to me like that in my house!"

Cody ignored the command to go to his room and kept glancing at his dad to see how he would react. His dad took the remote and changed the channel to an action show about a CIA operative.

Cody's mom opened the front door, shutting it quickly behind her to prevent rain from getting inside, wiped her feet on the door mat, hung up her soaked coat and umbrella, and trudged into the house, her body bent the way a double shift in a restaurant can bend a person. The father and son kept watching television. She waved a calloused hand, worn down from so many years at work. On the TV, American flag draped coffins were being loaded onto a massive C-130 transport.

"Hi boys, what are you watching? Oh, Lord, please turn this violent stuff off. Now look at this! What is this mess? The whole rug is wet!"

"It's not real, Anna. Just a TV show. I told the boy to go to his room and say his prayers. It's past his bedtime."

"Are you senile? It's not even that late. I'm fucking nineteen years old."

"Watch your mouth."

Another silence. Both father and son remained mesmerized on the couch by the television. A commercial advertised antidepressants — there was a sad cartoon blob that hopped across the screen with a rain cloud following it. Everything was black and white, a blue bird appeared carrying a big pill held in between its beak, which it tossed at the blob that smiled and sang about being happy as everything turned to color. Cody cringed at the jingle and tuned it out. Five more commercials played, then the show resumed. He did not realize until then that his father had changed the channel once again from the action show starring a physically fit, bald man who worked for the CIA hunting down terrorists, to another action show with a physically fit man with hair who worked for the FBI hunting down criminals. His mom went to the kitchen for a towel then returned to dry the carpet off.

"It was just water, right? Would you turn this garbage off?"

"That's not very patriotic of you, mom."

"Don't you dare talk to me like that Cody. I've had a long day at work and come home to two fully capable men sitting on the couch watching other men make the ultimate sacrifice on TV night after night."

"That's not fair, mom, dad can't do anything right now, and I would love to make the ultimate sacrifice for our country, but you won't let me."

"I'm sure your father can speak for himself on that, well then David, did you call the doctor today and see when you can get this forsaken cast taken off? It's been over three months," Cody's mom ignored the part about Cody wanting to make the ultimate sacrifice for his country.

"Darling, I told you the appointment is in two weeks."

"You told me when? And did you call the lawyer today?"

"No, I called yesterday. I'm waiting for a reply."

"There's no waiting. You must keep calling. Call until something is done."

His mom turned the TV off and disappeared into the kitchen while his dad picked up the newspaper and began to read. Cody walked up the stairs with his newfound book to his bedroom in despair, knowing he could not go another night like this, that if he did, he would drown in a sea of mundane moments. He would waste away like his father.

His tiny bedroom held only enough space for him to sleep and work out. The twin sized bed took up half of the room, while next to it stood a small bookshelf filled with comics and pulp action books. He loved the mutant superhero comics, which he first started reading when he got into high school and could relate to his favorite character because his rage fueled his strength. The stories of these mutants who were outcasts in society, but who were tasked with fighting to save a world that despised them, resonated with him. He wanted to have superpowers, which was his main motivation in exercising so often in that claustrophobic room, that, and because he was short.

He used the only open part of the tan carpet, which was a foot longer than the length of his body, for sit ups and push ups. There were imprints where his hands and back made impressions from his nightly routine. He dropped to the floor and did twenty push ups. Got up, paced back and forth, and did twenty more. His dirty blond hair was wet with sweat. Each set became harder and harder, but he kept going until he hit one hundred total. At the end of it all, his arms felt like they were on fire, then slowly became limp. He had been doing one hundred push ups a night for a few months now, and tried pushing it to one hundred forty. That night was the first that he made it to one hundred forty push ups without fail.

He still was not satisfied after reaching one hundred and forty push ups and stared at his bookcase, panting. While scanning the comics he had read dozens of times, he looked at the book that had been left behind at his mom's job earlier, and he had only just put away. It felt familiar to him, like he had read it before. He tried to think of where he could have seen it and skimmed it in the past, maybe one of the giveaway used book racks down at the Woodville Public Library, where Cody often liked to escape from his parents and use the computer to browse the internet because his family did not have one at home. No, it was not from the library. It was from a dream he had recently. He shook his head. "No, that's not possible," he said. He was confused and unnerved with the odd feeling that he had experienced a fake memory of having seen the book on a library shelf before. Or in a dream about a library?

This was no ordinary book, rather some kind of handcrafted artifact that was conceived by a peculiar mind. The book was the only hardcover on his shelves, a black cover with gold letters for the title, The Jersey Devil. He picked it up off of the shelf and smelled the musty paper while opening up to the first page. The book was moldering. There was no author's name on the inside title page, and no publication information. Cody raised his eyebrows. He began to read.

The Pine Barrens existed long before humans arrived in what is now known as New Jersey. It is a vast forest that has survived since the end of the last ice age, around twelve thousand years ago. Glaciers retreated from the coast and left behind a varied landscape in their wake. Native Americans settled the swamps and woods of the east coast several thousand years later.

He continued skimming through the pages, having to wipe away his sweat that blurred some of the words, although they remained legible.

The woods are haunted. Not by the ghosts of the Lenni Lenape, but by something demonic. The natives who used to live here would try to avoid the Pine Barrens until they were driven into them by colonists in the middle of the 18th century. In fact, the first Indian Reservation in the United States was in the Pine Barrens. Highwaymen and various outcasts also lived in the forest in order to avoid detection by colonial authorities…

"Weird," Cody said in a drawn-out whisper to himself while yawning. He skipped ahead.

These woods sprouted through sand dunes and acidic soil. A vast underground aquifer that holds pure water lies beneath, one of the largest reserves of freshwater in America. Marl pits and swamps layer between surface and subterranean to hug the realms of these two worlds. A lost world of the past and that of the present which is haunted by all that preceded it. This allows the perfect environment for preservation, whether it be of bones, ruined architecture, or something more intangible. The colonists who lived in the pines were folks who harvested charcoal and bog iron before it was more efficient to do so elsewhere. This eighteenth-century industry can still be seen in the ruins that dot the country. Countless sandy paths lead to old, abandoned furnaces and forges where the birth of the American nation sprouted in the hardened hands of rural laborers.

He skipped ahead again looking for a part that got to the point about the legendary creature. Cody had heard stories about the Jersey Devil growing up and wanted to learn more about it. He found some pages at the end of the prologue that mentioned the myth.

As far as the Jersey Devil is concerned, he was born to a woman named Jane Leeds on July 9th in the year 1755 and would go on to wreak terror among the scarce populace that inhabited the one million acres of water, sand, and trees known as the Pine Barrens. There was an evil spirit known to the Lenape as M'sing long before the Jersey Devil was born to a white woman. Some think that these demons are one and the same, but this is not true. The white settlers mistook the Jersey Devil for a Lenape demon. What they did not know was that the Jersey Devil was of their own invention...

Exhausted, he put the book down and jumped into bed and under the covers while still dripping with sweat. The Jersey Devil could wait. While trying to fall asleep he imagined what it would be like to skip his boring job at the pharmacy and enlist in the Army the next morning. Basic training would be fun, he thought. His fitness would put him at the top of his class. The deployment in a desert on the other side of the world fighting terrorists would be dangerous, but it would be something thrilling to him. He wanted real adventure. All of the body counts and American flag draped coffins that he saw on TV were the price to pay for adventure. He thought that anything would be better than his monotonous life, and going to war was the easiest way out. He fell asleep imagining driving a Humvee through the Iraqi desert.

Cody dreamt that he was on a beach by the Atlantic Ocean. He knew he was in Wildwood, New Jersey because the beach was so wide that it felt like a desert. The sand was piercing hot against the soles of his feet. He looked down to see that there was a campfire in front of him. A white stag appeared next to him, nuzzling his coat while he stoked the flames, and he periodically fed the animal shrubs that were in his pockets. The creature raised its head and sniffed Cody's hair. He looked up at the beast, and once he made eye contact, it screamed and ran into the oncoming waves. It swam along the shoreline, shaking its pointy ears with silver liquid spraying off of its shining hair. Cody looked down again to see that the fire had gone out. When he turned his head back up, a tidal wave approached, reaching hundreds of feet into the air, until the ocean met the sky, while the beautiful creature flailed, drowning in the foreground. He wanted to run to help the stag and escape but could not move. The animal tossed and turned in the waves, then disappeared, and the colossal wall of water overtook Cody until he could not see anymore.

Chapter Two

The next morning Cody woke up and made coffee, then cooked some scrambled eggs and scrapple with toast for himself and his dad. His mom had already gone off to work. After breakfast, he immediately left home bundled up for his shift at the pharmacy a mile down the street. The Delaware Bay blew cold wind into his face until he could not feel his skin anymore. He passed boarded up businesses down the well-trodden, sidewalk-cracked path of an abandoned town, to the periphery of what was once downtown; he imagined a formerly thriving Main Street while arriving at his clerk job that he had held since he was fifteen years old. The four years he had spent working there seemed like a lifetime to him.

The pharmacy's shelves were half empty. Back in the 1960's the place was a successful business, or so he had heard. The bar would be full of families drinking soda and milkshakes, his boss, Mr. Johnston claimed. Three workers used to be needed per shift to keep up with the demand. Now

Mr. Johnston rarely came in to fill prescriptions. Cody would be lucky if the number of customers reached double digits during one of his shifts, so he spent most of his time reading the news to keep up with the war and the world, but most of the newspapers were tabloids full of celebrity gossip, or Bigfoot, UFO, and El Chupacabra sightings. There were no headlines about the Jersey Devil. Nothing to be said about the chilling increase of missing children in the tri-state area. Cody sighed and stared at the door, wondering if he would have any customers that day.

Just when Cody thought no one would enter the shop, Vinny cheerily poked his head inside, then sat at the soda bar on the creaky stool, with his lanky, scoliotic frame hunched over, and his shoulder length, dark brown hair swinging back and forth. His puffy blue coat was unzipped and hung off his body. He ordered a black and white milkshake. Cody worked the dusty machine and slid the glass down to him like they did in the movies. Vinny mixed the shake together, gripping the straw with his washed and well-maintained hands unscuffed by shoeshine and other tools of his family's dying trade. Vinny was the sole other high school friend of his still living in town and worked in the family shoe repair shop down the street. He would often walk through the door and joke with characteristic sarcasm about how the pharmacy was busy.

Cody wondered aloud why Vinny was so fussy and teased him about it. In contrast to his spotless hands, Vinny's face was covered in red splotches that were sometimes noticeable and other times subtle. Cody had never asked what the source of Vinny's skin condition was and assumed that his friend had let his beard grow out ever since hitting puberty in order to try to hide it. He could not grow a full beard himself, and was quietly jealous, wanting one of his own.

"Man, by the look of your hands you didn't do any work today."

"You know it. Another busy day at the office, mi amigo?"

"You know it, Vin. Just can't keep up."

"Yeah, we know it, don't we? Striving for the American dream, bro. You just keep working hard and one day you'll be able to open up a successful shop of your own just like this, here in paradise," he spread open his long arms at Cody's imaginary domain.

"You know it," Cody repeated their shared refrain, although he was too distracted by his Iraq War and Jersey Devil daydreaming to truly humor his friend's antics. He sighed.

"What's wrong buddy?"

"Man, I don't know. I'm just fed up with this town. I need to get out."

"Oh, here we go again."

"See, that's why I don't want to get into it with you."

"Get into what?" Vinny asked, while scratching his face. He picked a scab off and stopped the bleeding with some nearby napkins.

"You're gonna' think I'm stupid," Cody looked away from Vinny with an uncharacteristic shyness.

"Well, that's nothing new buddy."

"I found this book about the Jersey Devil."

"Okay?" Vinny raised an eyebrow, perplexed.

"It's weird."

"So what?"

"It might be bullshit, but wouldn't it be cool to like, go look for it?"

"Look for the Jersey Devil?"

"Yeah."

"So you believe the Jersey Devil exists?" Vinny laughed as he asked.

"I don't know, I'm not sure if it actually exists. I just think it would be fun to go look for it in the Pine Barrens."

"You're an idiot. Why would you go look for something that doesn't exist?"

"Because it would be fun? And who knows? Maybe it does exist," Cody shook his head, shrugged his shoulders, and laughed.

Sometimes they would end up bickering like brothers, but Cody never remembered having a bad argument with Vinny. The only time Vinny ever showed more loyalty to someone else was when Vinny's younger sister Bianca broke up with Cody after prom night. Bianca and Cody dated the last two years of high school. Cody and Vinny avoided each other for three weeks after the breakup, and although Cody expected Vinny not to show up to the pharmacy and hangout with him anymore, like clockwork one day, his friend took a break from his job and sat at the soda bar, mixing his milkshake until it transformed into the same old purple sludge. They acted like nothing happened and had an unspoken agreement not to talk about it. Cody remembered that episode from a few months before and appreciated their friendship.

"Forget that Jersey Devil shit, you know what's for real? My cousin Jose hooked me up with some fire bud. This shit is for real." Vinny pulled out the bag of weed and showed it to Cody. He smiled as the scent of marijuana drifted towards him. "Is it time for your break yet or are you too busy to smoke?"

"I ain't ever too busy to smoke, Vin, you know it. I guess I can close up shop for a half hour and go on a little trip down to the pier," he flipped the shop sign from open to closed, heading with his best friend a few blocks down to the waterfront where they would hold their ritualistic communion.

The path to the bay was covered in empty beer and soda cans and other sorts of trash. They both shivered but tried not to show it. It became colder as they got closer to the water. Bare and dying trees reached out to them as they climbed over broken logs and branches. Dead leaves crackled as they pushed through shrubs to get to the waterfront, their thin canvas shoes crunching the ground mixed with litter.

"I hope we're the only people down by the river today."

"What? Are you scared of a little scrap, Vin?"

"No, I'm just tired of that shit, man, we're not kids anymore."

There would often be fights between teenagers if one offending group crossed an imaginary line on the gravel shore of the Maurice River that led to the Delaware Bay. This part of the inlet belonged to Vinny's cousins. Cody and Vinny were generally safe when it came to them, and yet if they ran into a large group of Vineland teenagers who came from the northwest, they would get jumped if they could not run away fast enough.

The high school was farther west along the shoreline, and they could see a group heading their way from that direction. They both noticed and walked down to the end of the old fishing pier where they felt out of sight and safer.

"I've got something to tell you, buddy." Cody looked Vinny in the eyes.

"Yeah, what's up?"

"I decided last night for sure that if I'm not going to enlist in the Army, I'm at least going to leave this damn town.

I'm so sick and tired of the same boring ass shit, day after day. I need to get out. Won't you sign up for the Army with me? Come on, man, it will be an adventure."

"Are you fucking crazy, dude? That's some bullshit war over there in Iraq. You don't want to get mixed up in any of that."

"Yeah, but they got the best dope though, don't they? At least that's what they say. Think about it, you and me in the desert all stoned and shooting at terrorists."

"What the hell are you talking about man? It ain't Vietnam. They don't let you smoke weed in Iraq. If you want good weed, go to California. Didn't you want to be an actor or make movies or whatever growing up anyway? And who gives a shit about terrorists, that's not what this war is about. Bush just wants oil, man."

"Never mind about politics, look, just think about it. It's better pay than what we're making now."

"Nah, man. They wouldn't accept me."

"Why not?"

"First of all, I've tripped on acid before, which I think disqualifies you. Plus, I got diagnosed with some shit. It's called Lupus. I don't really know what's gonna' happen in the long run because of it and I don't wanna' talk about it right now."

"What does that mean man, sounds like you're just coming up with excuses, is that the disease where you become a werewolf?"

Cody pushed him and laughed, but Vinny stayed serious. His high cheekbones, cleft chin, sharp nose, and soft brown eyes gave him the appearance of a human crossed with a sparrow, which was accented by the thick beard he had for his age. He was often looking everywhere around his environment fleetingly like a bird, too, like he thought he was prey and needed to be on constant alert.

"That's hilarious, dude."

"Come on, Vin, I'm just messing with yah."

"I don't know man, besides all of that, it just seems like a bad idea, going to war. Who cares how much they pay?"

"Alright, well if not that, then let's move out of this place, and head up to New York, or Philly and live in a squat house or somethin'. I fucking hate it here."

"Listen, Cody, I don't know about that. I can't leave my family. We can do that camping trip in the Pine Barrens we were talking about though, move it up a few weeks. We could maybe even leave this weekend after I'm done work if you want."

"I don't know, man. If we're not leaving for good then I gotta' show up to my job. My parents are charging me rent now and I have to work the rest of the week. I'll let you know."

Once they got to the end of the pier, they let their feet hang over the edge dangling just a few inches away from chunks of trash sloshing around gray muck. The strength of the wind by the water was hard to withstand. They buried their chins into their chests and stared up at the uniform charcoal colored skyline of the bay beyond the river with bunched up umber blocks of brick and cement surrounding them, sitting among the ruins of interspersed industrial buildings from a bygone era. The two gazed far off at the bay's expanse while the wind jostled their jackets. They looked at a trio of nameless islands, all covered in abandoned shipping containers.

Cody's father had told him that the island in the middle was once the refuge of the famous pirate Blackbeard, and home to a treasure trove of buried rum and gold. His father had said that there was still buried treasure there, but that it was blocked by one of the shipping containers. They could see it from the shore, and it looked just as if it was one of the many mundane features in the landscape. Cody wondered if the myth of the buried treasure was real, or just a child's fairy tale his dad had told him.

"Isn't it crazy that Indians used to live here? And pirates used to sail up through here? Like there's supposed to be buried treasure out here, somewhere, on that middle island right there, actually. Blackbeard's rum and gold and shit. It's like some crazy fantasy stuff if you think about it."

"Nah, dumb ass, it ain't crazy. It's history. There's not really any buried treasure though. People found all that shit…" Vinny looked at the island, "and they're called Native Americans, not Indians. White people called them the wrong name."

"Whatever, man, who the fuck came up with the name America anyway? Wasn't it white people?"

"Well yeah, we learned that in history class. I think America was named after some Italian explorer dude, Ah-mehr-ee-go?" Vinny sounded out while quizzically staring at the bay.

"So Native Americans is a fucked-up thing to call them too, no? Because that's not what the natives called it — America," Cody spit into the water, "and now look at this place. It's filled with Italians," Vinny laughed. Cody smiled and gestured at the land behind them, "New Jersey is boring as hell. Even the Italians here are boring — they're not mobsters like they show on TV. All the exciting shit is somewhere else."

"Exciting like California or Iraq?" Vinny snickered.
"Yeah!"

"Listen, Cody. No people want to just up and leave, to move away from their land and family. People want peace and happiness unless they're broke or forced out of their home by some other people. You, on the other hand, are crazy and crave adventure. You got a Napoleon Complex, dude."

"What? Man, I just want to experience something better than this, for real. I'm tired of Jersey. I would hate to waste my life away working a shitty ass, meaningless job like some machine."

"You mean like our families?"

"Yeah. Exactly. Like my parents who can't even stand up for themselves. This boring ass town is driving me crazy. That's why I want to go to Iraq and fight, bro."

"All right dude, chill. Let me light this shit."

Vinny shook his head and stayed silent while pulling a small bible out of the inside pocket of his bulky coat and opening it to a hollow compartment that held a few grams of marijuana, and one previously rolled joint. The joint was coming apart, so he put it up to his lips and licked it over to seal the paper that came from a page in the Old Testament. Half of the pages had been previously ripped out for smoking weed. As Vinny's tongue rolled over the joint, the blurry letters on the paper darkened.

"You got a light dude?"

"Nah Vin, I thought you had one."

"I got matches but it's windy as shit."

"Just try."

"Okay."

He struck several matches before he was able to get one to light. Cody helped him by covering the joint from the wind with his cupped hands. The skinny spiral on the end erupted in a small ember. Vinny held the joint between his slender index and middle fingers and let the flame roll back and forth lightly over the paper so that it would harden, then moved it to the end again, and puffed and coughed as the tip of the paper burned until it hit the fat middle filled with weed.

Vinny passed the joint to Cody, who inhaled and let the warmth spread throughout his body. Even though he felt warm inside, his fingers were freezing, so he passed the joint back to Vinny and shoved his hands back into his coat pockets. Cody had lost his gloves the prior winter, and never got around to replacing them. Vinny wore blue wool gloves that were cut off at his knuckles. His fingers were clean and neat, while Cody's were chewed up, the cuticles ripped apart from biting. He placed his right hand next to Vinny's and compared them without him noticing. He took another drag. The word Babylon burned until it did not exist anymore.

The pier was bitterly cold. Cody realized how close they were to each other, their bodies naturally gravitating toward one another for warmth, then heard one of the few Spanish words he knew yelled at them from behind.

"Putos!"

They were familiar faces. It was Vinny's cousins, a group of teenagers led by a heavyset man with curly hair in his early twenties.

"Jose, mi primo, como estas?" Vinny asked.

"Since when do you know how to speak Spanish, pendejo?"

Vinny embraced his cousin Jose. Cody stood up and shuffled his feet around awkwardly. They could never be too careful, even if they were usually safe on this pier. Jose turned from Vinny to Cody.

"Hey white boy, you see where we came from just now?"

It was then Cody noticed the cuts and bruises on some of the kids' faces. They wore their injuries proudly, smiling and punching each other in camaraderie.

"Yeah, we saw you coming up to Leeds Hill from Pine Point Park. What were you doing over there?"

"We just beat the shit out of some morenos on the other side of the railroad tracks."

"What, why Jose? Now they're gonna' come over here and mess with us."

"Nah, they won't be showing their faces around here no more. Are you scared of a little fight, white boy?"

"No man, I just can't be fighting kids no more, I'm nineteen now."

They laughed, like that was a valid excuse. The police rarely cared about teenagers or young adults fighting each other on the outskirts of town. If the cops knew drugs were involved, that was a different story. Everyone would get arrested.

"You're lucky mi primo is here. I'm not gonna' beat up his novio. It would be too easy anyway," Jose declared.

Cody did not know what the word novio meant; he thought it was some kind of insult, but he was not going to take offense to it regardless. The other boys all laughed at this, as they did whenever Jose said something he thought was clever and would look back at his lackies for approval.

"Yeah yeah yeah. Here have some of this."

Cody gave him some of the fast-dwindling joint. He remembered his father once telling him on a car ride by the bay about how farther up the Delaware River the Lenape had offered William Penn a ceremonial pipe to share a smoke with them as a token of peace. He wanted to bring up the fact to sound intelligent and then thought better of it, not daring to make any comparisons because Vinny had just lectured him about Native Americans.

"Hold up white boy, I see some of your kind coming this way. Did you call up tu gente to jump us?"

"It's all good, Jose. You know Cody is cool," Vinny said.

Another group of teenagers approached from the east. They wore their hoodies up so that none of them were recognizable from far away, and the tallest one pointed at the pier.

"We'll see about that, I don't trust this white boy, no matter how long he's been friends with you."

"Come on man, you know I'm with you guys, all right? If these kids try and start anything with us, I'll be right there taking them on, believe me," Cody's words were not enough for Jose and his friends to be reassured. He knew it took action to earn their respect.

"Didn't you just say you don't fight anymore?" Jose asked. Cody did not respond, lighting a cigarette with the end of the almost finished joint he held.

The cousins turned and stood with their hands in their pockets, looking like they were reaching for something inside their coats, but were unarmed. Cody's heart started racing. Every few beats the organ in his chest felt like it was hitting speed bumps. He took a long drag of his cigarette. For all of his talk about bravery and enlisting to fight in Iraq, each time he encountered a simple fist fight on the street he would struggle with his initial instincts to flee. He had seen teenage violence go too far too many times, but he never saw anyone get killed. The other group got close and then stopped midway through the pier. One of them called out.

"Hey, any of you got some weed to sell?"

Jose turned and looked at the rest of the crew behind him with a raised eyebrow.

"That's one sorry ass way to ask for some bud," Cody said.

Jose and the other guys laughed at his offhand comment, even though Cody did not mean it as a joke. There were ten of them opposite their eight, including Cody and Vinny.

"We can take them," Cody whispered to Jose.

"Well if it isn't Woodville's most annoying midget," the tall one said.

As the group inched toward them, Cody realized their leader was none other than Michael Ciliberti, whose dad was the police officer that had showed up to his mom's job the day before. He wore a gold chain that hung outside of his coat. Cody and Mike had gotten into some fights as kids and Cody won on more than one occasion, something Mike could never let go, especially because of the height difference between the two. Mike's friends laughed and made obscene gestures at Cody while Jose tilted his head and poked him.

"You gonna' let him talk to you like that?" Jose sincerely asked.

"Yeah, bitch, what're yah gonna' do? My old man told me he saw you at the diner talkin' 'bout how you're trying to join the Army! That's the funniest shit I ever heard. You know they don't take pussies."

"Shut the fuck up you fat ass greasy dago."

Vinny's cousins laughed at Cody's insult. Jose's younger brother Paco clutched his belly while stumbling around in the slushy mud-covered pier for dramatic effect. Cody was enraged, but he felt momentarily both surprised and pleased at how well the cousins responded to his trash talk.

"You shut the fuck up you little bitch. I'm not here for your shit. I'll punt your short ass like a fucking football," Cody's knuckles turned white; he turned to look at Vinny, who was red-eyed and listless. Mike changed the tone of his voice as he approached Jose.

"Look, we're being for real. Are any of you holding? We need to buy an ounce," Mike said, while trying to maintain a sense of confidence and composure in his voice, although Cody could tell that he was getting nervous.

"Yeah, I can hook you up, but not if you're gonna' be a narc. I know your dad's a cop," Jose crossed his thick arms.

"My dad doesn't need to know shit. You know I'm good for it. I've bought from you before, dude."

Jose pulled a plastic sandwich bag out of his coat. "Okay, I got an ounce for you here, white boy. Three hundred. Got the money?" It looked like it was somewhere between half an ounce and an ounce. Mike spit in the mud.

"This ain't enough for three hundred fucking bucks. What the fuck kind of spic shit you tryna' pull on me?" He smacked at the bag and knocked it to the ground. Cody's eyes grew wide.

Mike stepped even closer to Jose. The wind picked up. Jose smiled. They stared at each other nose to nose for a moment. Somebody on Mike's side threw the first rock, and it escalated from there, with both sides throwing rocks and sticks at each other, and Jose grabbing Mike by the coat collar and punching him in the face while Mike swung wildly at his foe with no solid connection. Jose briefly let go of Mike after a chunk of concrete hit his eye and blood burst out of the socket. His burly torso slouched over, but he refused to go down and re-attached himself to Mike, then held onto him as a human shield so that Mike's friends would stop chucking debris at him. Jose's tactic worked, and he held Mike in a full nelson while trying to catch his breath. Specks of crimson spattered about as his captive resisted. Jose stomped on a weak plank in the pier and caught his foot in the hole. He pulled his leg out while maintaining his hold on Mike, but lost his shoe in the process, their bodies swaying back and forth in the struggle.

Cody ducked to the side of a few rocks, taking a step back and almost falling into the river. He realized they were trapped on the edge of the pier and running out of things to throw back at the rival group twenty yards away, with Mike and Jose grappling in between. Not knowing what else to do, he flicked away his cigarette and charged past Jose and Mike while they wrestled, latched together like lovers, and ran straight at the smallest kid in the bunch and let a haymaker fly. He sounded like a miniature berserker yelling and running through the fray and the cousins took it as inspiration. Paco, Pedro, Esteban, Carlos, and Diego charged in right behind him, and the two groups clashed like it was a medieval skirmish, slipping and sliding in the muck, their cumbersome coats and winter gear made for awkward movements in the mud.

Vinny stayed back from the fight. This was that rare moment that fear was fully unleashed into rage and Cody no longer felt like a coward. After he took out the smallest kid with one punch, the other guys looked shocked for a moment, so he swung his fist at the other closest combatant. He kept hooking upwards reaching for chins. Before he knew it, three of the guys he hit were on top of him and he was getting pummeled until Juan and Diego pulled them off. The fighting reached a stalemate once Jose turned the full nelson into a sleeper hold and knocked out Mike. Jose stumbled toward the fray with half of his face covered in blood and a mean look in his eyes. Mike's friends backed up and then sprinted away.

Mike came around and rolled on the ground writhing in pain. Cody helped the first kid up who he punched and felt remorse. Here was this red-headed teenager with a face full of freckles who was also short and wanted to prove something to his friends. He appeared as if he was in his early teens and gave Cody a look of surprise when he offered him his hand. The kid ran off stumbling after the others.

Cody shook his head then heard a commotion behind him. Mike was up and wailing on Vinny. When Cody ran toward them Mike shoved Vinny into the river. Cody punched Mike in the back of the head and immediately felt a sharp pain. His thumb had accidentally slipped under his index knuckle while he was forming a fist. Vinny flailed his arms in the dark water trying to climb back onto the pier, his winter coat hindering his movement. Mike saw an opening and ran back down the pier. Cody yelled for help, then got on his stomach, hanging over the pier while holding onto Vinny's hand. Vinny's glove slipped off so Cody extended his reach as far as he could and grabbed him from underneath his shoulders. He could not hold onto him for long. Cody's right hand was throbbing and felt like it was on fire even in the cold water. Vinny's mouth was agape like a fish. He coughed up water as he bobbed up and down.

"Hold on buddy," Cody kept trying to pull on the increasingly heavier body.

Just when he thought he did not have the strength to hold on to him any longer, Jose arrived and leaned in to drag Vinny onto the pier. Cody hung over the edge still, exhausted. Someone pulled him back from the brink and he turned and saw Diego's bruised and bloodied face and laughed out of desperation in a delirious adrenaline rush.

"Man, this kid is crazy," Diego said.

Cody walked up to the other guys, who were speaking in Spanish while crowded around Vinny. Jose was demanding something from Paco.

"Nah man I ain't doing that shit!"

Cody inserted himself into the scene, shivering and soaked. Vinny looked like he was playing dead. Jose turned to him.

"Hey man do that shit with your mouth on his to make him better! Hurry!"

"You mean like that mouth-to-mouth shit?"

Cody placed his hand on Vinny's gristly cheek, and he smiled. Vinny was only holding his breath and acting like he was knocked out, then burst into laughter. The cousins looked at each other in confusion. He was soaked, but he was okay. Cody knew Vinny was playing a joke on them, that he was not drowning because his head was above the water most of the time; he was just stuck in there and needed help out. They all began to realize this and laughed in relief.

"Vinny, what the fuck is wrong with you?" Jose asked.

"I was just having a bit of fun."

"Okay, sure pendejo, let's get back to my house and warm up. It's fucking cold out here. Cody, you come with us," Jose said. He had his right hand held over his brow to stop the bleeding with a grin on his face and placed his other hand on Cody's shoulder.

"I wish I could go and chill with you guys man, but I just realized I got to head back to the pharmacy. If Mr. Johnston showed up and I wasn't there, I'd get fired. He's caught me sneaking out on my shift before."

"Okay man. You're welcome around any time."

They walked away from the pier. Juan and Diego helped up dripping wet Vinny and carried him between each other marching back to Leeds Hill like they were soldiers who had survived an ambush by the Tigris River in a bizarro-world Baghdad. Jose handed Cody the sandwich bag full of weed that he had picked up from the ground. Cody was surprised the bag did not get smashed during the fight, and a minimal amount of mud covered the plastic. There were far fewer seeds and stems in it than he expected or was used to, and the buds looked good, plump, and bright.

"Woah, for real? This looks like some real heady bud."

"It's all for you. You helped us big time in that fight, and that gets my respect. Thank you for being a good friend to my cousin."

"What? Wow, I don't know what to say."

"Say nothing, just take it."

He went to shake Cody's hand and when he gripped it Cody gasped. The skin was already starting to swell.

"Damn man, did you break something?"

"Nah it's all right dude. I'll fix it up when I get back to the pharmacy. Thanks though."

"You sure you don't want to come over and smoke just a little?"

"Uh, sure. Yeah. All right, but I got to be quick, man. I have to get back to work."

They left the waterfront as the sun set over the bay, the star dipping behind the abandoned buildings in an array of battered yellow and orange caught against the purpling sky. Jose hobbled while wearing only one shoe, his lumbering foot limping, a white sock caked in mud. He never complained. The group walked through the small batch of wilderness back into the outskirts of town to Jose's home. He lived in a two-story brick apartment building that filled an entire block. It would be hard to believe that anyone else lived there, though, because from the looks of the courtyard and the hallways there was no one around.

Jose's apartment was a one bedroom that was sparsely furnished, with a couch, several folding lawn chairs, a coffee table, and a big screen TV in the living room. There were three different video game consoles. The table was covered in bags of weed and all kinds of marijuana related accessories: bowls, bongs, bubblers, grinders, one hitters, lighters, rollers, and papers. Jose went to the kitchen and grabbed a handful of ice from his freezer to throw into his three-foot-long bong and then packed it with weed.

"Why'd he do that?" Cody asked Vinny, who was sitting next to him on the couch with a towel Jose had provided wrapped around him while the other guys were lounging in the lawn chairs closer to the TV and starting to play a video game. He was excited to smoke out of a bong because he was used to only smoking joints and blunts. It was a special occasion.

"Just try it out, man. You're gonna' love it," Vinny said while shivering.

Jose handed the blue bong to Cody, who received it with both hands, the stem cold to the touch. The ice cubes clinked inside of the glass while jostling in the dirty yellow bong water. He lit the weed and pulled, the bubbles bubbling and the ice pleasantly passing its temperature from the smoke to his lungs. The feeling came instantly, and he held on then let go to float as pain left all parts of the body, especially his hand.

"Fuck, that's good," Cody exhaled and coughed as he looked at Vinny.

"See, I told you."

"You guys can smoke the rest of that. I'm gonna' go clean off my face," the blood had started to dry around Jose's eye. He walked to the bathroom, and they could hear him turn on his shower.

Diego and Paco were speaking Spanish to each other while playing a cooperative campaign in a first-person shooter trying to fend off alien forces who were shooting them with plasma guns while they played human space soldiers who had to use ballistic weapon technology.

"Have you guys ever heard of the Jersey Devil?" Cody asked Diego and Paco after he had taken another hit of the bong and watched them play the video game. Vinny rolled his eyes.

"Yeah, man," Paco said, turning around, "I seen it with my own eyes."

"Don't encourage him," Vinny responded to Paco.

"Nah dog, I'm being for real. One time I was eating a slice of pizza on the boardwalk, and the Jersey Devil flew down and snatched it out of my hands. Shit was fucked up," Paco insisted while chuckling.

"That was a seagull, bro," Diego said.

"That shit didn't look like no seagull I ever saw: the thing had black feathers, red eyes, and sharp teeth," Paco replied.

They all laughed. Cody passed the bong back and forth with Vinny while staring at the video game in awe. He lost track of time until Vinny asked him if he had to get back to work before Mr. Johnston noticed he was gone, and at that he cursed and got up to stumble out of the apartment and run back to the pharmacy, the freezing world flashing by him in a blur of street lights.

Chapter Three

When Cody returned to the pharmacy, he fumbled with his keys because of his swelling purple thumb. It was pulled out of place. He realized that the sign had been flipped from closed back to open and the door was unlocked. The owner, Mr. Johnston, stood behind the counter with his hands on his hips. A slender black man in his early sixties, he wore a freshly pressed white button-down shirt with a blue bow tie, crease-less trousers, and shiny dress shoes. His face was squinched and his large wire frame glasses hung low on his crooked nose that looked like it had once been broken. This was one of several pharmacies he owned around South Jersey. Cody often wondered why he did not shut the place down due to lack of business. Mr. Johnston moved his hands from his hips to fold his arms over his chest in disapproval.

"Where have you been, Cody?"

"I had to run back home and take care of my dad real quick, you know he's got his leg broken and all and can't move around so good. I'm sorry Mr. Johnston," Cody knew he was going to regret that lie. Mr. Johnston might call his house and speak with his father to ask if he was telling the truth.

"You've been gone for a long time. Why do you look damp?"

"I tripped and fell into a puddle running back here. I think I broke my thumb."

Mr. Johnston gave a look of concern and reached out his hand to check Cody's. Cody showed him the injury. His boss grabbed his wrist and turned the limp hand back and forth like it was some kind of specimen.

"I don't think it's broken; it would be more swollen if it were. It's just a sprain. Here, take some aspirin."

"Thanks, Mr. Johnston."

"If I'm not mistaken, this is the type of injury one receives from punching someone the wrong way," Cody's boss pushed the frames of his glasses back up the bridge of his nose as he looked at him.

"Is it?" Cody asked, trying to look innocent.

"Yes, I've seen it before. Did you get into a fight again while on the clock?"

"No, that's crazy, I mean…"

The phone rang. Mr. Johnston answered it immediately. Cody hoped that his boss would not call his parent's house to check on his lie. He worried about keeping his job, feeling like he was walking on thin ice with his boss.

"You're in luck. I've got some business to attend to, so I've got to run. Don't you dare think about closing the shop again before eight o'clock. I'll be back at closing time, or before then."

"Yes, sir."

Cody pulled his coat off with some difficulty and placed it on top of the warm radiator. There had to be somewhere at home where he could hide his prize of the day, but the more he thought about it the more he realized his mother would find the bag of weed and get upset with him. She often went through his belongings and his tiny bedroom had no hiding spots. That would be the last straw for her if she found the bag. He had been getting in trouble with drinking all summer long. Even though his parents needed his help to pay rent, his mother was strict, and he was worried that she would kick him out if she ever found him with drugs, even weed. Beyond the counter there was a door that led to some stairs up to an old apartment on the second floor. No one had lived there for years. Maybe he could find a spot to hide it up there.

He ran upstairs and looked around the abandoned space. The place was full of cobwebs. No furniture to hide anything inside. He walked to what was once the bedroom and felt the floorboards creak under his soggy sneakers. There was one board that was especially creaky, so he knelt down and was able to lift up the plank of wood easily. The sandwich bag full of weed fit snug inside the hole. He jumped when he heard a squeak and looked up to see a mouse in the corner of the room staring at him. After laughing at himself for being frightened by a mouse, he walked back downstairs to tidy up his workplace. It was difficult to grip the broom as he swept the floor.

Cody finished his shift, and Mr. Johnston returned to make sure Cody closed up shop properly, then let him go home. He felt confident after the fight. His hand was still sore, and thumb swollen, even after keeping ice on it after arriving home. He went to bed imagining the fight playing out in his mind before finally falling asleep.

"Damn," he cursed aloud when he woke up, rolling over onto his stomach in bed. Because of his hand he was not able to do push ups the night before. That broke months of a routine. An uncanny tingling washed over his body. He buried his face into the pillow then picked his head up and looked at the mysterious Jersey Devil book that seemed to stare at him from his bookshelf and turned over to avoid its view. He flipped over again and thought about reading it for a little while. Streams of sunlight filled his bedroom. He got up and skimmed through the book to pick out a passage.

Jane Leeds watched the militiamen drill in the town square with newfound hope. She had discovered that she was pregnant a few weeks prior. Several months before that she had given birth to her twelfth child. Each birth she gave deteriorated her body to the point that the last labor had almost killed her. Her husband made her womb the bane of her existence. She knew that in six months' time she was doomed to suffering a gruesome death at the hands of her unborn child. Unless she could put a stop to it. She was nearing thirty years old, and her cheekbones had sharpened with years of exhaustion, but her face was still freckled and fair.

The British governor of New Jersey, Jonathan Belcher, had sent a courier to the settlement of Woodville to conscript all men of fighting age. The French and Indian War simmered in the west, and although the British government had yet to formally declare war on France, the Indian allies of the French had early success in raiding the outskirts of the British colonies. Jane's husband, Titan Leeds, would be sent on an expedition to western Pennsylvania in order to help secure the Ohio Country from the enemy. In that was her hope, because with her husband gone, she would be able to visit the Lenape medicine woman deep in the Pine Barrens and put an end to her pregnancy. Her husband was usually a reticent man, unless he had his fill of whiskey instead of rum, the former having the particular effect of turning him violent.

Jane shuddered as she stared at her husband from under her bonnet. She was a child when her father, a failed merchant from New York, sold her into marriage to Titan Leeds. Having never traveled abroad from Woodville as an adult, the wider world was an abstraction to her, only heard of through rumors and gossip. Even the Indians whom these men drilled to fight were some faraway fantasy in Jane's mind, and she viewed them with condescension that she mistook for compassion. She privately hoped that her husband was killed in battle. As the daughter of an Englishman of some former means, she thought about how she belonged in a place of importance, not this backwater settlement where she was doomed to suffer a diminutive existence. Jane dreamed of living in the high society of London or Paris, or at least New York, not some marsh settlement named Woodville on the edge of the Province of New Jersey.

Sweat dripped from the men and dampened their variegated tunics as dust filled the air. Many of them were drunk on rum and had difficulty in maintaining discipline while failing to stand to attention, a heap of their muskets leaned every which way in the center of the square like a pile of fallen matchsticks. In spite of this, the townspeople cheered, and the militia gathered their weapons then marched off northwest toward the setting red sun.

Her husband stumbled by her without acknowledgement. He had kept impregnating her against her will in the hopes she would bear him a son. Twelve times she had instead birthed him a daughter, and he would make his wrath well known each time in response. He would beat her even as she would recover from childbirth, and even in front of their daughters. This time, she would put an end to his abuse. Jane smiled at her oldest daughter, Elizabeth, who nodded knowingly at her mother's plan. As a fourteen-year-old, Elizabeth was practically a woman ready for marriage, and it was decided that she would take care of her eleven younger sisters while her mother was away for a couple of days, as well as after, if anything were to happen to her. Elizabeth looked like her mother, except her face was round with youth. Jane would go by foot through the forest, packing light, leisurely picking wild blueberries along the way. She knew of the Lenape medicine woman through the whispers of her Quaker midwives, who traveled to what they called the Indian witch to learn new (to the Europeans) techniques in medicine. During her last childbirth, her midwife even gave her a detailed description of where to find the Lenape medicine woman in the Pine Barrens.

Jane left at dawn the next morning, walked barefoot down sandy wooded paths in a northerly direction, letting her intuition guide her. An ambrosial scent filled the air as she journeyed deeper into the forest. The weather was fair, and she was not worried about anything other than her mission. Wolves and bears were said to lurk in the deeper parts of the Pine Barrens, but Jane feared no beast except the one in her belly. She knew in her loins that something was terribly wrong. She had suffered through difficult pregnancies twelve times before, but this was different. This one was cursed.

The bark covered wigwam stood alone beside an orange creek. A white tail deer skin hung over the doorway. Jane warily approached the small building and called out a hello to no response. The air smelled of honeysuckle and smoke. She could hear movement inside. She called out again, and heard a woman say, "Hè! Kulamàlsi hàch?" Slowly, she pulled at the deer skin until the woman appeared from behind it and emerged outside. The white woman and the Lenape woman were face to face. Startled, Jane took a step back, but the woman held onto her, gently placing her hand on Jane's stomach, and concerningly whispered the word, "Mahtán'tu." Jane asked the woman if she spoke English and she nodded her head, saying yes. Then she questioned her what her name was, and the Lenape responded, "Weènchipahkihëlèxkwe." The Englishwoman introduced herself as Jane, then tried to repeat Weènchipahkihëlèxkwe's name back to her, and the Lenape demurred with a motion of her hand, beckoning Jane inside the wigwam.

It was dark save the light of the fire kindling in the center of the room, with smoke drifting out of the chimney opened up by an overturned hide flap in the middle of the roof that was otherwise made of tree branches tightly woven together. The medicine woman's home only had a few pieces of furniture made of fur mats and was filled with a myriad supply of bundled herbs, tree barks, roots, leaves, and dried, unrecognizable things, all organized in rows. Jane stood waiting for Weènchipahkihëlèxkwe to say something, but her host was already busy preparing a tincture. Weènchipahkihëlèxkwe turned her head to look back at Jane while bent over her work, her previously relaxed face suddenly seized in trepidation then settled as stiff as stone. A horse whinnied in the distance. The medicine woman said that she could heal Jane of Mahtán'tu's evil touch, and brought the clay bowl over to her, proffering it below Jane's pox marked chin. A chartreuse colored tea emitting an effluvium. Jane recoiled in disgust. "Please drink," Weènchipahkihëlèxkwe said, but Jane showed apprehension.

The sound of clopping horse hooves grew louder. High-pitched neighing and shouts from outside. Jane closed her eyes and prepared to drink. She lifted her hands up too recklessly out of nervousness. The vessel dropped to the floor, liquid splattering everywhere. When Jane opened her eyes, Weènchipahkihëlèxkwe hurried under a mat that led to a tunnel, signaling for her guest to keep quiet, then she crawled into the dark. Jane was frozen with the spilled medicine at her feet. The tea soaked through her shoes into her toes. A white man tore off the deer skin door, pointing the bayonet of his musket inside, while another man barked obscenities outside. The blade grazed Jane's shoulder, tearing off her bonnet, unraveling her hair; when the militiaman saw that it was a white woman and not an Indian, he pulled back. He demanded to know where the Indian witch went. Jane lied, pleading that she was entranced by the witch and captured to be led there against her will and needed to get back to Woodville to take care of her girls. As he grabbed her and led her out of the wigwam, Jane turned to look back at the spilled medicine, lamenting that she lost her one chance to halt the beast inside her that was waiting to be born. A pang spread throughout her abdomen. She watched as the men set fire to the wigwam, the flames devouring the house. The smoke reached into the sky with purple arms. They mounted the horses, the man dragging Jane up onto the animal and squeezing his legs against her while grabbing at her all over her body. The horses were uncooperative as a haze began to engulf the clearing. She could smell turpentine amidst the air, hoping as she was carried off on horseback that Weènchipahkihëlèxkwe was able to escape.

"Shawiskte ntàpi," a man called out. The smell of cedar smoke floated throughout the forest and Jane felt strangely cleansed by it while breathing it in deeply as she was jostled about by man and horse alike. She thought she saw people within the trees, vague figures walking slowly towards her and her captors as they rode away. A lean, long-haired man appeared by a cedar tree in front of them, raised his hand and made a gesture with his fingers. "Ateha në tëntay," he ordered with a booming voice. She turned back to look at the wigwam. Men ran toward the burning home with buckets of water and doused the flames. The fire faded, smoldering, extinguished. The militiamen's horses stopped, pulling back to stand on their hind legs while whinnying. The man in the trees raised his other hand, and a volley of musket fire shot at them from the bushes on a ridge to their left. Jane saw her captor's comrade reel back then crumple with his horse into a heap in the grass. The horse turned every which way, squealing and writhing in pain, while the white man screamed, crushed underneath it. Jane felt the militiaman grip her as he urged his horse to ride the other way. "It's an ambush!" He yelled, attempting to unsling his musket, then giving up after realizing it was too unwieldy while Jane was nestled between his legs. His bandolier fell into the grass. She felt like she was going to choke as he tightened his grip on her and wheeled around. Her captor hurried his steed through bushes before finding the road and fleeing south, the forest and the world quietly becoming mundane once again as Jane scowled. "I shall return with the rest of the militia and kill those savages. May they all burn in hellfire," the man breathed into her ear. She closed her eyes and shuddered, then looked to the sky wishing for salvation, and yet whispering curses. This was all her fault, she relented.

Cody closed the book. He grew interested in the neighboring forest that he used to care little about and imagined going on a journey with Vinny into the Pine Barrens: camping, drinking, smoking, fishing, and searching for spooky stuff in those mysterious woods. He had never known that there were Native Americans in the New Jersey Pine Barrens, and the idea fascinated him. Was she pregnant with the Jersey Devil? Could the Jersey Devil actually be real? He thought it over, and previously forgotten memories from his childhood raced before his inner eye. Waking up to paralysis and a strange, shadowy figure in the corner of his bedroom, the window opened, wings fluttering.

Another time as a small child he had stood in a field alone after wandering beyond an empty playground to approach without reason the beginning of the forest where a set of unnatural eyes stared back at him. These associations emerged from his subconscious in waves. Bewildered, he looked at his hands. His arms and chest felt so much lighter than usual, like they had invisible weights lifted off of them. He figured it was because he neglected to work out the night before. His thumb was sore and swollen. The fight had completely possessed him with a need for action. He felt confident and ready for adventure, so he loathed more so than usual the prospect of another boring day at work ahead of him, tossing and turning, throwing a pillow over his face and sighing, but finally, he got up out of bed. He planned on reading more of The Jersey Devil later.

After breakfast he walked down River Ave to the pharmacy to find that his key would not work in the door when he tried opening it, so he jogged back home to call Mr. Johnston. His dad, still reading the newspaper, did not even look up when he came back inside. Cody went to the kitchen, found the family address book, searched for his boss, and then dialed the number for Mr. Johnston's house. As the phone rang, he became more and more nervous to speak with him.

"Hello, this is the Johnston residence," it was Mrs. Johnston. Her voice was elongated and elegant in the way that Creole speakers talk in English.

"Hi, Mrs. Johnston, this is Cody. My key to the pharmacy isn't working, is Mr. Johnston around to talk?"

"Why, yes, I'll go fetch him for you."

As he waited to hear from his boss, his father called from the living room, "what's the matter, Cody?"

"Nothing," he yelled, while covering the speaker with his hand.

"Yes, hello Cody," Mr. Johnston said.

"Hello, Mr. Johnston. I tried opening up the shop just now and couldn't turn the key in the lock."

"Well that's because I changed the lock, son."

There was silence. A quiet static fizzled in his ear. In his naiveté, Cody did not really understand what Mr. Johnston had meant by that, so he pursued his incorrect line of reasoning.

"Okay, do you want me to come pick the new key up?"

"No, Cody. Listen here, I know you're a good kid deep down, but I can't do this anymore. I can't keep putting up with your antics. You're always sneaking out and getting into trouble while you're supposed to be on the clock. I'm not saying it's all your fault; the shop hasn't been getting any business as of late and needs to be shut down. I barely ever get prescriptions for that location anymore. That new Supercenter has taken up all of my old customers. It's just not profitable."

"I can't believe it. I don't know what to do. I need this job Mr. Johnston."

"Go get a job down at the Supercenter, son. I heard they're hiring opening positions as door greeters. I'm sure your parents can give you a decent reference. They're starting at a whole six dollars an hour for new employees. That's a dollar more than minimum wage. You can't beat that, son. Not in this economy."

"But Mr. Johnston..."

"Now Cody, I don't know what else to tell you except that when I was your age, I had to face a lot of adversity. Especially how things were back then, so I worked hard to get to where I am now. Times are changing again, and I tried to keep the store afloat for as long as possible, though there's only so much I can do," he paused for a few moments, and Cody stayed silent, "…just keep your chin up. Things will turn around for you. Now, I have to get going and look after some other business. Good luck to you, young man."

And just like that, Mr. Johnston hung up the phone. Cody was shocked to find tears rolling down his cheeks. He disliked his job down the street at the pharmacy, but he hated more the thought of having to work in the new Supercenter the next town over. He did not have a car so he would have to catch the bus. He quickly tried to wipe away his tears. Cody placed the phone on the hook and peered out from the kitchen to the living room to see what his dad was doing.

His father sat in the armchair he rarely left these days. He had not always been like this, Cody thought. Back when he was a kid he looked up to his dad, who had risen up from line worker to foreman in the soda factory. Some of his fondest childhood memories were of watching his dad play intramural baseball. Cody would sit in the bleachers by himself and cheer like his dad was a professional, his own personal hero. His dad's weekends were spent playing baseball with his coworkers in a local league that he and the factory team dominated. His dad was short but fast and held down the infield with his gritty defense at third base. His arm was strong enough to throw out even the fastest runners at first base. By the time he was in his early forties, however, his body was all but spent from factory work, at least too spent to be playing baseball anymore, and now he was even too spent to be working in a factory with his broken leg.

Cody wished he could talk to his dad and tell him all of his thoughts. He watched his father from the dark threshold of the kitchen, and wondered if he could ever share with him how he truly felt, why he acted so rudely to his dad and his mom. He could not completely understand himself. How he felt about his life being wasted. How he lied to everyone. How he betrayed his high school sweetheart, the love of his life, his best friend's sister, an episode that was too shameful in his mind to speak of to anyone, especially his parents.

He repressed those memories. Even though he was only a teenager, he felt like all opportunities had slipped past him, that the world had slipped past him. He did not want to sit in front of the TV with his dad. He could not bear to watch the people on the television talk about the war on terror and think about the other side of the world and listen to a casual report of violent death without him being able to take part in it. To have purpose. No matter what the cost. He realized that he had been standing in the kitchen silently crying for a while, so he went upstairs to try to go back to sleep, even though it was late morning, but could not do that either.

The Jersey Devil caught his eye on his bookshelf again as he was moping in bed, so he got up and retrieved the book then returned to lay down and read it. The book had started getting good the last time he picked it up earlier in the morning. He wanted to see what would happen when the Jersey Devil was born. He flipped forward and found the page.

The night of the demon's birth was filled with screams from the mother. She dreaded having to bring a child into the world once again, for the thirteenth time, and cursed the baby through her labor pains. "Let this one be the devil," she hollered. As she helped to wipe the sweat from Mrs. Leeds' brow, the Quaker midwife shook her head and whispered prayers. The older daughters of Jane Leeds were also on hand to do whatever they could and feared for their mother's soul after having heard her unholy lamentations. One of Jane's youngest wandered into the room and the midwife ushered her out. Elizabeth refused to leave her mother's side, even as the labor grew worse and the Quaker midwife insisted. Jane gripped the Quaker's arm until her nails sank into her skin and drew blood; the midwife did not have the strength to pull away. The contractions came quicker, until the yelling became constant. Jane pushed with all of her might and finally birthed her thirteenth child.

By all accounts the infant was at first normal and healthy looking, but as each day passed, the baby revealed one deformity after another. First, coarse mule hair sprouted upon the child's skin. Then, it developed teeth that turned to those of a wolf, growing large and sharp. Then, the spiral, bony horns of a goat pierced through its skull. By that third day, the Quaker midwife fled the Leeds cabin, fearing the devil had in fact been born, but that would not be the end of the transmogrification. Jane Leeds seemed to have suffered from terrible nightmares while remaining in a coma after losing so much blood during childbirth. Her daughters did their best to take care of their mother and were hesitant to even swaddle the infant. They were relieved at least that their abusive, drunkard father was away with the British Army fighting in the French and Indian War out west. The baby lay squirming in its wicker basket without so much as a blanket to cover it.

Afraid to go near the deformed newborn, the twelve bonneted daughters, ranging from teenage to toddler, would toss raw onions and potatoes, skin and all, to the infant for it to feed upon, which it did easily with its full mouth of capable canine incisors. Slowly, the baby's eyes changed from pitch jet black to a calcified crimson. The first three days after the birth revealed an incipient change, as the baby's skin hardened while it howled constantly. On the fourth day, its little human baby hands transformed into hawk claws. On the fifth day, it grew a reptilian wyvern's tail that twirled about in the air. On the sixth day, its face turned into a triangular shape, resembling a demented deer. Finally, on the seventh day, the baby's back burst open to reveal the leathery wings of an otherworldly bat, and at that it emerged from its cradle, screeching a skin chilling noise that strangely had the effect of forcing the victims of the demon to feel sadness and sympathy for it. The girls huddled around the bed of their comatose mother whimpering, fearing imminent death at the entity floating before them. It hovered over them, vomited steaming blood in a circle around them, and then flew up the chimney, screaming into the night.

"Holy shit," he said, then closed the book.

The idea of going to the Pine Barrens to explore and perhaps catch a glimpse of some strange, supernatural stuff solidified in Cody's mind. Maybe the Jersey Devil was real, he thought. He felt like the weight of the air would crush him into his bed, so he got up and went out of the house without his dad saying anything.

He walked for a long time until he came to the bus stop. He looked up at the looming storm clouds stretched out across the town that were racing almost organically toward the sea. He waited for a long time facing leeward to protect himself against the wind even though it was the opposite direction from where the bus would be coming. He thought for a long time. He could hear a dog yelping and whimpering in a backyard across the street. He saw the bus out of his periphery barreling towards him and worried that it would pass him. He felt the urge to jump sideways in front of it. He instead turned around and stepped up onto the bus as it slowed down, placing change in the meter and carrying his limp hand with his good one as he sat on the long, empty bench, and the driver sped off toward the shore. He could smell stale beer and urine. He was only a twenty-minute bus ride away from the closest recruitment center, and this was the moment needed for action, regardless of his sorry state, he concluded. He tried to gain his composure. He wiped his face dry as the rain continued to grow heavier outside. He considered his posture. He kept moving his fingers and stretching his bad hand so that he could pretend like it was okay. He began to become aware of his heartbeat. He pulled the rope for the last stop before the bus went over the bridge and found himself in a parking lot. He walked up to the recruitment center nestled between a tanning salon and a computer repair store in a drab strip mall. He strutted into the lobby that was empty save for a man dressed in fatigues sitting behind a desk with plastic stars and stripes everywhere as well as black and gold posters proclaiming the words "Army of ONE" adorning the otherwise bland room. He wondered what that slogan meant exactly while smiling at the recruitment officer, who stood up to greet Cody and offered his hand to shake. He felt his stomach lurch in agony, wondering if he could ask to use the bathroom in an emergency, although knowing he could not show any signs of weakness, and tried to not make a face when the officer gripped his sore flesh, but thought he must have failed from the look of disappointment in the man, his smile slightly lowering into a frown.

The officer handed Cody some forms to fill out. He breezed through it answering no to everything then handed back the first paper detailing his health history. The officer made a phone call. He told Cody that a doctor would arrive shortly to perform a physical. Cody read an Army recruitment magazine as the officer ignored him while doing work on a large desktop computer. The longer he waited the more nervous he grew, and he tried to hide it by intently reading the recruitment literature he was given. He was surprised at how quickly the doctor showed up, however, and how the grim man in the long white coat did not even look him in the eye when he told him to take off his shirt. At first Cody's heart thumped in even bumps and then began to skip every other round of beats. He took deep breaths, it was all in his head, he thought. The doctor placed a stethoscope against Cody's chest, scrunched his face, tilted his chin, and guided his instrument as if it was a metal detector, the cold steel moving up and down to the rhythm of Cody's breathing.

The doctor cleared his throat. "Sorry son, you have a heart murmur. Can't enlist."

The recruitment officer, who was wearing forest camouflage while sitting stiffly in the strip mall office, simply shook his head then leaned back and observed the scene end in his computer chair. There was a moment where the tenseness of the situation relaxed. Everyone said curt goodbyes. Cody could hear the officer's thumbs brush the tight bristles of his crew cut hair as he followed the doctor out into the parking lot. The doctor turned around after stepping off the curb and looked gravely at Cody.

"Kid, you shouldn't be enlisting in the Army right now anyway. They could ship you off to Iraq. Why don't you enroll in college?"

"Yeah, I guess," Cody said.

He could not help but cry again when he had to wait outside in the rain for the bus back home, which was made all the more uncomfortable by him being overcome with uncontrollable shivering. He tried to find comfort in the continuous movement of cars and perceived them differently, without having the ability to describe them so, to be automatons without human beings even inside them. He realized that a part of the reason he was so depressed was that he did not own a car himself. A real American man has a car and can drive anywhere he wants to so that he can get away and he does not ever have to be justified in any of his actions because he can just move along. He does not ride a bus or get driven around by his friends. He found relief in this reasoning. Maybe he could steal a car and run away. He entertained the thought in order to distract himself.

In the woods across the highway an animal bounded through bushes. He turned his head at the sound of a screech. His heart started beating quickly again. He contemplated the Jersey Devil. Could it be real? He kept asking himself. The rain mixed with his tears so he felt less self-conscious even though he was around no one, but he still put his hood over his head so far that it would cover most of his water-soaked eyes that looked like holes filled and overflowing with bloodshot pools. Red and blue mixed together made not purple but gray. He tried hiding inside his soaked clothes. If some demonic cross between a kangaroo and a bat wanted to kill him in a strip mall parking lot on the edge of the Pine Barrens, then so be it. His overwhelming fear was both of dying and of wanting to die. He considered the contradictory nature of both believing in something and disbelieving in something simultaneously, even if he did not have the intellect to put it into words. Luckily, the bus showed up to save him from his self-imposed doom just as he was becoming overwhelmed with his racing thoughts.

He bounced along on the bus ride and arrived back home to his dad asleep on the couch. His father's snoring was pitiful. Cody went back to his bed to try to sleep again, even though it was only early evening. His bed became damp underneath him because he had forgotten to take his jacket off of himself. He got up and covered his face. He had only just realized he had forgotten to take his rain drenched clothes off, and that it felt like it was stuck to his body. He feared for his life as he sat on the edge of the mattress. His fear was for himself and of himself, that he had become possessed with the impulse to kill himself and actually carry through with it. He stared at the white wall for a long time.

His mom opened up the bedroom door, surprisingly home from the diner shift early. That suddenly corked his eyes. He had been crying for a long time, and he did not want to have to explain himself to her. She carried a few shopping bags with a straight posture to maintain some semblance of respectability. He thought about how her fear must have been that no one respected her, especially her family. His dad seemed to have said something to her as soon as she walked through the front door about Cody acting strange after the phone call from Mr. Johnston, because she headed straight to Cody's room instead of the kitchen. The food swung in its plastic pouches. A brief silence.

Neither of them looked each other right in the eye. Her hair was straight and up in a bun, but her bangs curled down to the sides of her cheeks. His mother was beautiful even after having to work sixty-hour weeks for many years as a waitress. Work did not deteriorate her like it had with his father, even though it was as physically and mentally demanding, just in a different way. The only signs of stress on her face were some slight wrinkles around her brown eyes.

"I got cut because the diner was so slow. You know, I'd say that we no longer have the regulars like we used to, now that the drive thru fast-food joints the next town over have started serving breakfast. Wouldn't be surprised if the restaurant closed within a year. It's a crying shame. There's not many of the 1950's style diners left. They're all getting torn down."

"That sucks," Cody said.

"Yes, it's a sin. Just a sin. What a waste. The Woodville Diner is historic don't ya' know? I learned a lot about it because it's our fiftieth anniversary this year. It was once a dining car on a train before being converted into a roadside diner. That's why it's so long and thin and has aluminum siding," Cody did not respond. "Why don't you come downstairs, and I'll fix you something good to eat."

"Okay. Hey mom, remember how that crazy guy made a scene at your job?"

"Well, of course, that's not something I'd easily forget now, is it?"

"Right, so he left behind this book…"

She grew suspicious, "yes, I remember him reading a book. I'm sure it was perverted filth, whatever it was, that man was downright evil."

"Yeah, well, I took a look at it, but then threw it in the trash. It was about the Jersey Devil," Cody lied about throwing it away because he realized after bringing it up that his mom would probably end up throwing the book in the trash herself. He side glanced over to his bookshelf and figured that she would not recognize it being there because there was nothing printed on the spine of the book.

"An awful myth that is, a bunch of un-Christian hoopla."

"Yeah, I know. Just wanted to hear more about the guy that was reading it, though."

"There's not much more worth knowing; he was one of those immoral men who pass through towns causing nothing but trouble. Although now that I think about it, he was different; he spoke strangely, like he was from the past, and was goin' on talkin' about his life as a train hopper and all the sin it entails, how he was a Vietnam War veteran, graphically described some horrible war stories, and like I mentioned before he said he had acquired a mansion of sorts in the Pine Barrens."

"You said before it was a refuge from the apocalypse, but a mansion in the Pine Barrens?"

"Yes honey, but he was a liar. Told tall tales, told them to anyone who would listen. He had been bothering me and my customers all throughout my shift until Johnny the cook called the police."

"Wow, that's crazy… uh well, I'm gonna' clean up and then I'll head down for dinner."

When Cody came down the stairs, his father had moved on from reading to watching TV. His mom was in the kitchen. No one asked her why she was home so early, but still she explained that she was cut from her shift over and over to her son and husband, talking loudly at the house in general because neither her son nor her husband would directly acknowledge her. She said it was becoming more and more usual for there to be early cuts at the restaurant and that it was not a good sign. Cody had gathered himself by the time he went downstairs. His mother had set up the kitchen and placed the grocery bags on the counter. He could not help but stare at her as she unloaded the bags, still sluicing wet from the rain outside, seeing something in her appearance that he had never really noticed before, an air of quiet, unshakeable dignity. He finally helped her put away the food without her asking. His mom smiled, then put her hand to his cold cheek. He withdrew.

"What's wrong, sweetheart?"

"Nothing," Cody said, but she gave him a knowing look.

"Well if you're not going to tell me, then you might as well start peeling some potatoes for dinner."

"You're cooking dinner tonight, Anna?" Cody's dad asked from the living room with excitement.

"Yes, David. London broil steak and mashed potatoes and fresh vegetables. A proper supper. I'm sick and tired of microwaving frozen TV dinners. And we're not going to eat in front of the God-awful television tonight either. That horrific war on the news and those action shows will have to wait. You boys'll just have to put up with having an actual conversation at the dinner table tonight," Cody groaned in response.

While peeling the potatoes, Cody cut the thumb on the hand he had hurt the day before, letting out a small gasp. He turned on the faucet to try to clean up his injury before his mom noticed, but as the blood ran into the sink his mother appeared at his side and grabbed his wrist.

"Fuck, mom that fucking hurts. Leave me alone."

"Cody, how many times do I have to tell you not to speak like that! Don't use such foul language in my house! Look at you, you've done and gotten your hand swollen, and the thumb! Lord don't tell me it's broken. I can't believe you. Was it another fist fight? I can't afford to take you to the hospital again. You'll have to pay for it yourself this time."

"Mom, stop. It's just a sprain. Mr. Johnston said it's okay. I'll take care of it. Just leave me alone, please."

"Well, I guess Mr. Johnston knows a thing or two about injuries. What with that broken nose he got from Officer Ciliberti. He sure isn't a doctor, though, now, is he?"

"Wait, what happened?" Cody asked.

Cody's mom covered her eyes and shook her head, "nothing!"

"What's the matter?"

"Nothing, dad," Cody yelled out, his father was still in the living room armchair with his leg propped up in its cast on the coffee table.

"Don't lie to us son, it was another fight, wasn't it? Tell us what happened," Cody's dad called out.

"Listen to your father, now. Tell me exactly what happened," his mother had a way of extracting the truth out of him just by looking at him and using his father as leverage against him.

"It wasn't a big deal. Vinny and I were hanging out, you know, going for a walk or whatever on my work break, and there were these guys who were throwing stuff at us from far away, there was a bunch of them, and only the two of us. We weren't trying to pick a fight, but then they jumped us. It was just a scuffle that was made worse by all the muck. It wasn't that bad, really, I just slipped and fell in the mud and that's how I hurt my thumb."

"Projectiles raining down on you during a fight in the mud? Sounds like the Battle of Agincourt," Cody's dad remarked, then snickered to himself while watching the television.

"What?" Both Cody and his mother asked, annoyed at the obscure reference. His mother turned back to him and pointed her finger at him.

"Cody, what has come over you these past few months?"

"Nothing, mom. Leave me alone."

"As your mother I cannot leave you alone. I won't leave you alone because you're still under my roof. If you can't start acting like a normal young man who doesn't get into fist fights, then you will have to go it alone. You won't be allowed to live here anymore. Then you will regret that I left you alone. Do you understand?"

She turned away from him. Cody stayed silent and listened to his mother vent out loud to herself while she tried to cook dinner. She complained that his older sister Emma had abandoned them by going away to sinful California for college. She resented her son who got into trouble. She said to the stove that she wanted a normal family. She told the refrigerator that she would do anything for children who would go to church with her on Sundays. She lamented again to the trash can that her daughter did not settle down to marry and have children. At that point, Cody could not take it anymore. Instead of arguing with her like he used to, that Emma was right not to marry, but was right to get away from this dead-end town, to escape this frustrating family and go off to college, he took the first opportunity he could to slip away. He went to his bedroom and packed his backpack, then snuck out of his window and onto the roof. It was cold and slippery, and he was hungry, but he was able to climb down the tree, shimmying like a clumsy bear cub because he was careful of his thumb, into his front yard. As he jogged toward the pharmacy, so many thoughts raced through his mind that he nearly broke into a sprint. He needed that bag of weed and the sense of calm it offered. Everything was too clear and overwhelming.

Once he got to the building, he noticed that Mr. Johnston had already put up a for sale sign on the front lawn; he shook his head and then snuck around the side to look through the window by the back door. It was dark inside, and he thought if he broke the window, he would be able to reach in and unlock the bottom lock of the back door undetected. He knew there was not a security system alarm in the building but was still reluctant to act. No one was around. There was more than just a physical barrier between him and his prize. All he wanted was not to be a coward.

He stood there for a few minutes smoking a cigarette and building the courage to break into the pharmacy, his thumb throbbing with pain. The smoke built up inside his lungs until he felt like he was full. The nicotine dulled his hunger but made him jittery. Once he had worked himself up, he pulled a rock out of the garden with his good hand and smashed the window, then reached in and unlocked the door. He opened the cellular phone that he never really used for lack of purchased minutes, pressing its buttons for a faint green pulsing light that looked like morse code in the dark and found his way stumbling up the stairs, hoping Mr. Johnston did not somehow find his weed and that it was still there. After he got up the stairs and entered the room, he pulled up the floorboard and sighed in relief. There was his green treasure basking in the green cell phone screen light.

Cody grabbed the bag and sprinted as quietly as he could out of the old pharmacy, hopping the backyard fence, then headed towards Vinny's house. His thumb was in constant pain because he kept smacking it into things, but he did not care. His sole focus was conveying to Vinny his new idea. He was going to convince him that it was time to take their camping trip early. Maybe he could even get his friend to run away with him to look for the Jersey Devil. Maybe they could finally escape this town for good.

Vinny's house was a duplex with a large porch and a Puerto Rican flag hanging by the stairs. Cody was worried that when he knocked on the door his ex-girlfriend Bianca would answer. He had not spoken to her since they had broken up at the beginning of the summer. There was a silent understanding between Vinny and Cody that they would not talk about how the latter had dated the former's sister throughout high school. Of course the face that appeared was hers, making Cody immediately forget all the words he had prepared to say in case he had to talk to her. Her eyeliner flared in the cat eye style. She pouted her full lips, gloss shining, and squinted in disdain.

"Well look who it is — are you gonna' run away again? Or are you man enough to face me this time? Don't worry, I won't bite your little head off now."

"Yeah, no, hey Bee, look, I'm sorry about everything…"

"That's lovely Cody. Everything's better then. That's all I wanted to hear."

"Really?"

"No you fucking asshole. You're a piece of shit. You cheated on me on fucking prom night. You weren't even man enough to fess up to me. I had to find out on my own weeks later," she clenched her fists as she spoke.

"Do we really have to go over this again?"

"Wow, that sounds like you're really sorry."

"How many times do I have to apologize?"

"Thousands of times. Millions of times. For years."

"Okay. Fine. I'm sorry, I really am. I'm so sorry."

"No, actually I don't want to hear your voice that much. It's small. It's a tiny little bitchy baby boy voice that only whines and complains and lies and cheats and steals then pretends to be the victim."

Cody was silent. He could not come up with a good response. He used to scream and yell at Bianca when he knew he was wrong. He had been able to use her insecurities against her. He was not consciously manipulative at the time, but that was what he had done. He wanted to be right all of the time. He started to cry. He did not want to cry. It was the last thing he wanted to do, show weakness in front of his former girlfriend, but instead of the ridicule that he expected from her, he was surprised to feel her hand on his shoulder.

"Ay bendito. Come here, Cody." The warmth of her body sparked a flood of memories. How they awkwardly lost their virginities together. She smelled of something beautiful that he could not name, which was ambrette seeds. As they hugged Cody could not help but to start to have an erection. His attraction to her was interminable.

"I'm sorry."

"Shut up. I still hate you."

"Is there a way I can make things up to you?"

"No, Cody. I just started my senior year. I have my whole life ahead of me, and you're a bum who's still stuck at that boring old pharmacy." She flipped her hair over her shoulder.

"Nah, it closed." Cody lowered his eyes in shame.

"Well maybe that's a blessing in disguise. Why don't you go join the Army like you always been talking about? You're a shortie but you're still tough. Look at those arm muscles boy, you're like a pit bull," Cody laughed as she squeezed his toned biceps, the tears had dried into sticky patches on his cheeks. Her manicured, red polished nails felt good against his skin.

"They wouldn't take me."

"What, why?"

"Well, they said I didn't pass the eye test."

"You don't wear glasses or nothin', I thought your eyes were fine."

"Yeah, but I'm... color blind."

"You lying to me? How did I not know this?"

"No, I'm not lying to you. I just never realized it because it's like a different shade type thing or something like that I think."

Cody could not bear to tell her that the Army would not let him enlist because he had a heart murmur, which was something he was not aware of before. He did not know why, but for some reason he found it more embarrassing to have a heart murmur than to be color blind. He was not sure if the color-blind rule was even real, except for enlisting in the Air Force. He had seen it in a movie once and figured Bianca would not know any better.

"Well I guess your dumbass is gonna' have to start reading some books and go off to college like everyone else because you know I sure as hell ain't playing around with your broke and short self no more."

She had let go of him, and for good. He watched her walk back into the house. Her curly dyed blonde hair bounced as she turned to look at him, her silver hoop earrings swinging in tandem with the motion of her bare thighs that peeked out from below her black and white polka dot skirt.

She looked back with a scowl, "I'll get Vinny for you."

"Fuck," Cody whispered.

Vinny came to the door and squinted at his friend with tired eyes, "Cody, what's up man?"

"Your sister, man."

"Hey, we had a fucking deal. No talking about my sister. I don't want to know shit."

"All right Vin, right, well anyway, it's a long story, but I think we got to leave for that camping trip tonight," Cody had a furtive look about him, hunched over, head owlishly swiveling to make sure no one else in the family, parents, cousins or otherwise, would make an appearance on the front porch. He was still anxious that someone had called the cops on him for breaking into the pharmacy.

"Yeah, but nah, buddy, I don't think I can swing that tonight," Vinny looked behind himself, "I've got a ton of work to finish up this week for my old man. I gotta' help look after my family, but we can go for the weekend, I promise. I already got all the fishing supplies and stuff packed up."

"I don't want to go for just a weekend though, dude, I want to go for good."

"You want to go to the fucking woods for good, bro? Like a piney? Live in a shack in the forest and eat squirrels and shit? You can't even fish, let alone fend for yourself."

"Well that's why I got you, man. I'm not a redneck Pine Barren person; I don't know how to do any survival stuff, but I want to go to the woods because I found that book. Remember I was telling you about it before we got into that fight? It's about the Jersey Devil. Says there's a bunch of abandoned buildings and shit in the Pine Barrens and there's demons and witchcraft shit. I know you think it's all made up, but I have an idea. I was thinking, maybe we could steal a video camera from the Supercenter and make our own movie like that witch project shit that we saw in theaters when we were sophomores. Remember that? We could try to find the Jersey Devil, and if nothing happens, we pretend that we get attacked on camera and make it big with that shit."

"Yeah, that was a good movie. So you're saying you wanna' make like a documentary about trying to find the Jersey Devil?"

"Yeah, why not?"

"Well, I mean, it could be fun I guess, but how are we going to steal a camcorder from the Supercenter man? Their security is pretty tight in there."

"I thought about that. I've got a few different ideas. I've had some free time. Long story short, I got fired from my job today. Mr. Johnston is shutting the pharmacy down."

"I'm sorry to hear that dude."

Cody thought for a moment, "I tried to go to the recruitment center too, but they…"

"They didn't accept you?"

"Nah."

"Well because you're too fucking short, man. What the hell did you think was gonna' happen?"

"Shut up dude. I'm more fucking fit than most of those dumbasses that enlist."

"Yeah, sure."

"It wasn't because I was too short either, it was because of my heart." Cody did not mind telling the truth to Vinny, as opposed to Bianca.

"Yeah, sure," Vinny said, even more sarcastically this time.

"Anyway, can you just hear me out? Maybe the Jersey Devil is linked to all of the children that have gone missing lately."

"What the hell are you talking about?" Vinny blurted.

"Don't you watch the news? Maybe the Jersey Devil is real, maybe it's not, but just listen to me: every time another kid goes missing there's another sighting of the Jersey Devil."

"Dude, you're fucking crazy."

"Look, I don't really even believe for sure that it's the Jersey Devil for real, I'm just saying, there could be some kind of creature out there that people think is the Jersey Devil. Wouldn't you want to find out? It would be like an adventure, even if we don't find anything, you can go fishing."

"You and your fucking conspiracies. Yeah, sure man, I'm down to go camping and fishing with you, it's just that I can't leave right now. How about we go to the woods next weekend? I'm pretty sure I can take off for the rest of the week after so we can get away and you can unwind from all this shit."

"Alright, well, I think I came up with a good plan. Since I gotta wait for you anyway, I'm going to apply to work at the Supercenter. Get a job there. And then steal the fucking video camera. Like an inside job. What do you think?"

"I think it's a stupid fucking idea but hey what the hell? Go ahead. Then you can make your stupid bruja devil movie while I go fishing."

"Sounds good dude. See yah later."

Cody took off to go home, and on the way realized his mom would be angry with him for skipping out on dinner. Sometimes it was tricky sneaking back into his own house while avoiding his parents. Luckily, they were asleep and had ignored out of exasperation for the time being that Cody abandoned dinner and snuck out. He went to bed hungry, staring in a trance at the black and gold book while thinking about Vinny and his upcoming camping trip. How even if there was no connection between the missing children and the Jersey Devil, that he could become famous if he made a documentary about looking for the Jersey Devil in the Pine Barrens. He fell asleep in a hopeful mood.

His dreams were painted with vibrant images. He was in the middle of the woods alone at night, but it was not dark. A silver light spread throughout the forest. He could see for miles around him through translucent tree trunks. He walked down a sandy path between pine trees that stretched as far as the horizon, until he came to a river that barred the way between him and the rest of the road. He wanted to return home. He walked up to the river and crouched down and cupped the water to drink it out of desperate thirst. When he gulped, he felt iron in his throat and understood that it was not water, but that it was sharp blood stabbing at his esophagus. He swallowed the liquid with difficulty and turned his head downstream to see a conflagration approaching him. A wall of fire stretched to the sky and expanded around him. An incongruous tree emerged from the flames unscathed. It was a towering white cedar. He focused on this tree as he felt himself become consumed by fire, a shining golden light enveloped and blinded him, and he could hear birds chirping. He opened his eyes and could see again. All of the burnt wood was made anew, spiraling in the air in cylinders, then building themselves into domed structures. A brown village stood where the barren forest once was, the sand replaced by a green field, and the red river expanded into a blue freshwater lake. His body levitated over the surface until he could feel a rush of wind above plunge him into the depths of the water. He struggled, water rushing down his throat as he felt a claw snag at his pants and pierce his leg before it dragged him through an icy whirlpool to the sandy floor while darkness overtook him. Cody shook in his bed and woke up gasping for breath.

Chapter Four

Cody walked from the bus stop to the Supercenter. The large building loomed over him, and the word Supercenter adorned the wall in big bright blue lights. He shook his head and took a hit of a joint. No, he refused to actually work here. This was all just a plan to steal the video camera, and yet the idea of a steady job, maybe leading to a raise and a promotion was attractive to him. This is how they trapped you, he thought. The false promise of comfort and safety. He finished the thin, shoddily rolled joint, stomping it out in the parking lot behind a car before striding through the automatic doors.

While he walked inside, he could see through the window that they had recently finished building the pharmacy section, where lines of sick and elderly people formed to pick up their prescriptions from a counter manned by one white lab coat clad worker filling bottles with pills. Behind the building loomed the beginning of the Pine

Barrens. It was there that some of the people who hobbled into the Supercenter made camp. Just beyond the parking lot stood a variety of makeshift shelters protruding from the edge of the woods. As long as the dirty tents, wooden lean-to's, and propped up tarpaulins remained technically off the property and far enough away from the parking lot, they would not be torn down. This colony of modern-day lepers had sprouted around the same time as the Supercenter was built. They came from various backgrounds, but their faces had the same desperate look: the need for a fix above all else. They came for pain killers.

Cody looked at what he would call junkies with disdain if not physical revulsion. He feared them because he was afraid of becoming one of them; they looked like zombies to him. It had happened to his once handsome cousin Max in the past year. When Cody graduated from high school, Max had suddenly reached out to his little cousin, supposedly to offer congratulations after having not talked to him much in the previous two years. At the time, Cody's parents had told him to be careful of Max and not to hang out with him anymore but would not explain why or where he had gone. What he had become, they said. Max claimed to have won tickets to a Phillies game through a work raffle and offered to take Cody as a graduation gift, and even to buy him beers, as he was three years older. All he needed was for Cody to front him fifty dollars for some reason, Cody could not fully recall Max's irrational explanation, but he would repay him at the game. Fifty bucks was no small sum for Cody, more than half his paycheck at the time.

Max had swung by Cody's old job one day looking haggard but excited, talking about how much fun they were going to have, and that he was going to buy a new pickup truck with all the money from this apprenticeship he had been working in Philly, that soon he would make it into the steamfitters union, and that they would be going to more and more baseball games in Philadelphia together at the beautiful new ballpark they were building. He left the store carrying away a bill imprinted with the face of Ulysses S. Grant, who suffered many scandals during his presidency due to him blindly trusting his friends, a fact that was lost to Max, but Cody knew because of his father's habit of spouting random bits of knowledge to his son, especially if it had to do with a president's failure. The day of the game came and went with no word from Max, the fifty bucks gone forever. That was when Cody's parents revealed to him that his cousin was addicted to heroin. "It's fitting that you gave him a fifty, son," his father said, "Grant was a great general, but a terrible president." His dad's focus on this seemingly irrelevant aspect of the episode and not the theft itself angered Cody.

There was a period of time in their childhood where Cody and Max grew up under the same roof, as both of their parents had simultaneously fallen on hard times and needed to have the kids stay with their grandparents in order to avoid being homeless. A key difference was that Max's parents never came back for him. His mom was Cody's dad's sister, and her and her husband had both been incarcerated on drug related charges. David's parent's house was a shoddy rancher situated on the banks of a meager, nameless creek by the pines. Max and Cody's grandparents fought each other daily. Once, their grandmother ripped the entire telephone out of the wall and threw it at their grandfather's head, and he drove off never to return. The cousins slept on the floor in front of the fireplace like it offered some kind of protection, even in the steamy summer months. This is why Cody and Max felt like brothers, experiencing trauma they did not know was trauma, bonding by playing catch in the yard. Their hand-me-down baseball gloves were so worn that the tan leather had turned black.

He treaded to the back of the brightly lit, gigantic shipping container that was the Supercenter, his mind returning to the present, staring at shelves filled with every kind of consumer good imaginable. There were Supercenters in every county of America. The chain company was fast becoming the number one employer of Americans. Each section of the whitewashed maze was what used to be the focus of a store on Main Street or River Ave in Woodville. There was a whole hardware section that put the old hardware store out of business. There was a supermarket that put the produce store, the bakery, and the butcher out of business. There was a toy section that put the toy store out of business. There were clothing sections that put various clothing stores out of business, except the shoe store that Vinny's family still somehow maintained, probably more out of pride than profit. Not for long. Soon that last small business would fail like all the others, leaving Main Street thoroughly abandoned like some kind of old wild west ghost town.

Cody knocked on the manager's office door and waited while leaning against the frame for a long time, daydreaming again about his childhood, remembering a falling out he had had with his cousin Max during Freshman year. It was Cody's first at bat of the high school season, and he looked into the stands hoping to see a familiar face. Anyone from his family would do, but all he saw were acquaintances, fellow classmates, and their parents or siblings. The diamond was well maintained, and the grass freshly mown. There was not a cloud to be seen, and the air was still. The blue expanse was overwhelming. His stomach had been aching and he thought he could feel the milk he drank earlier curdling inside him. He was worried that he would have an accident right when everyone's eyes were on his body, that a sudden, uncontrollable spasm would projectile launch human waste out of him, the pinstripe white pants he wore making him feel especially vulnerable.

When he took the first pitch, he heard nothing, and it was a relief because he was not even paying attention to the pitcher perched on the mound in front of him. The pitch was off the plate, high and outside.

"You're crowding the plate, puny asshole," the catcher hissed behind him. Cody looked back in response and the next pitch whizzed by his chest.

"Strike," the umpire bellowed.

"Come on, pussy, swing the fucking bat," the catcher barked while staring at him through the bars of his mask.

Cody swung at the next pitch before the ball even crossed the plate. The catcher laughed. Another strike. Cody looked at the uninterested audience watching behind the fence, then towards the mound again. It was too late. The grown man behind him screamed strike again and young Cody sulked back to the dugout, expecting to be berated by his coach or teammates, but it was even worse. No one looked at him.

He walked all the way to the back of the recessed bench made of unfinished wood, over the trash strewn dirt with his cleats digging into empty paper cone cups, and turned to see his cousin Max, a Senior who liked to hang around younger girls, on the other side of the fence being distracted by a couple of Sophomores. They both stood about a foot shorter than Max and wore their hair straightened and down, bangs perfectly trimmed, one brunette and one red.

"Hey cousin, what's up man?"

When Max didn't turn around, Cody looked back at his teammates to make sure none of them had heard or seen his cousin ignoring him. One of the girls pointed over towards the dugout though, and Max finally seemed to notice

Cody, who stared off into the distant forest, pretending not to see Max and the girls. He saw a figure bolting back and forth in the trees. A vicious wind suddenly picked up, blowing from the woods to the dugout, shooting pine needles and dust at the teenagers, briefly pausing the ballgame as people coughed and rubbed their eyes before play began again without a word. Cody looked around, surprised that no one seemed to think anything different of the raw world.

"Yo cousin, what's up man? Didn't see you there. Hey, you know Sam, and what's your name? Jen?"

"Ew, you're a freshman," Jen said, ignoring that Max had forgotten her name.

"Yeah, hey Max, did you see my at bat? I was wondering if you could give me some pointers on my stance."

"Nah, dude, but I'm sure coach will set you straight. He got me my first All-Star appearance for Varsity in just my sophomore year."

"Yeah, I remember going to your games. You were awesome, but it sucks you tore your ACL in the playoffs, man. You would have had college scouts at all of your games the next year."

"Yeah, whatever, cousin. See you around," Max sneered at Cody and walked away with the girls.

Max and Cody had stopped hanging out after that, and Cody assumed it was because he had embarrassed his cousin in front of the girls, although the real reason was that there was a new, shadier crowd Max had started hanging around after his surgery and his many pain killer refills. Cody wondered whether Max was now in the forest behind the Supercenter. There, littered among the needles, were numerous bodies of human beings who were either high or coming down or dead or somewhere in between. He thought about searching through the tents and tarpaulins and crude shelters calling out Max's name, scanning the zombified faces for fear of being jumped with a knife, or somehow contracting hepatitis or worse from rummaging around through the trash trying to find his missing cousin. Syringes dotted the landscape as if fallen from the pine trees in some kind of unnatural unfertilization of the earth with poison. What he would actually do if he found Max, Cody had no idea, but in his mind, he would become the savior of the older brother he never had, their bond breaking the latter's addiction; they would be together again playing baseball. It was not so.

Disassociation stopped, snapping Cody back into the present as the office door opened towards him, the edge of the wood smacking him in the side of the head, striking his temple and spreading pain in invisible shockwaves throughout his brain – a sensation Cody was familiar with from having been punched there several times throughout his childhood. The manager peeked out from behind the door and then waved Cody inside, sitting at a desk the length of the room itself. He was a fat man who did not seem to care how much his belly flopped over his waistband, his hair combed over a bump on the top of his scalp in much the same manner. What little hair he had left floated on his cone shaped skull in wispy silver strands. He wore his size like an aristocrat proud of his gout, regarding his new charge as if he was livestock. The man giggled at having hurt his new employee, as the pain in Cody's head dulled, bringing the room into focus.

"Well, hello Cody! You're that young man that interviewed the other day, may I call you Cody? Welcome to your new family, Cody."

"Yeah, that's fine thanks," Cody said with a dry throat.

"My name is John Ladder. You can call me Mr. Ladder, but don't try to climb up me," he laughed at his joke and Cody forced a smile.

"So here's the deal, bucko, you will start as an employee here under probation, as we do with all of our new hires. This means that we can terminate you at any time without cause for the first three months. We're going to be watching some films today on why you're joining the best company in the world and how you're going to fit in here. Okay?"

"Okay."

"I'm gonna' need some more excitement from you, young man!"

Cody shifted his gaze away, not out of shyness, but because there was nothing else to look at besides the blotchy pastilles that inhabited Mr. Ladder's skin like leeches left to suck away any signs of life from him. The intrusive thought of picking off and eating these candied legions infected Cody's mind and was reflected in the look on his face.

"Why don't you give us a smile? You know, that's a requirement at all times here in the Supercenter family!"

Mr. Ladder laughed soullessly, stood up and guided Cody towards another closet, beckoning him to sit in the solitary chair and turning on a TV situated on a tiny cart. He popped the unlabeled VHS in and closed the door behind him for the new employee to watch three hours straight of store policy and propaganda, half of which being the evils of unions and unionizing. The actors in the corporate film seemed to be reading their lines from cue cards beyond the camera.

The manager opened the door to Cody being jerked awake but pretended not to notice that he had slept through the video and handed him a blue mesh vest with his name pinned onto it.

"Now it's time to get to work, isn't it?"

Cody walked back out into the blinding lights of the Supercenter and winced, shielding his eyes with his forearm for a moment. He wondered why his new manager kept asking him questions that weren't meant to be answered. As he turned the corner of the aisle, he almost ran right into the hulking frame of a giant man in a trench coat wearing a cowboy hat. The figure stood over a foot higher than Cody, gripping the arm of a small child and holding it aloft so that it was levitating several inches from the ground. Little shrieks emitted from the kid, but no one paid any mind because the Supercenter was constantly filled with such sounds to the point where parents gave up on placating them. Obelisk pupils turned toward Cody, and the great slab of a gravestone face smiled, revealing abnormal cracks in the skin. His face was gray, and he did not seem human, standing in the harsh light of the store with an amber aura around his figure reflecting phosphorescence from short wavelengths to long wavelengths. Cody shivered, his skin rising with goosebumps.

"Pardon me, art thou employed here?"

"What, uh, yeah."

"Indeed. Where shall I depart from thine labyrinth?" The child did not look like he belonged to the strange entity that spoke to Cody but continued its indecipherable shrieks.

"You mean the exit? It's that way, all the way on the other side of the store."

"Verily. Until next time, Godspeed thee," the stone-like face shifted when it winked at Cody, who felt his throat clench with bile bubbling up from his stomach through his chest in a burning sensation. He covered his mouth with his hand and could smell the putrid acid resting on his tongue, then swallowed with difficulty.

The child floated behind the figure like a paraglider trapped in the air attached to a speedboat. Cody stood there wondering whether or not he should stop what he saw occurring or say something to Mr. Ladder about the suspicious character. He reassured himself that there were just strange people who came into the Supercenter and that nothing was wrong. The man spoke as if he was from the Old Testament. He must have been an Amish guy, he thought, but the man was clean shaven, which was not very Amish of him. Cody stewed over this until he heard a shopping cart crash into a shelf and out of his periphery another one of the grotesque approached. A bulbous woman glided up to him riding a motorized scooter and almost running him over to exclaim the word bathroom in a loud declarative statement.

"What?" Cody responded.

"Bathroom!"

"What about it?"

"Where!"

"Where is the bathroom?"

"Yes!"

"Uh, over there."

She skidded away in her struggling machine at a cool five miles per hour, knocking over a plastic barrel of cheese puffs in the process with her pudgy red splotched elbow that stuck out like the wing of a steroid-fed chicken. The seal popped off as the container smacked against the linoleum floor and the orange balls unleashed themselves from their vacuum sealed prison, bouncing in every direction and leaving trails of artificial cheese dust in their wake.

"Jesus fucking Christ," Cody whispered to himself. He got to his hands and knees and began to gather the runaway snacks into the jug, the label staring up at him: it depicted the face of a cartoonish clown transfixed with a devilish grin that was supposed to be advertising. Cody's necklace chain fell out from under his mesh vest, the cross dangling as if Jesus was being hanged from a golden tree uncovered by a corporate uniform overlooking a sea of fiery cheese balls — the hill of Golgotha bearing down on a hellfire of carcinogen infused junk food.

Mr. Ladder peered around the shelves at the end of the aisle, "looks like we're going to have to dock that from your first paycheck! Hurry along now Cody."

Cody could not tell whether Mr. Ladder was joking or not, but finished gathering the cheese puff balls into the barrel, and, not knowing what else to do, screwed the cap back on and placed the jug on the shelf with the rest like nothing happened. His hands were smothered with orange excrement. He walked away while wiping the remains off onto his jeans, leaving brownish streaks along the front of them. His thumb was looking better, still bruised but not swollen anymore.

CCTV security cameras lined the high ceiling rafter at periodic intervals. There were several in the electronics section keeping watch on the expensive consumer goods: televisions, video games, CD's, DVD's, computers, speakers, and, at the end of the aisle, cameras and video recorders. Cody enviously eyed a brand-new silver digital video camera recorder. It was behind glass, though, so he looked at the product number and made a mental note of where it would be in the stocking room. The intercom blared throughout the Supercenter, interrupting tranquil piano music.

"Attention shoppers! If anyone has found a lost child, please report it to customer service. I repeat, a child is lost. Thank you."

This was his opportunity. He made for the nearest set of "employees only" doors, pushed the metal bar to open the door with surprisingly no resistance, and came out into the back of the Supercenter, a space filled with boxes to be stocked later. He searched around until he found the matching product number on a box at the edge of the rack near the open delivery gate and gave a cursory glance around. No one was in sight. No security cameras to be found. No sound except the distant hum of cars driving along the highway.

Cody took the box and walked out of the garage to shamble past the shantytown without giving it a second thought this time. Bodies remained unmoving, hidden beneath blankets and tarpaulins. It was as if those people no longer existed. The only thing that was on his mind was trying to act natural as he quickened his pace to avoid the front parking lot and made his way through the homeless encampment. No one noticed him.

He went home and ran immediately upstairs to open his prize. A brand-new video camera. It was the most expensive thing he had ever owned. Cody smiled a genuine smile for the first time in a long time. The Jersey Devil sat on his bed next to the empty box and instruction manual and Styrofoam and plastic and paper miscellany that was inside. He turned on the camera to the sound of a tinny digital jingle. He pressed record, then took a shot of The Jersey Devil, opening it with his bruised hand and letting the pages cascade one after another, zooming in with the telephoto lens while his eyes adjusted to the parallax of the video versus what he saw in his peripheral vision. Then he closed the book and shut off the video camera.

He was anxious to get to sleep. He and Vinny were going to the Pine Barrens the next day. He was excited about making their Jersey Devil movie. He rolled around in bed back and forth for a while until he felt a sharp pain in his chest that he knew was indigestion, but worried it was the beginning of something much worse. The book beckoned him. A child is lost. Please report to customer service. A child is lost. The pain spread throughout his body until he fell asleep.

Chapter Five

The waning light of the evening was obscured by fog and thickets of oak, cedar, and pine. Cody sat scrunched up in the passenger seat of Vinny's blue pickup truck as they raced through the edge of the Pine Barrens, where the forest meets the ocean, anxious about having no call no showed at his new job. He worried they might find a way to get in touch with his parents and say he was wanted by the police for stealing the video camera. He had left the wrong phone number on his application form and had not signed any official documents yet, so he kept telling himself that he would be okay. It would not matter anyway. He had no plans on returning home anytime soon, let alone the Supercenter. Doing so would turn him into someone else, someone devoid of a meaningful life.

The moon through the mist looked like it was about to fall out of the sky and crash into New Jersey, sinking the land back into the unfathomably deep Atlantic Ocean it originally rose from. Cody felt high. New Jersey was the only state he had ever known, but there were still so many secrets hidden there, especially in its dark, wooded heart where they were now driving. He was both excited and terrified about the future and about where they were going but refused to say anything about it to Vinny. He did not want to seem afraid. All of the crying he had been doing lately made him feel like a coward. A half smoked blunt rocked back and forth in the car ashtray like a pendulum sweeping cremated remains. The Jersey Devil and the video camera sat on the floor between his sneakers.

Cody kept nervously playing with his crucifix necklace, which glinted in the fading light. His sister Emma had given it to him as a birthday gift before she left for college in California. Whenever he felt like his body was going to break gravity and be recklessly sucked into the sky, he sought comfort in the necklace's physical solidity against his chest, fingering the jewelry as if re-grounding himself in reality. Emma was the only one who understood him, and it helped that the west coast time difference meant that she could answer him late at night when no one else was around to talk. He suddenly wanted to text her but was so sunken into himself from a combination of weed and whiskey that he was too anxious to look at his cell phone.

Vinny popped a cassette into the car stereo. Creedence Clearwater Revival's "Born on the Bayou" droned on and on and Cody wondered what a hoodoo was exactly. He imagined an old hound dog chasing an apparition through the woods and pictured a domesticated animal running after the ghost of a wild beast. What would happen if the specter were caught? The fog cleared. Vinny's shoulder length dark hair flowed along with the song and wind in such a way that Cody could only see strands of it through the vague light of the dashboard and lavender dimming sky already pierced by a few stars, like the light was never enough. Like he could only see partially.

"What's up, dude? You been lookin' like you seen a ghost since we left Woodville."

"Nothing. Just kind of high, yah know. Actually, I'm pretty fucked up, man."

"Word. I can't wait to actually get wasted myself. We should kill that first bottle of whiskey and a case of beer by sunrise."

"Yeah man, I can't wait to get wasted in the woods and catch the Jersey Devil on camera, too."

"You're an idiot. I can't believe you broke into the pharmacy for the weed dude, that's crazy. Plus how you went berserk during the fight at the pier. And then you stole that video camera. When did you turn into such a badass?"

"Well, I needed my weed, and those guys pissed me off and I want to catch the Jersey Devil on video," he said matter-of-factly.

Vinny laughed, "you and this Jersey Devil shit all of a sudden."

The bag of weed sat on Cody's lap. He thought about how Vinny had stopped drinking and driving ever since his grandfather was killed by a drunk driver his Senior year of high school, so it was just Cody sipping on the bottle of whiskey and chugging back beer with his feet on the seat and his knees tucked up to his chin.

"Remember that time we had to drag your big ass cousin through the woods because he blacked out chugging a bottle of cheap vodka and when we almost got to the top of the hill,"

"Jose slipped out of our hands and rolled all the way down!" Vinny interrupted Cody.

"And he still didn't even wake up! Man, that shit was hilarious."

Cody and Vinny laughed in sync with one another, as they had since they became friends. It was in the darkness of the very same woods, under an old roadside oak tree, where Vinny's grandfather was found pressed between hunks of metal, his limp body smoldering, having been ejected through glass – his bloodied vessel crumpled like ink-soaked paper – yet somehow with his pack of cigarettes unscathed in his pocket. Cody felt wet inside his boxers, and worried that he pissed himself, but realized he had only accidentally spilt his beer all over his lap. The beer seeped into his jeans, and he felt cold. In a display of vulnerability, Vinny relayed aloud to his friend the shame he felt about drinking and driving so much in the past. Cody half listened.

"You know, when my grandfather was killed, my family fell apart."

"What do you mean? You're super close to your family."

"I definitely try to be, but after he died, my uncle went to prison, my mom became super depressed, my dad won't talk to anyone, and my sister and I started fighting all the time. That's why I feel like I have to stick around and help out."

"Is that why you don't really let me inside your house anymore?"

"Yeah well, I'm just kind of embarrassed, you know?"

"Yeah man, I can relate."

They had most of their equipment stashed in the garage at Vinny's place, so it had not been too difficult to leave in a hurry: preparing a tent, two bottles of whiskey, three cases of beer, a carton of cigarettes, all of Vinny's fishing equipment, two bags of weed, and a whole bunch of snacks and sandwiches. It was a forty-five-minute drive from Woodville to the Winslow Fish and Wildlife Management Area, about half the distance from one end of the Pinelands to the other, traveling south to north up the Parkway along the shoreline, then west down the Black Horse Pike. They had left before sundown. It was cold for the middle of autumn and the smell of burning wood permeated the air. After the fog let up, the final light of the setting sun reached over the pines and onto the road so that Vinny had to wear his aviator sunglasses even though it was almost dark. Both the sun and moon were briefly suspended at the same time on opposite ends of the sky.

Twilight occurred just as they drove over the giant concrete arc that was the Great Egg Harbor Bridge. Cody shifted in his seat so that he could see the orange star sink into the brackish bay water to the west while Vinny's angular face stuck out in the foreground. When the truck made its descent to the bottom of the bridge, what was left of the sun rested for just a moment over Vinny's head, so that it looked to Cody like his friend wore a halo.

"Why the hell are we going to this exact spot anyways?"

"There's a little something there called the Blue Hole. It's a small lake that's always clear down to the bottom and never freezes even in the coldest winter."

"Why Blue Hole? Just because it's pretty good for fishing?"

"Yeah, well there's apparently some weird fish in there that you can't get anywhere else, but also there's something else there."

"Oh, shit dude, is this like the best spot to find the Jersey Devil?"

"Yeah buddy. Blue Hole is the home of the Jersey Devil."

Cody started to crack up. "I thought you didn't believe in that shit! How the hell can you not believe in God, but you believe in the freaking Jersey Devil?"

"First of all, I never said I believed in the Jersey Devil. You did! I'm only doing this shit for you to cheer your sorry ass up. Second of all, the Jersey Devil is more believable than God. Maybe it's some weird animal or a big bat or something. Like Bigfoot. That shit is probably real, I think. Have you ever seen the videos of Bigfoot? They show that shit on that one TV show all the time… what's it called… whatever, I'll believe it if I see it. I think it's possible for the Jersey Devil to be seen. You can't see God. I don't understand how you can believe in all that Christian crap anyway." Vinny grabbed Cody's cross necklace, but Cody pushed his hand away.

"I don't, really. I just wear this because my sister gave it to me as a gift. So you're actually going to help me try to capture some video of the Jersey Devil?"

"Yeah man, maybe we'll run into Jesus chilling with some pineys and the Jersey Devil by the Blue Hole. I always found pineys interesting, man: people who live off the grid in the middle of the woods. That shit is cool."

"You better not be fucking with me, I can't stand you and your bullshitting sometimes," Cody was intoxicated to the point where he could not tell if Vinny was being sarcastic or not, but he began to appreciate him playing along.

"No bullshitting here, Cody. And guess what the Jersey Devil does at the Blue Hole?"

"Does he have sex with magical fish people?"

"No, he swims to the bottom of the lake to eat fish, sure, and if anyone ever jumps in there while he's doing his hunting and disturbs him, he will drag you all the way down and you'll never be seen again."

"Dude, you drank too much cough syrup as a teenager. You're seriously lacking in brain cells."

"Says the idiot who's slurring his words."

At that moment the truck lurched as Vinny stomped on the brakes. A loud thud coincided with a high-pitched screech and Vinny pulled the steering wheel, veering to the right until the vehicle bumped off road and came to a halt beyond the warning tracks but before hitting any of the trees.

"What the fuck was that?"

"I don't know. Shit."

Cody's stomach churned and he felt like his insides were going to explode out of his rear end. He tried to ignore the feeling while stepping out of the car. Blood covered the windshield and the two of them stumbled out of the truck to find a deer twitching behind the pickup on the side of the road. Vinny walked around to the front to inspect the damage while Cody crept back to the dying deer, its eyes solid black balls sunken into its head. Its hooves shook and Cody stood over the animal, frozen by the sight of such violence. Vinny ran over, his mouth agape. The doe slowed its breath and stopped shrieking after a few minutes; the two friends looked at each other speechlessly before pulling the corpse off the road and resting it on the grass.

"We should leave," Vinny said. Cody agreed.

There was minor damage to the truck: a crack in the windshield and the sideview mirror taken off, but still dangling from the side of the car by wires. Cody pulled a water bottle from his backpack and emptied it onto the glass, then wiped off the blood with his coat sleeve. They got back in, and Vinny sped off.

"You're a fucking moron. Why would you wipe off the blood with your jacket sleeve? I could have just sprayed it off with my windshield wipers. Now you look like you murdered someone."

"I don't know man, I'm pretty drunk and high," Cody laughed a nervous laugh. The road was spinning in front of him.

The drive into the dark and the reemerging fog aroused a primal fear. Something about swooping into grayness that felt like being swept up into a void. Unknown birds screaming in their ancient dinosaur tongues and a sharp pang in the ribs reacting to visceral awareness that can only be drowned out by digital ephemera.

Cody played a video game on his mobile phone to try to distract himself from haunting anxiety. Big blocks shooting little blocks at other big blocks in a supposed vacuum of projected space and scrolling signifying the passage of time. Vinny turned off the Parkway and drove inland into the heart of the forest. True darkness fell around them as they sped along the desolate tree lined highway toward the place the Jersey Devil was supposed to inhabit. Still playing his video game, Cody sensed the book between his feet expanding like a claw and pressing against him. Unable to ignore it, his breathing quickened until it became uncontrollable, all sense of reality collapsing as his combination of inebriation and disassociation reached an apex. He was panicking but trying not to show it to Vinny. Deer blood coagulated on his jacket, transforming from a sticky liquid to a thick paste to a hardened cake. He tried to brush the solidified blood off but only bits of flakes fell from him.

"Fucking stop getting that shit all over my car, dude," Vinny implored. They were nearing the turn onto the dirt road that led towards the campsite.

"You ever feel like you're going to die, man?" Cody stared beyond Vinny's blurry figure.

"Yeah, every time I smoke an entire blunt to my fucking face and drink a half of a bottle of whiskey."

"You do?" The world was spinning.

"No, Cody, I don't fucking do that. You just did that, which is why you're so fucked up right now. You're one hundred and twenty pounds soaking wet, that amount of shit would kill a kid less stubborn than you. Just close your eyes. You're going to have a massive hangover tomorrow morning, but all you have to do is smoke a little bit of weed and drink some beer when you wake up. Everything is going to be fine, man. We're almost there."

The dilapidated truck creaked its way off the paved road and onto a dirt track, its tires stumbling over old soggy boughs until it veered around a bend where there used to be a campsite, the remains of which were now a wooden outhouse and fire pit situated by the quarry lake with a two-hundred-year-old brick furnace towering over the placid water. This was one of the countless clearings of sand for which the Pine Barrens are named. Vinny turned off the ignition and swiveled toward Cody with a smirk and eyebrows raised. The engine purred to a halt.

"We're here."

Silence enveloped them as Vinny slammed the door and Cody tumbled out of the pickup. Gradually, however, as the sound of the engine left their consciousness, this initial quiet faded, as they became aware of the steady hum of various insects chirping. Vinny turned a flashlight on and scanned the area with its wide light. A twenty-foot-high brick tower, roughly four people in width loomed over them, the ancient foundry remaining impressively erect while other structures had fallen and disintegrated around it. Once used to smelt bog iron, its forgotten forge had created cannonballs for revolutionaries and pirates to shoot at the great hulking bodies of British warships. Cody and Vinny set up their tent. Cody, who was too drunk to be of much help, crashed down onto his sleeping bag as soon as Vinny laid it out for him, and he slept a dreamless sleep.

Chapter Six

When Cody finally woke up, he lay before the ancient iron forge, a structure of which he was uncertain of its purpose, but then he recalled a passage of the Jersey Devil describing abandoned furnaces in the Pine Barrens. He grabbed his head, moaning because of a piercing headache. Vinny sat on the monument's mouth, its individually crumbling bricks doing nothing to lessen the sense of its inviolable solidity, then hopped off his old seat and stood over his friend. Cody blearily eyed a haggard and lanky form who looked like Prometheus teleported through time inspecting an alien world, a Neanderthal flung too far into the future, bearing witness to the technological ruins of a lost civilization. Vinny let out a sigh, then fished out one of the bags. Indica dominant. Perfect for the occasion. They needed to relax and smoke off the hangover.

"Holy shit."

"What's wrong?"

"Vin, I just had the weirdest déjà vu."

"Okay, so what?"

"Like I've seen and felt this moment before, of us waking up together in this strange forest, but our bodies were all changed. Like we were completely covered in hair. And that when I had this experience originally, I thought that we had died, but we didn't. We're reborn. I saw this the last time we ever hung out at the Hamilton Mall."

"Ah yes, the good old days, when we first tried cigarettes and alcohol and weed and chased emo girls."

"Don't you understand what I'm saying? This forest, this is it, it's where we've been headed our whole lives," Cody turned around suddenly and gazed off at a crow squawking on a jagged branch nearby them.

"You and your fucking déjà vu acting like you're some kind of psychic."

Cody frowned at his friend, "shut up and roll the blunt, Vin."

"No, but you're right. I feel different too. I can't explain it. Maybe it's the Jersey Devil. He must have been in our dreams last night."

"Yeah, right," Cody rolled his eyes.

"I mean just look at that water. It's so blue and magical."

"That's funny dude, it's practically red."

"What? You have to be joking! It's super clear. That's how I'll be able to catch so much fish, man. I can see right through the water."

"I can't tell if you're being sarcastic or not. The water literally looks like blood to me."

"Wait, are you fucking with me?"

"No, I thought you were fucking with me."

"Get your eyes checked bro, maybe you're color blind."

"That's funny, that's what I told your sister…"

"Man, how many times do I have to tell you to shut the fuck up about my sister?"

"Okay, man, I'm sorry. Let's just get high and forget about it."

The hard, cheap cigar broke open easily between Vinny's fingers. He cracked the inner shell after soaking the outer leaf with his tongue, unwrapping it deftly, then tossed the stale tobacco to the side, which blew in clumps into the woods. Vinny opened the grinder and distributed broken down buds evenly throughout the brown sleeve then unscrewed the bottom of the device to sprinkle the fine powder known as kief, the potent part extracted to make hash. Vinny and Cody had an understanding that they would only use this precious substance in times of real need. This was a time of need.

"Oh, so we're starting the day off right, huh?" Cody asked with a smile.

"Yeah buddy, need to take the edge off, especially since I'm feeling a flare up coming on…"

"A what?"

"Remember how I told you that I have Lupus? That's why I get these rashes on my face, and sometimes I get flare ups of pain in my joints, like my knees or elbows. Kind of like arthritis. It hurts like a bitch," Cody understood for the first time why there were red splotches on his friend's face.

"I thought you were joking about having a werewolf disease. I didn't know that Lupus was an actual thing."

"It's not a werewolf disease, dude. It's a real disease that like, fucks up your immune system and shit."

"Aren't you a bit young to have some arthritis type shit?"

"You don't gotta' be old. The shit got so painful that my doctor finally believed me that something was wrong for real."

"Is there a cure?"

"Nah man, but smoking weed helps."

Vinny rolled the blunt, wrapping the wet tobacco leaf around it just tight enough. He lit his green lighter and dragged the yellow flame gently all along the outside of the blunt in order to dry and strengthen it. Then he placed the blunt between Cody's lips and burned the other end for a solid few seconds until a cloud of cobalt smoke grew between them and was cleared by coughing. The air filled with the smell of tropical flowers and fruit foreign to the northeastern swamp forest they now disturbed with their presence. They puffed on and passed the blunt back and forth, listening to the sound of birds and enjoying the fresh, pine scented air. Cody took his sneakers and socks off and dug his toes into the cool sand.

"Man, I'm glad I didn't get shipped off to Iraq. But I'm still bored as fuck, and wanna' get the hell out of my parent's house for good. Maybe if we make this movie, I can use it to submit like a portfolio to art school and get into film making."

"Yeah dude, I don't want to shit on your dreams all the time, I know I bust your balls a lot, but joining the Army, especially to go fight in Iraq, was a dumb idea. This Jersey Devil shit is stupid too, but at least it won't get you killed."

Cody laughed, then coughed out smoke. Trails of refuse strewn about. Trash littered the landscape even in the wilderness. The flotsam of a decadent civilization. A paper facsimile of a king's crown from a fast-food restaurant rotting in the grass. A dragonfly landed upon the shoddy golden diadem, buzzing softly. The black insect spread its rainbow-colored wings in a yawning motion. On the shore of the quarry lake washed up detritus defiled nature. If the Jersey Devil lived here, it was not evident. Vinny caught a carp, a light gleamed in his eye because he was finally proud of a catch, and he showed Cody how to filet a fish. He pronounced it flay. Cody practiced filming by shooting Vinny cutting open his catch, zooming in on the purple guts oozing from the knife wound and blood shining in the sun. He realized only at that moment that he could not charge the camera battery out in the woods, not having planned ahead, so he stopped recording to conserve the energy as much as possible. While Vinny was fishing, Cody cracked The Jersey Devil open to a random passage in the middle. He had not read much of it in a few days and wanted to get to a part that had featured the legendary creature more prominently.

She was healthy again, reinvigorated, the color back in her cheeks. When she woke from her coma there was no one else around. Her bed was surrounded by a circle of ash. Where were her daughters? She had remembered the excruciating pain of giving birth and nothing else. Jane rose wearily from her stained blankets and searched the pantry for anything to eat. She found some stale bread and a clay jar full of cider and dipped the crust in to soften it and devoured the food then chugged the sour alcohol. The woman then struggled into her clothes. Feeling a little drunk and not used to using her legs, she stumbled out of the cabin into the blaring sunlight.

Jane walked into town to face the contemptuous stares of her neighbors. A shining white building loomed over the square; its steeple adorned with a plain cross. It was taller than all of the other structures, which were wooden and unpainted. The church had a foundation of stone, also painted white, and the white paint was fresh. An old, bearded man turned to look at her while he touched up some of the wall with a brush. Lifting her dress while stepping up the stairs, Jane pushed the doors open with a shove of her shoulder and marched right through the vestibule and into the sanctuary. Dark wood throughout the room. No ornaments, nothing to adorn the altar. An austere place of worship.

The pastor immediately stopped reading the bible, rising from his chair, his spectacles falling off of his face. Jane approached him until they were inches away from each other and demanded to know the whereabouts of her daughters. "Somewhere safe, away from the Mother of the Devil," sneered the puritan. No longer fearing his threats of eternal damnation, she spit at his feet in defiance. They heard a screech.

Glass crashed and a ball of darkness bounded into the sanctum. The shape unraveled in the air to reveal a demon floating above the two astonished humans staring up at certain doom. The beast lunged toward the holy man and opened its mouth to enclose the circumference of his head. Its teeth scraped his skin off the face and sank deeper into the back starting at the nape of his neck until it tore into flesh and scalped the pastor so deeply that his brains protruded from the top of his skull in ribbons while he howled in incomprehensible agony. Then there was silence.

Jane backed away. The creature swallowed what it had bitten off, tilted its triangular, hairy face at her while emitting a wet, reptilian clicking sound; there was a countenance of recognition, the beast smirking with gore dripping from its mouth. She almost expected that it would speak to her. The Jersey Devil held the corpse up by its claws so that the man's decapitated body stood as if it was still alive. The demon gnashed and chomped through bone while staring at Jane and intermittently smiling at her, like a wolf pup looking at its mother while feasting on freshly caught meat, then it unclutched its grasp, launching itself upwards and bursting through the ceiling of the church, flying off with a howl. The clergyman's headless corpse crumpled to the floor. Jane ran outside covered in the pastor's blood in a panic, passing the stunned townspeople, to the first horse she found. She untied the nervous mare and pulled herself up onto the saddle to ride away from Woodville for the final time before anyone could stop her.

"That's fucking cool," Cody said.

"What?" Vinny looked over while leaning back with his fishing rod.

"Nothin', I just got to this part where the Jersey Devil bites this priest's head off."

"Oh, well that actually sounds pretty interesting," Vinny said, "maybe you can read some of the book out loud at the campfire tonight. You should practice first though, you probably forgot how to read well since we haven't been in school for so long."

"Very funny," Cody replied without laughing. He kept reading.

Jane rode the horse north through fields, looking behind her constantly to make sure no one was following her, and keeping off the road until she got to the forest where she had made her trip to try to stop the pregnancy six months before. She did not know where else to go, having never traveled farther than that in her entire adult life. Weènchipahkihëlèxkwe's wigwam was burned down by the militiamen, but perhaps she rebuilt it after the other Lenape fended off the white men. The sand path led to the creek where Weènchipahkihëlèxkwe once lived, but there was nothing there. Just as she lost all hope, she heard a bird call and the hairs on the back of her neck stood. She turned around to see a man with dark hair who was wearing a deerskin breechcloth and a colorful bandolier pointing a musket at her. "Aimalàxàmuk," he said.

Weènchipahkihëlèxkwe crept up behind the man and lowered his gun while whispering in his ear. "What are you doing here?" She asked Jane. "I'm sorry, I know the last time I came they burned your house down, but I swear no one followed me this time." Weènchipahkihëlèxkwe looked incredulous and then slowly her face changed to be more sympathetic. "Did you give birth?" She asked. "Yes, it was a demon," Jane replied. Weènchipahkihëlèxkwe motioned for Jane to follow them, and she got off the horse, patted it on its behind to be free, and walked into the copse of trees.

He closed the book and took a swig from a beer. They spent the day sharing blunts and drinking beers to try to decompress from the previous night. Cody had thrown up profusely that morning from all he had drank the night before, even spitting up blood after excessive dry heaving. The vomit had hardened into the sugar sand overnight. It was Vinny's intention to go back home, but not Cody's. He did not know if anyone cared about his absence. Even though Cody did not want to leave, he did not feel entirely comfortable with staying either.

The forest spoke to him. He thought it was how high he was at first, and then changed his mind. Something was different about this place. He could hear voices in the distance. The leaves of many of the trees were sharp needles that could break skin and shed blood. Animal noises sounded like human beings. The earth itself was sand, something Cody was used to from his many beach trips growing up, but this sand was different. Instead of it being solid ground, the sand would make you sink down to your ankles. It was not quite quicksand, which Cody was used to seeing in the movies, but something close to it. A seagull cried a skin tingling cry. He kept chewing on his fingernails and would often wander about twenty yards away to relieve his bowels. His diarrhea was frequent, but they had prepared well for the trip and brought plenty of toilet paper.

Their cell phones could not get service in the forest. Sometimes there would be one or two bars on the signal of their phones, but they still would not work, and other times the signal would come up empty. During the day they had the energy to set up camp around the tent in a clearing in the woods about forty yards away from the old truck, settling in a small patch of grass with just a slight canopy of pine needles covering the sky like giant translucent green spider webs. When evening came the two grilled hot dogs while finishing the bottle of whiskey and case of beer between them. Before they knew it, they were both fast asleep inside the tent before the moon had risen. Strange dreams crept into their minds in the night.

A roustabout runt and cobbler scion adrift upon an inland sea of sand. A fisherman perched upon a terrestrial wound where purity escapes the aquifer at an oasis never meant for fishing. A filmmaker capturing a mythical beast. A desert forest encompassing both outer and inner worlds. A demon circumscribing the campsite. A cat corpse festering in a cardboard box, the feeling that one has done this before but with a different outcome of lifting the fragile cage and the dead feline staring up with living eyes. A revelation of both truths existing. A quantum superposition.

Cody poked his head outside of the tent because he could hear some movement. A black man wearing a gray suit and a leather apron sat at their camp. He was boiling water at their fire, and the flames were blue. Cody watched the man place herbs in the pot and stir the liquid around. The frock he wore became translucent as it touched the pot. Cody asked him who he was, but did not speak with his mouth, making him wonder whether he was dreaming or not, and when the man responded to him without speaking as well, he could tell that it was not a living person. He was immobilized by the apparition but thought-asked a question.

"Hello. Who are you?"

"My name is Doctor James Still," he said.

"I'm Cody, what are you doing?"

"I hope you don't mind me using your campfire. I'm making a tincture of lobelia."

"What's that?"

"It's a medicine for people with asthma. There's a little boy down yonder who'll be needing it. Gonna' be a big fire."

"So, is it like a magical potion?"

"No," the doctor chuckled, "it's a natural medicine."

"Oh, okay. Well, are you aware of any magic, or supernatural stuff in the woods? Like, say, the Jersey Devil?"

The doctor frowned. "No, I'm not aware of any such thing. I have studied botany, the laws of nature, and I am aware of the earth's beneficial properties through many years of study."

"Oh, cool, where did you go to school?"

"Schools are not necessary to learn," he told Cody.

"Yeah, I agree," Cody said, and then put his hand to his forehead, feeling a headache coming along.

"Here, drink this," the doctor insisted, and poured what was in his hip flask into a cup for Cody and offered it to him. Cody was expecting it to be some kind of medicine, and he felt a comforting coolness spread throughout his chest after having a draft.

"What's this?" Cody asked.

"It's fresh spring water. You shouldn't drink so much alcohol, you know."

Cody laughed, then took a sip from his cup, "yeah, I know. Sometimes I feel like I'm going to die, and I'm afraid. Other times I feel like life won't end, but I want it to end. I feel like I'm just stuck being a nobody. That's why I came out into the woods to look for the Jersey Devil."

The doctor shook his head when Cody mentioned the Jersey Devil. "I don't believe in magic. I believe in God and nature."

Cody was worried that he had said the wrong thing. "I found a book about the Jersey Devil. I thought you might know something about it."

The doctor continued to work on crafting the medicine in silence until he looked at Cody a final time and then gazed up at the stars. "I wrote a book. You should read it sometime. It's the story of my life. There's a part of it that you might find useful where I wrote this: The laws of nature are justly executed. The rich, the poor, the learned, the unlearned, the king who rules a nation, or the beggar upon the wayside, all meet on the common level of humanity at the grave," he said while scrutinizing the sky.

Cody looked at the man from another time as the pine trees rustled quietly. He closed his eyes to think of a response while finishing his drink. When he peeked up from his cup, the man was gone.

Cody was surprised that he still felt hungover when he woke up. His head throbbed and his mouth was dry. Vinny was already outside boiling water for instant oatmeal in the same pot that the doctor had used in his dream. He swore at first that he saw strange footprints in the sand, but when he moved closer, the marks were not discernible.

"Man, I had the craziest dreams last night."

"Yeah?"

"Yeah, the first one I can't really describe. There was like this dead cat inside this cardboard box. It was weird. The second one was really cool though, there was a doctor cooking something at our camp; he looked like he was dressed like from the 19th century or something, like he was a ghost, and then he had me drink some water."

"Was it some magical bullshit?"

"Nah, there was no magic. He just gave me regular water; I thought it would cure my hangover when I woke up, but it didn't. I feel like shit."

"You had a dream about a ghost of a guy from two hundred years ago giving you water and you thought it would cure your hangover in real life when you woke up?"

"Yeah."

"I'm surprised nothing crazier happened in your dreams. You've been believing more and more in this Jersey Devil bullshit to the point where I'd expect you to actually believe in supernatural shit."

"I thought you said the Jersey Devil could be possible?"

"Yeah, well, I was just joking around; it's not possible. There's such a thing called science," Vinny laughed.

"Why is it so impossible for you to believe that the Jersey Devil could be real?"

"Because it's fucking not dude. I was just playing along with believing the Jersey Devil could be real on the drive up here because you were so fucked up and I was just messing with you. Now I think you're losing your fucking mind."

Embarrassed, Cody waved off Vinny's response and then walked away to go sit on a fallen pine tree trunk and read his book where his friend was not looking, though only consuming brief passages. He sipped on a beer for breakfast.

The Jersey Devil was here, somewhere, the book said. It mentioned the Blue Hole as the demon's hiding place. That the Jersey Devil would drag unwitting victims down to the bottom of the pond. He looked around, besides the Blue Hole, all he could see were pine trees and sand. The water was still. In the distance, a dog barked three times. Cody closed his book and stood up to try to see where the noise was coming from, then the barking resumed, only closer, until it was nearby. He turned his head toward where the pine trees sloped up a hill. At the top of the barrow a dog stood looking down at him. It was a snarling, short-haired black lab. The dog slapped its paws against the sand and barked at him once more. Cody froze. He eyed a big stick between the animal and him. The dog barked again and turned its head back, then began wagging its tail. A little girl with blonde pigtails who was wearing a pink dress emerged behind the dog, scratching it behind the ears. Cody called out hello to the golden-haired girl, who waved at him, then turned and skipped through the trees while the black dog pranced along with her.

Cody returned to camp to find Vinny with a blunt hanging out of his mouth staring off down a trail that they had not yet walked down. Without so much as a word between them, they ventured away from the Blue Hole and into the depths of the forest. Cody felt like they were both in a trance. He wanted to tell Vinny about the little blonde girl and the black dog that he saw but could not find the words to speak.

They trekked uphill for almost an hour while sharing the blunt between them. Cody became hungry enough that he felt like he could faint. He lit a cigarette to stem the hunger and kept walking silently beside his friend while feeling light-headed. At first the sandy path was lined with sassafras, pitcher-plants, and skunk cabbage, then all of the vegetation except for pitch pine trees disappeared, and the smaller plants were replaced by enigmatic, multi-colored cairns. The stones were stacked neatly on top of one another and were painted bright colors: yellow, green, blue, and purple. Dark red sap dripped down the trunks of the trees like they were bleeding.

At the end of the trail was an escarpment that was home to an unnatural cave. The deteriorating entryway looked like it was carved into rock by a blast of dynamite. Cody and Vinny shared a glance with each other and then turned on their flashlights to walk inside. The walls were made of brick that had been overcome by slime. It did not take long until they reached the end, where they heard a steady drip. Vinny shone his light upon the carcass of a large black dog splayed upon an iron patera with a hole at the bottom that had relieved its sacrificial contents of blood to form a crimson pentagram on the engraved rock surrounding it. Cody pointed his video camera at the gruesome, illuminated sight. The blood was fresh. He both clenched his muscles and quivered, feeling a thrill in the terror that was laid out before them.

"Let's get the fuck out of here," Vinny whispered. Cody agreed, and they ran out of the tunnel back toward camp, stumbling downhill, while Cody still had the camera rolling, the video depicting their trail, bouncing senselessly along the path, an upside-down image of pine trees with their bushy bottoms scraping the sky. They arrived back at camp and dove into their tent, gasping for air and grabbing for beers in the cooler.

"Why would anyone do that?" Vinny was panting as he sincerely asked Cody the question.

"You already know the answer. I didn't want to tell you I told you so, but…"

"I was just joking around with you about the Jersey Devil man, but now I'm starting to think that something fucked up is out there. Not like supernatural shit, but some Satanists or something, some kind of brujeria. There's gotta' be like, some pineys out here that worship Satan."

"I know, I started feeling that too after finding the book and coming here. Dude, I saw that same fucking dog right after I went off to go read alone. It was with this little blonde girl. I wanted to tell you about it after it happened, but I didn't for some reason. Maybe the little girl is like a demon or like a ghost or something. This shit is fucking freaky." They both kept panting with their hands on their knees.

"Yeah, like I said, I don't know about any of that supernatural shit man, but there's definitely some fucked up people out here doing bad stuff. Like, Satanists or cultists or whatever. Brujeria."

"What's that?"

"Witchcraft."

"Yeah dude, at the very least. Do you think the little golden-haired girl sacrificed the dog to the Jersey Devil or something?" Cody sincerely asked.

"No, dude… or maybe? I don't fucking know, man the shit is just weird and it's creeping me out. Whoever did it is fucked up in the head."

"You're right. I don't think the little girl could have done that… I hope she's all right. Should we go look for her and make sure she's okay?"

"What? No man, what the fuck is wrong with you?"

"Hey, I just want to make sure there isn't some little kid wandering around lost in the forest with fucking dog killers wandering around. It was her fucking dog. The Satanists, or whatever they were, probably kidnapped the little girl!"

"Cody, your imagination has gotten out of hand. Let's just take it easy."

"Fine. Let's have some drinks and eat and chill for a bit before going too far from camp again."

"I'm about to drive the fuck back to Woodville and leave your ass out here all alone if you keep trying to make us wander off again."

"Hell no. You wouldn't do that… look man, you win, we don't have to leave camp again. We can fish and do whatever you want, let's just hang out here at least for another day."

"All right bud, but if anything else crazy happens, I'm driving us the fuck home."

The waning moon rose over the Pine Barrens and reached through the trees with its strong light into the tangled branch canvass sheltering them. They ate a meal of bologna sandwiches and drank beers by the campfire. Vinny opened another bottle of whiskey, and they took turns passing it back and forth slugging shots until they could not remember ever being afraid, both falling into a heavy, dreamless sleep. In the morning a light drizzle woke them up. They opened up the tent and looked around at the misty woods, chugging water bottles and smoking cigarettes in the cold. A fog hugged the water of the Blue Hole. A crow cawed repeatedly.

"The Blue Hole sucks," Vinny said.

"Yeah, it's kind of like a murky ass pond, nothing special. But I thought you thought it was like a magical clear blue?"

"I was just fucking with you dude."

"Oh, sometimes when I'm high I can't tell if you're joking or not."

"My bad, man. But seriously, there's no fucking good fish in there. I only caught that one carp. Let's head down that ways' a bit, where there's a bigger lake and we can find better luck."

"You sure you're not afraid?"

"Of what?"

"Of the shit that we ran into yesterday? I'm serious, that dead dog got me spooked, for real. I thought you said you didn't want to wander off again."

"Dude, it was probably just some hillbilly ass teenage pineys doing that shit. We were all freaked out because we were super high. I'm gonna' cut back on smoking weed. That new shit my cousin got is too strong."

Cody laughed, "yeah, sure. Okay buddy."

They made off with their fishing gear away from the Blue Hole and walked along a sandy path to find a lake shoreline in a deeper part of the woods, in the opposite direction of the cave where they found the dead dog. The fog was thick enough that they could not see the other edge of the lake. Vinny nodded at the water in approval and unloaded his gear. It was quick work finding the first catch, but their hot dog bait attracted just a few small fish. They built a fire by the shore and shoved sticks through the fish, roasting them over the flames until the gaping mouths were burning from purple to black. Cody pulled some scales off of one and tried to pick it apart so he could eat what little seared flesh he was able to tear off, to no avail, instead he chucked the bones back into the water that ebbed toward the beach. They opened a couple of bags of potato chips. Their fingers were sticky with beer and crumbs latched onto their skin. Cody's hand was no longer sore or swollen, but when he moved his thumb, it clicked with a sharp pain. It popped out of place inwardly and he gasped, prompting Vinny to ask if he was okay. He said he was fine and popped it back into place.

Vinny went back to fishing and for a while was only able to catch some pirate perches that he threw back, then he became excited when he pulled up a two-foot-long chain pickerel. Cody grew bored with the fishing, only feigning interest so that his friend would decide to stay and agree to help with making the film, pretending to hunt for the Jersey Devil later that night. Maybe he could get him drunk so that he would have the courage to go back out again to that same cave they had run away from even after the incident, he thought.

"Here dude, have another beer and a shot," Cody handed the whiskey bottle to Vinny and cracked a can open for him.

"Yeah, sure." Vinny slugged the whiskey and sipped the beer, tottering by the water with his line lax.

"So you know I've been telling yah, I got this plan where we can fake an attack in the darkness of night with the video camera. There's this nighttime mode on the camera that looks cool because it's green. It doesn't work really well but with flashlights I think it could be better. We can set up a false attack on ourselves and act like we are getting chased by a monster in the woods with the camera shaking. Like what happened yesterday, and we can add that to the video that I took."

"Uh huh," Vinny nodded, spacing out while sitting up fishing and Cody was talking.

"So I was thinking we could go back to the sacrificed dog and take it and use it as the Jersey Devil, people won't be able to tell because it'll be blurry, like hide it in some bushes or something, or like light it on fire in the old furnace, and make it look like a supernatural effect or something.

"Dude, I don't know, that sounds dumb," Vinny said, drowsily.

"Well it was cool how the weird ending was done in the found footage witch project movie thing, and we could throw in some humor in ours."

"How would the fuckin' plot and the dialogue go if we haven't written any of it down?" Vinny asked.

"We could just wing it man, our conversations are interesting enough that people would want to watch."

Vinny rolled his eyes, "yeah sure, I'll play along, but I'm not gonna' fuckin' go nowhere near that damn cave again." He gave up fishing, dropping his rod as he stumbled to the log as they sat back around the fire and drank beers. Vinny yawned. "I'm bored. Why don't you read a lil' of that Jersey Devil book out loud while we smoke some more weed. Cody could tell that Vinny was almost at his limit with alcohol intake. He just hoped Vinny would be able to make it back to their campsite without too much trouble. Vinny scratched at his beard while slightly swaying with his eyes half open.

"Okay cool," Cody said, as he opened the book to a new chapter in the middle and began to excitedly read aloud.

The world's newest incarnation of the devil soared over the Pine Barrens, spinning and flipping in the air, performing somersaults in apparent joy for having been gifted a newfound freedom. For far too many centuries it had languished in the smoky depths of hell, feeding off the souls of the damned. It longed for the sweeter taste of the living. Blackish drool slopped from its jaw. It knew it had to kill humans in order to survive in this plane of existence. Sickened, however, by the overwhelmingly pure scent of pine, the demon flew west, darting high over the forest to avoid smelling the trees, speedily reaching the Delaware River. It hovered for a time over the water, watching for the lights of colonial Philadelphia, wanting to wreak havoc upon the city, but understanding that it had to shed the blood of a certain man who was farther west.

The demon sniffed the air and looked towards outer space. Untethered from gravity, the full moon rose quickly over the ocean and close to the earth. Its silver light reflected off of the floating demon's leathery skin. It did not look at the scarred lunar surface but somewhere else. Somewhere beyond. Mars was on the other end of the heavens, towards the west. The sky's bright red dot pierced the darkness. The beast stared at the planet with its otherworldly eyes, transfixed by the aura of Mars. It sought to transform this world into an anareta of its own —

"What's that word?" Vinny asked.

"Anareta?" Cody looked up from the book and shrugged his shoulders.

"What does that mean?"

"I don't know man, you're the nerd I thought you'd have an idea."

"Nah man, I got nothin'. Go on…"

It sought to transform this world into an anareta of its own, a barren ball of desolation where nothing but destruction and ultimately death thrived. The wooden and brick settlement that was the nascent colonial city below had to await its doom. The citizens of Philadelphia knew nothing of love. The beast laughed in the air, and then took off into the night towards the coming battle.

The Battle of the Monongahela began with a British salvo of musket fire into a patch of shrubs that overlooked a highway they had just built called Braddock's Road. Lieutenant Colonel Thomas Gage ordered his men to maintain their formation and steadily advance upon the enemy in spite of not being able to see them for more than periodic instances when the Indians and French popped out behind their cover to fire down at the British. The enemy were fewer in number, but they had the high ground. French and Indians used trees as cover while shooting at will. Every other man in the British column crumpled over and morale buckled, until the commanding officers ordered a retreat. Chaos ensued, and any remaining discipline eroded as the sight of war painted Indians and grizzled French marines emerging from their cover and whooping loudly, the awful sound of their battle cries, instilled panic in the soldiers.

Titan Leeds marched along with the other American militiamen bringing up the rear of the advance guard British soldiers. They sneered at their allies who were attempting to fight in the standard European style of warfare. It was time to show the English how wars were fought in the New World. Taking up position behind trees on the side of the road, they waited for the enemy to come upon the retreating redcoats. Colonel George Washington led the ambush, only firing upon the enemy when they had advanced within close range. The first volley was deadly for a dozen of the enemy, but the remaining Indians disappeared as soon as they had arrived. Titan Leeds watched as Colonel Washington and Lieutenant Colonel Thomas Gage convened about how to follow up after the attack. What they did not know was that a supernatural entity was watching them, its bloodlust curdling in the darkness of the night while floating above the paused battle. The officers agreed to advance with the regulars on the road and the militia flanking through the woods. Titan Leeds crouch-ran alongside Colonel Washington until they could hear voices speaking low in French only a few yards from them, a voice yelled "Avancez sur l'ennemi!"

Cody butchered the French pronunciation and Vinny laughed in response. "Keep going," Vinny said, "it's getting good." Cody continued, chuckling.

Figures charged from the ridge. Torches danced in the night. Scalps were nailed to the trees along the hillside. Blood dripped down bark and shined in the starlight. The Jersey Devil swooped down and ripped the heads off several of the soldiers, French and British alike. The American militiamen saw the demon feasting as it zoomed back and forth between scurrying men, cries of "Indian demon" echoed through the forest. The Jersey Devil descended upon Titan Leeds as he leaned against a tree for cover. It pinned him against the trunk and swiped off his head from the neck with its claws, eating his face then piercing his scalp into the bark. Colonel Washington drew his sword and charged at the creature, swinging his saber at the beast. The demon flew around in a circle, doing cartwheels in the air as Colonel Washington chopped and stabbed wildly at the beast, but in an instant, it was gone, flying off with a screech into the night. The body of what was once Titan Leeds crumpled over in a heap of wet flesh. The top of his skull stayed pierced into the trunk of the tree, the blood dripping down onto his body.

"Wow, that was intense. George Washington fighting the Jersey Devil!" Vinny laughed, "no wonder you wanted to come out here."

"Yeah man, it's a good book."

"Who's Titan Leeds? And why did the Jersey Devil want to kill him specifically?"

"He was the piece of shit husband of the woman who gave birth to the Jersey Devil. He beat her up and forced her to have thirteen kids."

"Oh, word, so is the Jersey Devil actually the good guy?"

"Uh, I don't know. No, I don't think so."

A rustling of pine needles and sand. Because of the drinking and the storytelling, Cody and Vinny did not notice anyone approaching from the trail. They suddenly turned to look in alarm at a little boy standing in front of them. A boy in gray sweatpants, dirty sneakers, and an oversized hoodie had walked up to their camp in silence and stared at them with his tiny fingers grasping a rifle almost the length of his body. His eyes shape shifted colors: first they were a soft hazel, when he turned his cheek, they looked green, and when he moved his chin back to them, they were brown, his sharp cheekbones giving him a gaunt, undernourished look. The child held the old hunting rifle with the kind of unknowing grace that only small boys hold guns.

"Hi, what's your names?"

"Oh, uh, I'm Cody, and this here is Vinny."

"Whatcha' readin' there?"

Vinny shot Cody a concerned glance. Two young women approached several yards behind, seeming unconcerned that the little boy was conversing with strange looking young men drinking beer and cooking fresh caught fish like castaways stranded on a desert island.

"Do ya'll got a banged up truck parked a ways back there?" The tall one said this as if she was inquiring about a car that was double parked in the city, a bit of annoyance in her tone.

"Who are you?" Vinny interjected before Cody could reveal more information.

"I asked you a question first, boy," the tall one exclaimed. She was physically fit, green eyed, with golden rings around her pupils that looked like sunflowers set against a field, raven black straight hair with bangs, pale with freckles, shorter than Vinny but taller than Cody.

"Do I look like a fucking boy to you?" Vinny was apoplectic. His face was filled with red splotches.

"Vinny, stop. Don't curse around the kid," Cody placed his hand on his friend's arm.

"Yeah it's a kid with a fucking gun."

The boy laughed, "it's cool. I'm eleven, so I've heard it all before. That's my sister Sara. She's just worried because there's been some weird stuff happening in the woods lately."

"And I'm Erica, nice to meet you two," Erica was just about Cody's height with blonde hair and brown eyes like him. She was the younger of the two girls, in her mid-teens, and smiled innocently yet warily at them with her wan face.

Sara was carrying a rucksack, and a large rifle was slung across her back, her long ponytail resting across the shiny wooden hilt at her waist. She wore camouflage pants with a matching jacket and old black boots. All three of them wore orange vests over their camouflage. Erica's face was round and unblemished, she was the only one of the five who wore makeup, her hair also pulled back, and she donned a similar but newer camouflage outfit and was carrying a rifle as well. She offered her hand to both of them and shook them as if they were about to sit down for an interview in an office lobby instead of the desolate forest and lonesome lake that was set before them.

"You two must have gotten in an accident or something. Want me to call a tow truck for you?" Erica was the congenial one.

"No, no it's just a beat up old truck, it still runs fine," Vinny stood up nervously when he replied. He seemed to regret getting so angry with the child. Sara looked suspiciously at him.

"Is there something wrong? You've got dried blood all over your coat," Sara stood pointing at Cody with her boots planted firmly in the dirt and her crossed arms resting below her ample chest, tilting her right wrist to point in a lackadaisical accusation.

Vinny answered after a beat because Cody seemed unable to speak, "everything is fine. Yeah, we had a little accident, I was, I mean, I crashed into a deer. Look, we don't want to get the authorities involved or anything."

Sara laughed in response, "Authorities! Ha, you're in the Pines hun, barely any cops round these parts."

"Right. Well that's comforting."

"That it is, I guess ya'll are all right enough. We don't care 'bout none of that marijuana ya'll are smokin' neither, you can smell it from a mile away boys; we're just on our way to do a little bit of huntin' so your secret is safe with us."

Vinny and Cody looked at each other with relief. They were not sure what to expect at first from this armed family of pineys, but all seemed well after Sara's initial aggression subsided.

"Sorry for being a dick, here, have a couple of beers," Vinny said. The girls laid down their guns and sat on fireside logs at the invitation, accepting the cans that Vinny offered.

"You can sit down too, buddy, here, have this," Cody produced a bag of cheese curls from his backpack, "what's your name little guy?"

The boy took the snack with a look of awe, like he had never seen food that was packaged. He joined the group on the grass by the fire, plopping down with his knees tucked into his chest and his soon to be orange crusted fingers popping open the little tin foil bag. His gun rested on the laces of his shoes.

"I'm Steve. Thanks! I haven't had these in forever. They're my favorite," Steve smiled before he munched on the snack.

"No problem, kid."

"Sara and Steve are my sister and brother. We live a few miles down the road. When we saw the bashed-up truck, we thought something bad had happened, but now I'm glad to see it's just a normal accident," Erica spoke to them as if she was eager to make friends.

"What do you mean by just normal?" Vinny asked this question with an air of confrontation, but he was not aware of it.

"Normal as in normal. Look, ya'll can keep on doin' whatever it is that you're doin' out here. Ain't no good fish around these parts," Sara seemed like she was distracted by something that was far off in the distance.

"No, it's fine you can stay," Cody said, "we've got plenty of beer to go around."

"Let's hang for a bit, we don't wanna' be rude," Erica replied.

Off in the distance the sounds of rifle shots cracked the air. Sara and Erica chatted quietly while sipping their beers, uncaring about what was happening around them, whether it was close or far away. Vinny and Cody traded concerned looks with each other, realizing that their escape from civilization was not as isolated as they originally thought. It was hunting season. Cody and Vinny kept glancing at each other out of wariness for their new guests. They had known each other long enough that they could have a kind of unspoken communication. A flare of the nostrils and slight movements of their mouths could express a range of emotions.

"There's evil men and wild dogs in the forest," the kid had been watching Cody and Vinny's every movement and could tell they were worried.

"Shut up, Steve," Sara said, while punching his arm, "he's just being a dumb kid."

"But you said…"

"Hey, look it's cool," Vinny interrupted the boy, "we're just here for a little bit of camping and fishing, not to cause any trouble. Relax with us for a bit, have another beer."

"Yeah, Cody said, trying to relate, "we actually ran into some weird shit earlier, like some kind of Satanic sacrifice type stuff."

"What the hell are you talking about?" Sara asked.

"Nothing, Cody's just pretty high, we were actually tripping earlier on some mushrooms."

"What?" Cody mouthed, but Vinny elbowed him.

"Hey, do either of you have any bud left that y'all would like to share?"

"Seriously, Sara?" Erica looked annoyed.

"What?"

Cody laughed, "yeah we can roll up a blunt or two, if you're cool with smoking in front of the little guy," they're just white trash pineys, of course they would not care about smoking weed in front of a child. Hell, the kid has probably gotten high before, too, Cody thought. Vinny looked at Cody thinking the same exact thing and snickered.

"Hey, I'm not that young. I'm almost twelve. I've been around weed before," Steve was defiant as Vinny and Cody laughed.

"Yeah, but you still shouldn't be around it," Erica frowned at him.

"It's fine, Erica, it's not like he's going to have any. We've had a long day huntin' without much to show for it and I need to take the edge off anyway."

"Sorry you guys haven't had much luck. You're welcome to share the fish that we caught. We're about to cook some more now."

"You mean what I caught," Vinny nudged Cody.

Sara laughed at them, "That there water's got too much iron in it for big fish."

"Yeah well, I nabbed a two-foot carp earlier."

They sat conversing around the campfire at the edge of the beach. Dusk arrived slowly in the forest. The lake reflected different colors depending on who was looking at the water. They counted the hawks that circled high above them swinging like pendulums. There were seven in total. A few fish periodically jumped out of the water, but the birds of prey never swooped down for them.

"That's a lot of hawks. I wonder what they're all doing up there if not hunting for fish," Vinny observed.

"They's a huntin' for somethin' else," said Sara.

The autumn air shifted its tepid breeze toward the group by the lake shore. More rifle shots sounded off far away, and they learned to ignore the noise as just another part of the forest. They spent some time smoking and drinking and politely conversing, the evening growing colder and the fire dwindling until it was just smoke hissing. The boy grew restless.

"So, you guys know of any good ghost stories from around here?" Cody asked.

"Yeah, everyone knows about the Jersey Devil of course, but there's other legends in the Pine Barrens," Erica said.

"Cody wants to make a horror film, like that witch project movie that came out a few years ago," Vinny explained.

"I'm actually making a documentary about the Jersey Devil. What are some of the other stories?" Cody leaned forward on his log.

"Well…" pondered Erica, "there's a few. And they're not all evil like the Jersey Devil. There's the legend of Captain Kidd, a Scottish pirate from colonial times who is said to have buried his treasure in the woods close to Barnegat Bay. No one ever sees him; he's supposed to be guarding his treasure chest somewhere, wherever it is, but he has a black dog that's friendly, and if you follow it, it might lead you to where the buried treasure is and will even help you dig it up. If Captain Kidd likes you, then he'll let you have all of his riches. Sometimes you see old men wandering around the Pines with metal detectors trying to look for it."

"I like that story. It's so cool that there were actual pirates around here way back when," said Steve.

"Oh yeah," replied Cody, "off the coast of our town, in the Delaware Bay, Blackbeard was supposed to have buried his treasure on some island. My dad told me about it."

"That's a stupid kid's story; Blackbeard wasn't even real," Sara interjected. Vinny realized that Cody was also about to chime in and fully tell them the story about how they saw a black dog that was sacrificed in a Satanic ritual, but Vinny nudged him to keep quiet.

"So what?" Erica continued, "then there's also the ghost of the black doctor of the pines. He was a real person in these parts over a hundred years ago and was supposed to heal people with herbs he found in the forest."

Cody could not keep quiet anymore, "I had a dream about him! His ghost was in our camp. He was making some kind of medicine at our fire. He gave me some water to help with my hangover and then I woke up, but I was still hungover." The piney siblings looked at Cody quizzically, and Vinny put his face in his palm, shaking his head and sighing. Cody took a furtive gulp of his beer.

"Hey, is it okay if I get more wood for the fire?"

"Just stay within earshot, Steve," Erica said in the soft tone of a loving big sister.

"So, how old are all of you?" Cody asked Erica, who was sitting beside him on the log. He wanted to lean closer.

"I'm sixteen, Steve is eleven, and Sara is twenty-two."

"Wow, those are big gaps in age."

"What of it?" Sara asked.

"I don't mean anything by it. Just saying."

"They're my half siblings on my father's side," she retorted.

"Oh okay, I guess that makes sense."

"Ain't none of your business to begin with…"

An awkward silence. The boy left his gun on the ground by the fire and wandered off to the nearby woods. Slowly, small talk ensued. Smoking weed bonded the four otherwise strangers. They laughed and shared stories about camping and fishing while making jokes about the Jersey Devil, the myth which could not be avoided. Erica said that it was a good story, but that she did not actually believe in the existence of the Jersey Devil; Sara stayed silent when they spoke of it. Cody and Vinny continued their own imperceptible conversation throughout the exchange. Getting high can have an effect on the perception of time in that an hour only feels like a few minutes, so that when that hour had passed without anyone becoming aware of Steve's prolonged absence it was not due to negligence on the sisters' part, nor was it ignorance for Cody and Vinny, until a few gunshots echoed through the trees and the two young men snapped out of their daze.

Erica let out a yelp, "where's Steve?"

Everyone jumped up and ran towards where the boy had disappeared into the woods. Cody patted his coat to make sure he did not forget to put his book and his camera inside of the big pockets on the inside of his jacket. They wordlessly combed the forest for the first few minutes until Sara started cursing furiously, blaming the boy for his carelessness, and trying to hide her growing anxiety. Cody and Vinny tried to reassure Erica and Sara that they would find the boy's trail. The group hiked up a gradual incline until they stood atop a hill overlooking what looked like an abandoned cabin in a large clearing with a dirt road ending in the building's driveway; this had two parked cars, a large windowless white van, and a cop car.

"Look, there must be a police officer who lives here. Let's go knock on the door and ask for some help," Cody said.

"No, this place ain't look right," replied Sara, "let's sneak over to those bushes on the other side and get a closer look through yonder window first."

They all followed her lead, crouch jogging down to a copse of oak trees and half dead mini sweetheart and hog bushes that lined a small ditch that surrounded the ramshackle house. Cody had his video camera at his side and lifted it pointing at the window. He zoomed in on the figures inside, not initially realizing what was happening. The four of them had poked their heads above and in between the branches of the bushes. With a view a bit farther than thirty yards, the group saw the figures of two men in the window gyrating maniacally as if operating an old-fashioned misery whip over a small log. Cody turned off the video camera. They heard the unmistakable cries of a little boy.

Sara unslung her rifle from her shoulder and rested the butt on her collarbone in one swift motion while shutting an eye to take aim at the first large figure that came into her sights. Before anyone else could react, she flipped the safety off, then squeezed the trigger and the man her bullet bore down did not even hear a sound outside of his own groan, his tongue hanging out of his mouth. The bullet tore through glass, skin, flesh, and bone, creating a crater in his forehead.

No one knew what to do, eyes wide open, huddled behind barren branches bearing the view. The man's body fell limp after an instant of stillness. The other man watched the fountain of blood erupting upon the bare skin of the child and himself, then stumbled out of the cabin while pulling up his pants. Sara stood and looked down on her companions, urging them to follow her lead once more. They heard the revving of a car from the other side of the house, and watched the man covered in blood speed away in the cop car down the sandy forest track, a shower of red speckles trailing him.

It took a few minutes for them to cross the ditch and reach the cabin. Erica opened the door and rushed inside to encounter her little brother in a fetal position on the floor soaked in blood. At first, she thought him dead, then noticed he was breathing. Part of the man's corpse rested crumpled on top of the boy, its pants around its ankles. Excrement pouring out and onto the child's feet. A cascade of brains spilling out of the other side onto the dirt floor which had become a slough. The room smelled like an abattoir, with brain matter strewn about like discarded offal. The cabin's interior was a mess and not just because of the blood and corpse in the middle of the room. An old oak table was the only furniture besides a couple of fold up lawn chairs, and the kitchen was completely stripped. A few rusty shovels and other tools leaned against the wall. What was not covered in dust was smothered in black grime. Blood and flesh adorned all objects.

When the boy realized he was safe, he kicked the body off and turned his head to see his sisters standing over him, Erica with tears streaming down her cheeks, the black of her eye mascara flowing like oil slicks, and Sara with her face cast down to the ground, grasping her gun as if it could console her. Erica took her jacket off and wrapped it around the child, the camouflage sticking to his skin like wet leaves after rain. Sara walked over to the corpse and dragged it by the arm to the other side of the room, then proceeded to kick the cloven stump of a head in with her boot until the neck nearly split in two.

Cody and Vinny stood at the doorway witnessing this scene after they returned from their short diversion outside of seeing in what direction the escaped man had driven.

Erica tried to look into her brother's eyes. He spat and yelled.

"I need a fucking cigarette," Sara stated toward Cody and Vinny.

"Uh, yeah, sure, I got you," Cody pulled out his pack and tossed it to Sara, "keep it. We got a whole carton."

"This is fucking insane," Vinny said, pointing at the dead body while walking over to Erica and Steve as if he could offer some form of help.

"What was I supposed to do?" No one answered Sara. "Was I supposed to just let it fucking happen?" She asked the room. No one argued with her.

"Stop," Erica held out her hand while kneeling by the gore, palm outstretched in Vinny's direction. Her red nail polish double coated with blood. The boy shook in the cradle of her other arm, his neck resting on his sister's bicep.

Cody noticed the pistol laying on the table and went over and grabbed the gun, inspecting it and placing its mouth in the back of his jeans after checking to make sure the safety was on, the handle sticking out of his lower back like the metal tail of some strange beast. He had only ever shot a gun in video games and bee bee guns in real life, but in his hubris figured it would be similar, just something only needing to be taken a bit more seriously.

Sara took a long drag of her cigarette, "you know how to use that thing?"

"Of course I do. I've been shooting all of my life, just like you," Vinny gave Cody an incredulous look but did not contradict his lie.

Though Steve remained silent, Erica kept hushing "shhh" while rocking his head back and forth as if he was an infant.

"We have to bring him back home," Erica implored.

"Are you fucking crazy? We can't bring him home like this, just look at him! We ought to take him to a hospital," Sara stood over them pointing the cigarette at the broken boy while leaning on her rifle with the other hand.

"Dad is passed out. We can bring him back, clean him up, and take care of him. What else are we supposed to do?"

"But how are you even gonna' get him back home in this sorry state? And what do we do with the body?" Sara asked no one in particular, staring down at her kill, no longer fuming with rage.

"I can walk," Steve said. Everyone stared at him.

"Okay, Erica, you take him home. I'm gonna' dump the body."

"Don't touch it!" Erica shouted.

"It's too late for that," Vinny noted.

"We'll take care of it," Cody blurted. He looked at Vinny for approval, but his expression was the opposite.

"How do we know which one was the cop?" Sara asked.

"I think it would be safe to assume that the cop was the guy who drove away in a fucking cop car," Vinny said.

"Yeah? And in what way will you two idiots figure out how to handle this situation? How do we take care of the fucking dead guy, and some fucking monster who just ran away? What if the dead guy's the cop? And why should we trust you? We just met, and now this shit happens, and we're fucked."

"You mean you're fucked. You just killed a guy, I'm getting the fuck out of here," Sara slammed the butt of her rifle against Vinny's arm. "Ow, you bitch! You're lucky you're a fucking girl or I'd beat the shit out of you."

"Go ahead and try me, asshole. I'd whoop your scrawny ass."

Cody came up in between Sara and Vinny with his arms extended.

"We're not going to leave the woods. We can take Vinny's truck and go have a look around, see if we can try to find him. He couldn't have gotten far from here. Sara, you come with us. Erica, we can help you take your little brother home first."

"What? No," Vinny interjected. Cody stared at Vinny in response. "Fine," he relented.

Erica cried on Steve's shoulder as he winced. Sara furrowed her brows and looked down. Steve was motionless, still in shock. Sara turned to Vinny and Cody.

"We can't just leave all of this here for tomorrow morning. We need to either burn or bury this body and then we have to go scout out where the other motherfucker went. There's this old house about ten miles up that road the cop car drove down. The drug den. I knew that car when I saw it. I've seen it before parked outside that there drug den that's farther up north. The cop car says Woodville on the side of it and that town ain't around here."

"Wait, what? Woodville? That's where we're from, how did I not notice that?"

"She's right Cody, I saw it and thought it was weird that a cop car from Woodville is all the way up here."

"I reckon that's a crooked cop who comes all the way up here to get his rocks off in the pines. That drug den up there ain't nothin' but trouble. I'd bet a million dollars that's where the piece of shit drove off to, and I guarantee the fucker went to hide out there. That's where all sorts of shit is said to happen. It's not just a drug den, but like a meeting place for scumbags who come into the woods to do bad shit," Sara leaned against her rifle while deep in thought.

"Alright, we're just going to have a quick chat outside," Cody replied.

Cody and Vinny walked out onto the porch with the woods looming over them to confer with one another, their ears still ringing from the gunshot.

"What the fuck Cody, this is crazy. Are we really doing this? I know you feel the need to help because something terrible just happened, but this is too much. This isn't a video game. This is real life."

"We're in this mess. We got to get out of it with them."

"Yeah, but something's going on, man, it seems like Sara knows more than what she's leading on, like, what the fuck is this drug den she's talking about? And how is she so sure that's where the cop is heading? And why the hell are we gonna' help these pineys we just met? There's a fucking dead body in there!" Vinny had his hands raised up to the sky and then shook Cody's shoulders.

"Dude, I don't know, but did you see what just happened to that poor kid? We gotta' help them out. Plus, what if that Woodville cop was Officer Ciliberti? I didn't get a good enough look at him, but he looked familiar from far away. Let's fucking nab his ass."

"I don't believe it man. This shit is crazy. Your beef with a childhood bully and his dad is gonna' get us in big trouble."

Sara walked out of the cabin with a couple of shovels. She tossed one to Cody.

"Come on, we don't got time to fiddle with ourselves boys, let's get to work. We can't do nothin' else without burying the body."

"You're right, we need to clean up this whole mess. I'm not trying to go to jail," Cody said.

"We don't got to do anything, dude. How about we just call the cops like normal fucking people and be done with it," Vinny raised his voice.

"We can't call the cops asshole, then I'll go to fucking jail. And the guy who, who, fucking, fucking hurt my little fucking brother was a fucking cop."

"So what? Then he'll go to jail. You won't. It's like self-defense or something."

"No it's not, asshole. Cops protect their own. Even if they were to believe us, I still killed a man and I'm not going to fucking abandon my little brother and sister. You're not going to squeal, are you?"

"Nah, that's not what I meant. I just was trying to think of our options because this is fucking ridiculous, and I don't want to go to jail either."

"Then keep your fucking mouth shut," Sara yelled.

Cody looked at Vinny with a raised eyebrow and shrugged his shoulders.

Erica emerged from the door with Steve, holding his hand in silence, and walked with him, her flashlight guiding their path. As they passed by Sara hugged them then looked at Vinny.

"I'm driving them home, right? While you guys uh, bury the body or whatever?"

"Yeah, but you better come right on back here for your little friend…" Sara looked at Cody and Vinny nodded in response. "Now ya'll be careful. My cell is out of minutes, but I'll call you, Erica, from one of theirs or a pay phone later. Make sure you answer." Erica nodded.

The moon and the stars cast light between the branches while they walked into the woods. Vinny trailed the siblings and gave a concerned glance back at Cody.

"Are they going to be all right by themselves?" Cody asked Sara.

"Well, what worse thing could happen?" Sara responded. "Your friend isn't gonna' abandon us here and rat on me, right?"

"No, I swear. He's like a brother to me."

"Erica knows her way around here. Our house is in that direction. Your friend will be back here in no time if he doesn't run away, and we can't waste a moment cleaning this mess up. It's possible the fucker who got away could come on back here with back up."

"Shit, I didn't think of that. Now I'm worried about them running into anyone."

"They don't have far to go, and she knows how to use a gun."

"What is this, the wild west?" Cody asked Sara, which she ignored. "It might as well be," Cody said.

They leaned their shovels up against the wall, then grabbed a faded blue tarpaulin that was stuck in mud to the side and ripped it out, shaking it off and then spreading it like a blanket onto the grass. Back in the cabin the stench had begun to spread throughout the room. Cody coughed and gagged as he helped pull the body out, holding the shoulders where the head used to be, and dragged the corpse onto the tarp to wrap up like a giant, festering burrito.

They pulled the body a few hundred yards east into the woods until Sara told him to stop.

"This is the spot."

The soil in that area was typical of the Pine Barrens, loose and sandy, easy to dig. They worked for what felt like a long time, until the lengths of their shovels were well below the surface level. They got out of the hole, Sara climbing easily, then helping Cody with a hand. He was embarrassed to need help, especially when Sara did not ask for any. They picked the body up and swung it into the makeshift grave, then began to dump the dirt back onto the tarp. Cody's thumb throbbed from the fight that had happened the week before, which now felt like it was years ago to him. He thought that the sprain was almost healed, but shoveling aggravated the injury.

"So what are we going to do about all the blood and shit back at that cabin?" Cody asked.

Sara looked up at him while continuing to shovel the sugar sand onto the corpse, her bangs sticking with sweat to her pale forehead.

"I saw some bleach and stuff in a pile of junk in the corner of the room. We'll dump the bleach everywhere and give it a scrubbing." Cody stared at Sara in disbelief.

"What?" Sara stopped and turned to look at him.

"Have you done this before? You seem to know what you're doing,"

"Are you accusing me of something?"

"I'm just saying. You got an answer for everything."

"What, because I'm a piney you think I'm some kind of redneck murderer?"

"No, of course not."

"I've never killed another human being before tonight, but if I have to I will again."

Cody put his hands up and backed away, "Sara, come on, we're on the same side here. It's a stressful situation. Let's just keep it moving."

"I don't mean you. I mean I'm gonna' find the other guy who did this and make him pay."

"Oh, right," he chuckled, then helped her finish burying the body.

They trudged to the shack and put their shovels where Sara found them then dug through the trash to find old sponges and bleach and got to work scrubbing away the blood from all of the hard surfaces. It was easier work than they thought it would be because the floor was made of dirt and all they had to do was turn it over with their feet while dumping the plastic jug everywhere. Once they finished, they took turns washing themselves in the dark stream that ran by the cabin, and everything looked the way it was before except their clothes that were covered in dirt. The blood came off fairly quickly because they acted fast, and they were satisfied with the cleanup. They hiked back to where Cody and Vinny made camp. Vinny was leaning against his truck smoking a cigarette.

"I'm glad you didn't run away," Sara said.

"I wouldn't ditch my boy Cody like that."

They disassembled the tent and gathered their belongings to throw into the bed of the vehicle, with Sara hiding her rifle behind and under the seats.

"I'm fucking starving," Cody said.

"There's this bar with a kitchen open late on the way to the drug den called the Mud Hole Inn, we can stop there and see if we can find a way into the drug den through someone who's hanging out there so that we don't just go in blind," Sara responded.

"Wow, everything's a fucking hole around here. Sounds delightful, except that we all look like a mess, our clothes are dirty, and Cody is covered in blood, which, I know is deer blood from earlier, but still doesn't look good," Vinny said.

"It's all right I'll just take this jacket off before we walk in, even though it's cold out."

"Dios mio, yeah, okay Cody, brilliant plan, but our clothes are still covered in dirt."

"You two ain't much different than half the guys around here looking like that, even with blood on you, but yeah, Cody, take that jacket off when we head in there."

"You really think it's a good idea to go out somewhere in public after having just killed a guy?"

"Yeah, it will give me an alibi. They know me there. Plus I need a drink. We'll be quick."

"Okay, but will they serve us? We're underage and outsiders here and not to mention Cody looks like he's fifteen years old because he's five feet tall."

"Shut up, dude. I'm not five feet tall. I'm five foot five."

"Yeah, sure. I'm serious man, just looking out for you."

"I've got a fake ID bro, don't worry about it."

"That piece of shit thing? That's funny! Show Sara." Cody took out his wallet which had only a few dollars in it, what looked like a military identification card, and a potpourri of various pieces of paper. He pulled out the ID and showed it to them.

"I mean, it looks like you, yeah, but it don't even got a birthdate on it," Sara squinted at it as Vinny laughed.

"It's on the back. That's what it's like with a military ID," he turned it around to show her. The picture of the man on the card was blurry, but he did indeed look like Cody with dirty blond hair, brown eyes, a round chin, roman nose, and high cheekbones.

"How did you even get that?"

"I took it from this guy who left his wallet at my job."

"Okay well, between Vinny being super tall with almost a grown man's facial hair and your, well, whatever that is, I know we'll be all right. Besides, I know the bartender real well; she'd probably let me bring anyone in, no matter how young they look. Let's go."

"Yeah, but I ain't drivin' into any town. I'm too drunk. I don't wanna' get pulled over after all that. It was bad enough dropping off your brother and sister at your house in the middle of nowhere. I almost got lost on my way back, these dirt roads all look the same," Vinny said.

"Oh come on man, you've had to have sobered up by now," Cody elbowed Vinny in the stomach.

"Yeah, what are you some kind of little bitch? It's okay, I'll drive. Gimme' the keys," Sara insisted while poking at Vinny and grabbing at his pockets.

Vinny frowned and pulled away, "no, fuck you. It's fine. I'll drive. That whole thing fucking sobered me up. I'm hungry as hell and I just want to get out of here anyway."

The pine tree branches were drooping over the road and the needles scratched the roof of the truck. Sand drifted through the air in gusts as they jostled along the winding dirt path. They came off the sand road to turn left onto a paved street and head north.

Vinny turned the radio on, but it was just static as he switched the knob to change the channels. Cody leaned forward to check on Vinny and make sure that his friend looked sober. He was worried about getting pulled over with the gun that he took and the body that they had buried in the woods. His hands were shaking but they looked clean. The warmth of Sara's body pressed up against him felt good and he closed his eyes to imagine her in a way that he knew was wrong at the moment. Cody was uncomfortable because of all of the stuff inside of his jacket pockets and so he pulled it all out and placed it by his feet. Sara noticed the black and gold book sitting on the floor mat of the passenger side.

"What is that, a bible?"

"It's Cody's unholy bible."

"What?"

"It's the book about the Jersey Devil. The one I was reading out loud by the fire when your brother came up on us…" Cody trailed off and cringed at having mentioned her brother. Sara stared straight ahead at the road.

"So ya'll really were serious about this Jersey Devil nonsense?"

"Yeah well, I wanted to come to the Pine Barrens to look for the Jersey Devil and make a movie about it. Vin just wanted to fish, but then I had all these crazy dreams, and then I saw the little girl who was lost with her dog, then we found that same dog's corpse from some kind of Satanic sacrifice in this weird cave, and then that crazy shit happened with your brother."

"Jesus Christ, so ya'll really are in the pines to try to make a movie about the Jersey Devil?"

"Yeah, that's why I brought the video camera."

"Wait. Did you take a video of what happened to my brother?"

Cody was silent. He forgot that he took footage of the scene before Sara shot the man. First, he thought about lying to her and then he came to a realization.

"It's evidence. To clear your name. I mean just in case you get caught. I won't look at it or show anyone, I swear."

"I guess it's a good backup plan… Did you get me shooting the guy?"

"No, I turned it off right as I realized what was happening. It's only a few seconds long."

Sara grabbed the camera from Cody and opened the digital viewfinder to look at the video. She stared at the blue lit menu screen for a moment and then shook her head.

"You know what, never mind. I don't want to see it. Just swear to me that you will keep it secret and safe unless I get arrested."

"I swear."

"All right. Here Vinny, make the next turn. We're getting close."

Chapter Seven

The wind blew litter along empty roads. They encountered scarce stop lights temporarily erasing memories of what had happened earlier in the night. It was as if staring into the red and yellow and green somehow hypnotized the three of them, whose stained jean legs were pressed against one another inside the cramped cabin of Vinny's pickup truck.

The rural road and thicket of pines suddenly gave way to the town. While taking directions from Sara, Vinny slowed while driving through the only large town in the middle of the Pine Barrens, Hammonton, "The Blueberry Capital of the World," and kept north, straight into the largest, most isolated part of the pines, the Wharton State Forest. None of the houses had lights on, and they saw no other people. They all tensed and kept an eye out for police cars. The pickup truck rattled as it hit a deep fissure in the asphalt, the tires kept turning. They made it through the town. After fifteen minutes of driving through civilization, they drove through the blueberry fields to the north of Hammonton. A building by itself in otherwise wilderness. Where those who are lost gather.

The Mud Hole Inn was a wooden structure on the side of a two-lane highway running north through the center of the Pine Barrens. Unpainted, it blended in with the forest surrounding it. They pulled into the dirt parking lot of the bar that had several cars and a few trucks parked in it. On the front lawn there was a cluster of bombed-out vehicle frames. A single streetlight illuminated a part of the cranberry bog across the street. A firefighter's jacket hung on a wooden post in the field like some kind of enchanted scarecrow deliberately placed to ward off forest fires. The light bounced off its yellow high visibility reflectors. They could hear the shrill, skin tingling sound of a beast screaming in the pines beyond, but ignored it, for what else could be done other than leave unacknowledged what cannot be controlled?

No signs adorned the building so that passerbys would drive past without knowing what it was if they did not already know the inn was there. An old pay phone stood a little ways from the entrance and Sara walked up to it without saying anything to her companions, placed two quarters into the machine and held onto the phone solemnly and spoke into it in a low voice. The pay phone's dial buttons were rusted out so that the caller would have to almost punch each square with a knuckle in order to press them properly. Sara anxiously stroked the cord while she spoke with her sister. Vinny looked at his watch while Cody inspected the bed of the pickup truck to make sure everything was set in place.

"I should call my family, but it's a little too late right now. Cody, do you have any cell phone service out here?"

"Nah man, I had a couple of bars on my service when we drove through Hammonton, but they went away as soon as we drove back into the woods."

"Shit, dude, aren't you worried about your parents?"

"Nah, man I mean I told them we were going on a camping trip this weekend, but I didn't say goodbye when I left. I'm sure they're happy not to hear from me."

"I wish I could say the same. My mom is probably worried because I haven't checked in with her today."

When Sara was finished on the pay phone she motioned for them to follow her into the bar. Dim lights escaped the blinds of the windows, and a country song could be heard coming from inside.

"Hey, I'm going to call my family real quick. I'll meet you guys in there."

"I don't think so, Vinny, we're going to wait right here until you're done," Sara said.

"Why? You don't trust me?"

"No, I don't and there's nothing that you can say that will make me. Just hurry up, it's almost midnight and the kitchen is about to close."

"I just dropped off your brother and sister and came back for your asses. Gimme' a break."

Vinny placed his change in the pay phone and dialed the number to his house. He talked briefly on the phone with his sister Bianca. He told her that they were fine and was just checking in and Cody asked him to say hi to her for him, but he would not. He placed the phone back onto the receiver. When he turned around, he noticed a sign on the door that declared "NO COLORS" and pointed at it.

"What the hell is that?"

"They don't want your kind in here, Vin," Cody playfully elbowed him in the ribs, but Vinny did not laugh.

Sara rolled her eyes, "no, you fucking idiot, it means they don't want any gang colors worn in here. There's a lot of bikers 'round these parts, as you can see by the motorcycles yonder in the parking lot."

"Yonder?" Cody guffawed.

"Ya'll don't say yonder?"

"Ya'll?" The boys chuckled. Sara huffed and walked through the door.

"While Sara's kind of friendly for a piney, there's still probably a bunch of racist rednecks in there. We can't trust them. Let's be careful," Vinny whispered to Cody, who nodded.

They casually walked into the dark room. The bartender smiled as they sat down and placed her hand onto Sara's open palm extended over the bar. She caressed Sara's fingers and simultaneously flipped a rocks glass onto the bar and poured a shot of bourbon from the rail below almost to the rim and pushed it towards her. Sara drank it in two separate sups. Several men and a few women hunched over at the bar with half of them staring into their drinks and the other half staring at the young newcomers. Blue smoke filled the air and one of the older men coughed quietly but incessantly.

"Sara darling, how was the hunt? Looks to me like it was unsuccessful, unless you were huntin' for two boys. Kitchen is about to close if you're hungry."

"Thanks Joanna, I'm sorry I thought I'd be here earlier. Got a little sidetracked. We'd like to throw in some food real quick. These are my new friends, Vinny and Cody."

"Well hello boys. My, are you two handsome. A bit dirty though."

"Yeah well that's because…"

"I really don't care, you little cutie pie," the bartender gave Cody a wink and he blushed. He was relieved he did not have to show the military identification to her.

The bar was U-shaped with the kitchen at the mouth. Everything was made of wood. Exposed beams on the ceiling. The kitchen only served fried foods, an exposed scullery the size of a closet with enough space for a deep fryer and a place for the cook to stand. The cook was an old man in a blue apron, white shirt stained with grease, and a tattered maroon pillbox baseball hat with a P on it that used to be white but was stained yellow. He looked bored and frustrated to have new customers right before closing time. Cody eyed the cook's vintage Phillies hat with envy; he always wanted one but had to settle for a cheap knock-off Phillies hat that his mom had bought him at the Supercenter. He looked around at the bar and felt like he could be a regular there. Plywood boards covered up parts of the walls. Old neon signs for various beers and whiskeys half working, flickering. A man with long hair and a cowboy hat sitting in the corner was asleep with a guitar placed on his lap. Cody snickered at a big white sign on the wall that exclaimed "PINEY POWER."

"We'll get the platter," Sara said.

"What's the platter?" Cody asked.

"It's a big basket of everything, sweetheart: ears, tails, french fries, onion rings, chicken tenders, and shrimp," Joanna answered.

Cody's stomach grumbled, "sounds good."

"Ears and tails? What kind of redneck shit is that?" Vinny whispered to Cody who laughed in response.

They ordered beers and lit up cigarettes at the bar. Joanna poured their pints and came back over carrying all three in the palm of one hand, then emptied the black plastic ashtray that was filled with cigarette butts in front of them.

"Oh, sorry for leaving this here hon, I didn't want to empty that earlier because there was this creep who came in and was chain smoking there."

"I bet you have to deal with a lot of creeps," Cody was now feeling confident and trying to flirt with the bartender who looked like she was in her early thirties. She had big red curly hair that reminded him of an actress he could not name from an old movie. Her skin was leathery tan and slightly wrinkled but she carried herself with the specter of what he thought was a sublime, rustic beauty. Cody could not help but stare at her cleavage as she leaned over the counter until Sara noticed and silently kicked him under the bar.

"Yeah, this one was different. He was wearing a cop uniform, but I didn't recognize him from any police department around here."

They looked at each other with wide eyes. Joanna turned the volume of the TV off and put the radio on over the bar speakers. It was a modern country song that began with a driving hi-hat and an electric guitar riff.

"Was he tall and wearing glasses?" Cody asked.

"Yes, yes he was, and he didn't say anything, just stared at me smiling and whenever he needed a drink, he just pointed at the whiskey he wanted and kept shaking his empty glass at me."

"That's him," Sara said.

"How do you know? We didn't get a good enough look at him; we were too far away. It could be any cop. All I saw was that he was wearing glasses, he wore a cop uniform, but he did look kind of familiar," Cody scratched his head as he tried to make the connection. "Was that really Officer

Ciliberti? I couldn't make out his face from that far away," he said to Vinny, who shrugged his shoulders.

"Who?" Joanna leaned in and looked concerned on the other side of the bar while darting her eyes back and forth between the trio. Her hands were spread out while placed on the bar top.

"It's nothing. We just saw him at another bar earlier and he made a rude comment, I'll tell you about it later," Sara smiled. Joanna nodded and walked away to work on the other side of the bar for a moment.

"You know this guy?" Sara whispered.

"I think it might be this cop from my town. He was at my mom's job when some crazy guy caused a scene there recently."

"That's weird, but we have to be careful what we say to people," Sara implored to Cody.

"Right, sorry."

Joanna came back with a bottle of whiskey and her hand on her hip. She rolled her eyes. "That gentleman wanted to buy you a shot, Sara." A scruffy looking man from across the bar smirked.

"Gentleman's a stretch. Kindly tell him to fuck right off. I'll take the free shot though."

Joanna laughed and then poured the whiskey. "His name is Virgil, been hanging 'round here a few months now. I don't like the looks of him. How's Erica doing by the way? I haven't seen her in a while."

"She's hanging in there. A bit stressed out you know with dad sick and all."

"Yeah, she's a sensitive girl. It's a shame about your dad. I hope little Stevie is doing well too, he's a sweetheart."

Sara took the shot that Virgil sent over. "Mhm," she hummed while slightly choking, swallowing the burning liquid, and wiping her mouth with the back of her hand. Cody gawked at her, impressed with how much she could drink and how well she seemed to handle her liquor.

"What's wrong with your dad?" Vinny asked.

"Ain't none of your fuckin' business," Sara said.

Cody watched the cook fry their food. "I like your cook's Phillies hat," Cody remarked to Joanna.

"Oh that's Frankie, what a weird coincidence."

"What?" Cody asked.

"There's a cool story how Frankie got that hat, it's signed by Tug McGraw himself."

"Who?"

"Are you not a Phillies fan?"

"Yeah, I am."

"Well I guess you're a little young for that, but Tug McGraw was a pitcher for the Phillies back in the day; he helped win us a World Series in 1980."

"Oh that's right, yeah, my dad's talked about that. I grew up watching Kruk and Curt Schilling. I was bummed as a kid when we lost to the Jays in '93."

"How old are you?" Joanna asked Cody. Vinny side eyed him and Sara coughed after inhaling her cigarette.

"I'm 22, just kind of short, yah know? Anyway, what was the coincidence?"

"Oh yeah. You hear this song I just put on the radio? This is that new hit, 'Real Good Man' by Tim McGraw!"

"So what?" Cody asked, hoping Joanna forgot that she had asked him his age.

"Tug McGraw the Phillies pitcher is Tim McGraw the country singer's father! It's just a weird little coincidence, don'tcha think?" She tilted her head and batted her eyelashes, then walked to the kitchen.

"There ain't no such thing as coincidences," Sara whispered to herself.

"That was a fuckin' close one," Vinny said.

"Yeah Cody, real smooth. I don't want Joanna gettin' all pissy with me for bringin' underage kids up in here."

"We're not kids, we're 19, I thought this dive bar wouldn't care anyway and you said it would be fine?"

"You know, the drinking age used to be 18 during the Vietnam War," Vinny stated, while pointing his finger in the air to interrupt.

"Well it ain't now, just hush," Sara said to Vinny, then turned back and shushed Cody as Joanna walked over carrying their basket of fried food.

When their food came out, they picked their portions and placed them on paper plates while wiping the grease from their fingers with brown napkins. The basket was a heaping pile of hot fried food that was plenty for all three of them. They ate ravenously and burned the tops of their mouths in their impatience. Everything was covered in ketchup and hot sauce and salt. While he was eating, Cody stared at the man sitting closest to him because he was bragging about how he got away with beating his girlfriend by lying to the cops. Cody chewed harder and harder with his mouth open.

"You hearin' this dude? I wanna kick this guy's fucking ass," he whispered, accidentally spitting food onto Sara's lap. She wiped it off onto his leg.

"Ew dude, Cody, no. Can you chew with your mouth closed? Jesus Christ. It's no time to be a hero with this rando right now. Remember, we got priorities. We got to get goin' after this so we can get to the drug den. I bet that's where that cop is heading. I'm gonna' fuck him up and I could use some help," Sara said, and Cody's eyes lit up.

"Hell yeah."

"You guys are fucking insane. I'm not driving you to no drug den in the middle of bumblefuck nowhere so you could fight a cop. There's no way in hell," Vinny interjected.

Sara turned to Vinny. "Who said I was gonna' fight him?"

The man named Virgil who offered to buy Sara a shot overheard Vinny say the word drug and walked up to them. He wore jeans, a black leather jacket, and a trucker hat. Sara placed her palm on her forehead while shaking her head.

"You kids looking to score?" Virgil asked.

"Yeah man," Cody jumped up, "We're trying to score some hash my guy."

"Hash?" The man laughed. "How about some dope?"

"Sure!"

"Cody, I think he means heroin," Vinny said.

"What're you not into that?" Virgil walked over and leaned close to them on the bar, his cigarette smoke wafting towards them.

"I'm more of a hallucinogen guy myself," Vinny proudly stated. The man looked at him incredulously.

"I heard you kids say drug den. I know what you're talking about, and I can get you in there. It's a cool spot where you can get away from this lame shit and do whatever you want. Especially you, sweetheart." Sara interrupted Cody, who was about to step between Virgil and her, and pretended to be interested in the latter's advances.

"Great, yeah. Sounds perfect," she blinked quickly in exaggerated succession.

The other men at the end of the bar were talking about how baseball is not good anymore, that there are too many home runs and that everyone knows that the players are on steroids, but no one does anything about it. Frustrated by

Virgil, Cody walked over to them and tried to join their conversation. Joanna got close from the other side of the bar and looked at Sara and Virgil warily while pretending to clean. The older men Cody spoke to said they had been coming there for years and only tolerated newcomers and outsiders because it meant more money for them in selling their goods. Various knick knacks and carved trinkets sat by the wall behind the men as if they were itinerant merchants from a bygone era.

Cody suddenly remembered the gun in the back of his pants because he leaned too far over the bar and the handle pressed against his lower back. He pulled the back of his shirt down to make sure the gun handle was not sticking out. The pistol increased his confidence, even though he had never used one, and he was prepared to follow Sara and whatever course she led them on, no matter how foolhardy. He looked over at Vinny and saw how he was getting antsy, his leg jostling, shifting back and forth in his seat now that he was done eating his food. It seemed as though Sara and Virgil had come to some sort of agreement and that she had convinced Vinny to tag along even if it was just to drop them off.

"Be safe getting home!" Joanna called out to another patron as he left. "If not, you'll see me on the news," he retorted. The guy in his piney patois of a Jersey accent pronounced the word news like noose.

"That's not funny, Jim," Joanna scowled.

One of the other men at the end of the bar had been standing over two women in the corner of the room flirting with them. He did not speak or dress like a piney and he boasted about being an airplane mechanic. The younger woman slipped away from him and walked to the other side of the bar to whisper into the bartender's ear before leaving. Joanna looked over to see the man grabbing the older woman by the shoulders and shaking her while intensely speaking to her. No one noticed until the man had moved his hands to her neck and started strangling.

"Hey! Knock it the fuck off, John, or you won't be allowed back in here no more," John stopped and turned to Joanna to murmur an explanation as if he had only said something wrong and would be able to continue with his business after the bartender diverted her attention elsewhere. The woman said it's fine that they'll just go out to her car and finish talking there. Joanna went back to work but kept an eye on them as they walked out of the bar to the parking lot.

Sara left a wad of cash on the bar and thanked Joanna. Joanna grabbed Sara's wrist and whispered earnestly in her ear. Sara waved her off, giving her a kiss on the cheek and looking back with a smile as they all left. The man who was strangling the woman was now standing with his hand on the roof of her car peering through the driver's window as he pleaded with her. She sat at the steering wheel and looked straight ahead while listening to him.

Virgil passed by them, got into his jeep, and drove off into the darkness. Vinny, Cody, and Sara piled into the truck and drove after him from the bar parking lot down the highway until he peeled off onto a dirt track that led into the pitch-black forest. Vinny hesitated at first to drive off the road and into the woods, then Sara nudged him, so he turned on his high beams and followed the man's jeep into oblivion.

Chapter Eight

Vinny drove down the sand road. The glare of the truck's high beams reflected off sap sticking to the trunks of pine trees. They discussed what they were going to do when they got to the drug den. Virgil's jeep bounced along the sandy tracks ahead of them.

"Why don't I stay outside with my rifle while you two go in there to buy weed, then you can tell the cop you know him from Woodville, he'll feel threatened and bring ya'll outside to arrest you, that way I can draw him out and I can shoot him?" Sara suggested.

"That's literally the dumbest fucking idea I've ever heard in my life. How much whiskey did you drink? You're not fucking shooting anybody else. You're going to get us killed," Vinny implored while maneuvering the truck with the shaking steering wheel. Sara laughed, "yeah, you're right.

Best we all go in together and I lure him out." Vinny scowled as he side eyed her.

They hit a deep hole in the dirt road. "Damn it, my suspension's gonna' be fucked. Sara, I don't think you're quite the cop's type."

"Fuck off, I don't wanna' think about what happened to Steve. It's makin' me fixed on killin' the cop even more."

"I know, Sara," Cody said, "and we'll do something about it but not kill him. That's a bad idea. Not sure what we'll do, maybe we can just scout the place, and all go in together and figure out if the cop is there or not, buy drugs, and then leave and camp out to deal with the cop when he leaves, if he is there? I can videotape him and use it as evidence that he's a crooked cop. Maybe we hide in the trees, and I get a good, clear picture of his face this time?" The darkness was split by the headlights. Pine trees and their ugly bark disjointed and cloven by some unknown violence. The lights flickered.

"I don't want to go along with any of this shit, for the record. Sounds like none of you have an actual plan. I can't believe I'm even driving into the middle of bumblefuck nowhere for a person I just met, no matter what happened to your little brother. If you guys wanna' go to this drug den so bad, I can just leave you there and come back," Vinny said.

"You're not gonna' do that, that'll look suspicious. Just stick around, we'll be quick, and I promise I won't get you hurt. Anything weird happens, we can just run away," Sara's tone of voice changed to a higher pitch to be more endearing. She smiled.

"Yeah, come on, Vin. Let's just buy some shit and leave. If the cop is there, he won't even know it was us. I want to see if it's Officer Ciliberti or not. Whoever he was, he didn't even see who we were when Sara shot that other dude. We were hidden in the bushes." Cody looked at Sara's thighs.

"You guys are fucking crazy, but fine. I'm out of weed anyway and need to buy some more. As soon as any weird shit happens, I'm fucking out of there," Vinny sighed.

When they arrived, Cody and Vinny's jaws dropped in astonishment at the spectacle illuminated by gas lamps affixed to the walls and set about the property. Off this sand path in the middle of a foreboding forest was not the halfway house cabin or shack that they had expected the drug den to be, but an old manor house that still retained signs of its former grandeur, an abandoned mansion from the 19th century, when the region was rich from iron ore mining and charcoal harvesting. The big house and its satellite buildings had fallen into disuse when industry left the Pine Barrens, and the estate had miraculously withstood the fires that rage roughly every seven years in those woods. Its unpainted stone exterior was blackened by past infernos, but the house remained stately, with numerous spires and elongated arches. The windows were tall and thin and like those of a church, although boarded up from the inside. Green and yellow lichen caressed the masonry. The roof was upheld by dark flying buttresses on either side of the villa, with brick retaining walls in the foreground. Virgil's jeep pulled up to the front entranceway, which was crowned with a pointed archway. On it were inscribed faded words of some importance that were too obscured by time to be read any longer. The only other car parked around the front of the house besides Virgil's jeep was the same Woodville police cruiser that they had seen earlier in the night. Virgil got out and opened the gothic door, slowly turning the knob, and then gestured to them to get inside like he was in a rush.

The first-floor interior of the large house consisted of one massive room like an ancient mead hall emptied of its warriors and nobles. Walking through the foyer, they heard screams coming from somewhere further inside. The sounds were snuffed out when the front door closed. It was then that they noticed their guide's disappearance, just as the sound of a metal clang echoed around them, their exit barred. Vinny, Cody, and Sara looked at each other as they could hear slamming of other doors in the house. Echoes bounced around. They simultaneously tried to open the door they had just entered through, but with no success. Vinny banged on the wood with his fists. Cody turned back around to look at the room as his eyes adjusted to the darkness. Drywalls that had once separated the ground floor rooms had been taken out by a sledgehammer still propped up against the outer wall, leaving only the wooden skeletons of interior walls in place.

At the far end of the room was a hulking, pale man who was stark naked, sitting on a makeshift throne made of wood with crimson velvet cushions at the end of a long table. He was gargantuan, his skin folding over itself throughout his body with a combination of muscle and fat that made it tough to tell where one type of flesh began and the other ended, his torso a mound of layered excrescence. A smile crept across his broad face as they stepped into the room toward him. Each yellow tooth hung independently from one another. The incisors and canines were fanged as if deliberately sharpened with a knife, while the rest were solid monoliths twice the size of average teeth. There was no hair anywhere on his body, and he shined with sweat in the dim candlelight of the dining table covered in fast food bags: their contents splayed out in a greasy feast of cheeseburgers, fried chicken, tacos, Chinese food, and donuts.

The man raised his massive frame by placing his meaty palms onto the table. Cody had seen this creature before. He racked his brain. Was this the same person he had suspected of abducting that child at the Supercenter, the one he had mistaken for an Amish man? That man was cloaked in a long trench coat. This was the very same man, disrobed in all of his degeneracy. He was unmistakable.

Upon his head sat a paper crown like they give to children at a fast-food restaurant, his only adornment besides a priest's collar wrapped around his throat, as if he'd torn the collarino from the rest of the cassock. His purple nipples shined with excretion. The crown was covered in mock thorns drawn with green crayon.

Cody thought he remembered seeing the same symbol somewhere recently, although he was too overwhelmed to make any coherent associations. The figure stood leaning precariously over his feast as if about to fall forward; his penis, the size of a toddler's forearm, plopped onto a plate of french fries, becoming covered in ketchup that looked like blood in the room's dim lighting.

"Welcome, children," the man's voice was, shockingly, a countertenor that wholly contradicted his appearance.

At his right hand sat a rocking cradle perched upon a shining mound of flattened obsidian iron bog ore, its contents not visible at first in the unnaturally glaucous light. Beckoned forward, Cody approached the feasting table to see a desiccated figure in the soft ivory cushions of the baby basket, an ashen corpse that appeared to be comprised of an amalgam of creatures, a chimera of inhumanity and bestial marriage: hooves, twisted joints, claws, a hairy, triangular face and, what stood out most, a set of leathery wings attached to its torso and draping over the cot's walls.

"Holy shit," Cody gasped.

"Aye, thou hast admiration for mine prey, the progeny of Lucifer."

"What the hell is that thing?" Vinny asked.

"Ye know verily well what it is child, I shall not repeat myself."

"That's the Jersey Devil?" Cody approached the relic, mindful of the man sitting next to it and conscious of the gun tucked into the back of his pants.

"Is this guy for real? Nope. I'm getting the fuck out of here," Vinny said while turning around and rushing back toward the door. Sara and Vinny struggled again with the closed door, then searched along the walls for a crack in the boarded-up windows. Cody stood still just feet away from the man and the corpse.

"Do not yet approach the sepulchered demon. Thine eyes shalt see it closer yet. T'was mine aspiration ever since I set foot in the Pine Barrens to track down and slay this demon, and verily we are feasting in joyous celebration. Sit down and join us in our communion. The acolytes shall be here shortly."

"How do we know that thing isn't fake?" Vinny asked as he gave up searching for an exit and crept up behind Cody, who inched closer to the cradle and gazed at the corpse inside. "I mean, just look at it, all the body parts are sewn together. It's a circus act," Vinny said.

"It's real Vin, you said you'd believe it if you see it and it's right there in front of you!" Cody turned and stared at Vinny.

Vinny regarded both their host and Cody warily and backed up to the other side of the room. He changed the tone of his voice, "well actually, now that I think about it, it looks cool as shit you know? Definitely real. The Jersey Devil, wow. I can't believe it. My bad, that's a fucking dope ass corpse you got there, but I was gonna' say we're just here to buy some drugs man."

"There is the smoke of the furnace and the smoke of the land, yonder is the smoke of the land, I am the smoke of the furnace," the man responded, "there was once a time when the smoke of the land superseded the smoke of the furnace, that time has lapsed, and now is the time when the furnace shall hold sovereignty over the Earth. Now, I shalt not repeat myself, sitteth down for the feast!" The man's shrill voice echoed throughout the room.

"What the hell is he talking about?" Vinny said to Sara.

Sara turned her head from her search for an exit and saw Cody drift carefully toward the opposite end of the dining room table to sit down. Sara spoke for the first time since they had entered the house. "No thanks on the whole feast thing, we just ate actually. To be honest, we're in a bit of a rush and only came here to buy some drugs, so if we could do that and be on our way, I'd really appreciate it, mister?"

"Father."

"Mr. Father?"

"Just Father, a founding one at that."

"You're saying you're a founding father? Founder of what?"

"America."

Sara rolled her eyes, "oh so you're telling us here right now in the year 2003 that you're, who's the fat one, uh… Benjamin Franklin?"

"No, I am the Founding Father," Father said, sincerely. The guests could not help but to snicker, and Father noticed.

The sound of footsteps coming downstairs. Cody turned in surprise to see his cousin Max walk toward them. He had sunken cheeks and darkened eye sockets, and if the light were other than the chartreuse glow that enveloped them, Cody would be able to make out more clearly his cousin's jaundiced skin sagging from his bones.

"Father, I see that we have guests."

"Max, it's me, your cousin Cody. Don't you recognize me?"

"Yes of course I recognize you, Cody. I was wondering when you would make it."

"What are you talking about man? I had no idea you were even here. You remember Vinny, right? And this is my friend, Sara."

"Yes, of course I remember Vinny. We've been waiting for you. Don't mind Father's appearance. We were just having an orgy and we're all pretty loose with clothing around here."

"What?" Cody looked around, bewildered. "You knew we were coming?"

"Aye, I knew. From the fallen Firmament, I be," Father stated. His threatening aura receded. He sat back down in a gesture of relaxed satisfaction, his penis sliding through sauces on the ornate jade china dinner plate and causing it to crash to the floor and break without eliciting the slightest flinch from him.

"It's true," Max said, "soon you will see."

"Verily," said Father, "ask of me, and I shall give thee, the heathen for thine inheritance, and the uttermost parts of the Earth for thy possession."

"Wait, is he quoting the bible or something? This guy is fucking nuts," Vinny whispered to Sara. Cody stood listless, smiling at his cousin.

"Look, this is very generous and all, but we're not really into the orgy or swingers scene or whatever this is, really. We're just here to buy weed, like I said. And it's getting late, so how about it, then?" Sara pulled out a wad of cash and waved it desperately.

"How do you have so much money?" Vinny asked Sara, who elbowed him.

"I work for it," Sara said.

She tried to avoid eye contact with Father while talking to Vinny. Cody settled down at the long table opposite Father, who faded into the background as if he was some grotesque statue left behind by an ancient outer world for terrestrial ornamentation. Vinny was still visibly nervous, legs shaking, eyes shifting back and forth to make sure no one else came into the room with surprises. Sara backed up closer to the door. Suddenly, Father raised his hands while humming as if he was about to break out into singing a hymn. He gestured to the cradle with the shrunken, desiccated body in it, then opened his black eyes wide and fierce.

"This here is not the only token of mine power that ye' witness. Not even a fortnight hath passed since your Lord hath uncovered the buried treasure of Captain Kidd. This wealth shall be distributed amongst mine followers, and even the three of thee shalt receive a share, if ye' join us for the night," Father pulled out a burlap sack from under the table and emptied its contents out. A pile of gold doubloons spilled onto the fast-food feast set out in front of him, precious metals clanking off the wood. Vinny and Cody looked at each other in awe. Their host continued, "tis' this good fortune, which is not only of a material nature, but also a symbol of mine divine providence, that hath blessed us and proveth eternally mine authority on all things in these lands."

"We are grateful for your generosity, Father," Max said as he bowed.

"Tis' coming together quickly, everything under me, and all shall be right with the world. Earlier this very evening we came upon the beast in the pines, who, in its unnatural wrath, bore down on us with utmost malevolence, and yet we defeated the devil's child, so that I shall now wield its power. This night shalt be remembered as the beginning of the end. The cycle of history hath been broken, and all shall be made anew."

"Hear! Hear!" Max rejoined.

"Initiates of the Golden Dawn, heed mine words. Thou shalt abide by the authority of me, of each level of tree layered over which I rule. Thou art neophytes with no position. Zero upon zero. The three neophytes standing before us shall proveth themselves yet. Neophytes know not how to suffer the four elements. I shall unleash these elements upon thee. Whomsoever therefore resisteth the power, mine power, resisteth the ordinance of me: and they that resist shall receive to themselves damnation!"

"Initiates? This is insane. I didn't agree on joining any cult. This guy is crazy and quoting lines from the bible, or whatever is the bruja version of it, and these are probably the same Satanists that sacrificed that dog in the woods," Vinny leaned forward and mouthed as quietly as he could to Cody. Father heard and shifted his gaze over to Vinny, not knowing what else to do, Vinny started an awkward, slow clap. Cody and Sara joined the applause, which seemed to please Father and Max. Father lowered his bare head. Cody figured that Father was on drugs and fell back asleep, because he kept his head lowered in a trance for a while after his speech.

Max whispered to them. He said that they had acid for Vinny, and plenty of weed of many different strains for the trio to buy cheaply if they pleased. Sara still stood at a distance while Vinny and Cody were gathered at the close end of the table with Max. She was wary and not entranced by the theatrical performance of Father, nor the drugs nor food; she noticed in her constant scanning of the room that another door was hidden on the other side of the stairwell and crept toward it in a casual manner, as if she were pacing around because she was bored. A tiny latch snap. Sara was gone and the lumbering, naked being awakened from his trance.

A train of acolytes filed down the staircase. They wore the same clothes: new white sneakers, sky blue jeans, and black polo shirts tucked into their pants. They were clean-shaven and bald. Men of different ages, all the same, drone countenance. Father rose from his seat at the head of the table and welcomed the twelve of them. They sat down around Vinny and Cody without paying the young guests any mind. Father said grace, "each and every one of ye' shalt give me thanks. The bountiful feast and wealth that I hath bestowed upon thee is generous. Recognize my almighty reign and thy soul shall become one with me, and the moment I consume thee then thou shalt complete thy service to humanity." A silence, then Max and each acolyte thanked Father.

Vinny stared at Cody. The acolytes dug in, scarfing down cheeseburgers. Father massaged the mound of golden coins in front of him, smiling. Cody realized that the cultists, now that they were closer, had hands stained red with what looked like blood, and he recoiled. He looked toward Father, who swiveled his head back and forth watching his disciples eat. They sucked on their fingers loudly as they finished.

Another acolyte joined, this time from a hatch in the floor, holding in his bloodied hands a silver tray covered by an ornately engraved lid. Father rose again from his chair, coins spilling about, his penis becoming erect. Vinny covered half of his face. The new disciple lowered his head, kneeling to the floor, and raised the offering to his leader. Cody straightened up in his seat and craned his neck to see what would be uncovered. The servant lifted it to reveal a mound of slimy spheres. Father reached for the eyeballs and shoved a handful into his mouth, chomping messily. The audience kept their heads down.

A clanking of metal. The front door opened. Virgil rushed into the room, his face bleeding from his brow. Everyone turned to look at him except Vinny, who was high and staring forward, still stunned by the scene.

"Father, the girl escaped," the man approached Father with deference, chin lowered, kneeling by the head of the table. He held in one hand Cody's video camera, in the other The Jersey Devil, and raised them up to the figure. Cody tried to get out of his seat, but the acolyte sitting next to him held him down by his shoulder.

"This is my book," Father said, "and what is this device?"

"It's my video camera," Cody replied.

"Do'st thou mean to make a mockery of me and mine flock?"

"Uh… no, sir, I was just trying to make a movie about the Jersey Devil."

Father rose from the table and paced the perimeter, with all who were seated at it forcing their eyes downward so as to avoid looking at his naked body. Cody lifted his head to look at Father loafing over the congregation. Father whispered in Max's ear, his tongue touching the skin. Cody cleared his throat.

"Not to interrupt," Cody said, "but uh, I actually know about another buried treasure in New Jersey."

"Jesus Christ, Cody, dude, what are you doing?" Vinny whispered.

"It's all right bud, I got this handled," Cody told him.

"Proceed, child. If thou withholds thine secret from me, thou shalt be punished."

Cody confidently straightened his back and shrugged off the man who was holding him down. "There is an island that my dad showed me off the coast of Woodville, my hometown. Blackbeard's buried treasure is there, in the Delaware Bay, right by an abandoned shipping container. I know exactly which one. I could tell you if you let us get out of here."

"Verily, child. In due time. Thine wisdom in sharing this knowledge will grant thee mercy. But first, I must insist, thou shalt feast with us. Thy food remains untouched, you must eat it."

"Thanks," Cody winked at Vinny and gave him a thumbs up, "but, like we said, we literally just ate right before we got here, so we're good."

"I insist," Father raised his voice. Cody and Vinny picked up their cheeseburgers and looked at each other.

"So, are you the guy that left that book behind at the diner in Woodville? I was trying to return it to you actually, been looking for you this whole time. In a good way, I mean. Like, that's why we're here, also to buy the weed of course. Sorry that our friend was so rude and left, but I think she was just a little freaked out…"

"Cody, I think you're only making things worse," Vinny said.

Father glared at him, silent, turned his layered fleshy back to him, and walked to the wall to retrieve something that Cody could not see above the heads of the solemn acolytes. Cody began to sweat from his forehead so that the drops obscured his eyes. Vinny and Cody attempted to eat the burgers before them, even though they were full. Cody's chest grew in weight. He could hear metal dragging across the wooden floor. A slow, heavy heaving, then silence. Cody's retinas burned with salt. Everything was blurry to him.

Cody saw Max's eyes shoot toward Vinny, who was frozen with a wide gaze looking down, unaware of any movement around him, fixated on the burger in between his fingers, not daring to eat the meat itself. A cracking of a skull as Cody turned his head in terror to reveal the sanguine image. The moment stopped as if fixed upon a medieval painting of a martyr, eyes rolled into the back of his head, Vinny sat frozen while truncheoned by Father with a sledgehammer. Steel weight splitting brains.

Father posed naked over his prey in macabre ecstasy. Cody felt cold metal slap against his wrists and realized that his cousin had tried to handcuff him but missed. Besotted, Father lay upon Vinny's broken head. Max, who was bigger but weaker than his younger cousin, was too frail to restrain him, so he followed Cody silently among screams and reached after him and pulled the exposed gun out of the back of Cody's waistband. The two wrestled over the gun, and Cody accidentally pulled the trigger as he wrenched the weapon from Max's hands. The crowd of acolytes who had gathered around the fighting cousins scattered as one fell screaming from having been shot in the shoe, red spreading throughout white leather. The gun dropped and Max kicked it across the wooden floor. It was out of reach. Cody lunged at the beast, intent on taking him down. Father backhanded Cody across the temple and darkness overtook him.

Chapter Nine

A chain link fence no higher than five feet surrounded the perimeter of the cemetery, intended to keep out or in who knows what. Some humans thought it necessary to delineate the ground arbitrarily. Even the home of the dead has been deemed private property, and yet the earth still finds a way to reclaim. Vine swallowed steel forming an enigmatic bond between nature and man-made structure. The sun cast its own gloom upon all objects that day. Every shadow extended until penumbras merged with one another in metastatic totality.

The empty hearse moaned as it drove off with the other cars in tow. Only a few figures remained, all distant from one another for fear of having to hold a conversation. The sexton and graveyard workers chain smoked while impatiently perambulating the perimeter, waiting for the last of the bereaved to leave. They inhaled and exhaled plumes of smoke, sucking in carcinogens and blowing out gray cones, sometimes rings, the circles created out of boredom. The sexton inexplicably peered at the sun while covering his wide brow with his wrinkled, veiny hand. His skin became translucent, underneath blood flowed like lava.

The graveyard was mixed between new and old headstones in a seemingly random order of hereditary plots. There were some stones so aged and weathered that no words were visible any longer. Slanted, faceless slabs crying out blank words in decrepit anonymity. Some even dated back to the Civil War. Polished monuments worth many thousands of dollars loomed over simple oblong shapes in the ground. There was not enough time for a headstone to arrive. The newest plot lay nameless and naked on the day's burial.

A stone Virgin Mary stood at the end of the grave aisle with her arms outstretched. It could be seen even from far away that bits of rock had been chipped from the statue. Half of her face was shaven clean off and the mantle and tunic were tattered at parts, pockmark holed as if shot with buckshot, revealing not skin but the sky beyond her, like the heavens were her bare body. The azul firmament piercing through colorless stone.

A mother emerged from the internal void of her stunned grief to see the scene set out before her, holding a white handkerchief to her mouth. The casket was lowered into the grave with a pulley and ropes. There was nothing else to the ceremony. Whatever stragglers that were left began to leave, with only the family staying behind. A small tractor emptied dirt into the grave. Fresh soil blanketed the casket in cold suffocation. She stood by the grave as it was covered. The earth was flattened by workers using shovels. No tears marked her face, but her skin sagged, weighed down by the knowledge of loss. There was no temperature to the air, only a sense of grief.

Her funeral dress was beautiful but archaic, a Victorian gown of black lace. A veil covered her whole head, and she stood completely still, so that from far away she looked like a midnight obelisk projected outwards in defiance against the sun.

"Son, where are you?" She called out, feeling that her boy was still there, even seeing his figure in spite of everything, and finally wailing in lament. She choked on her tears until she felt like she was drowning.

"Mom."

Her husband had not made it to the burial. She cursed him in her thoughts. Men and their intransigence.

"Mom."

"Who's there? Son, is that you?"

"Mom."

The voice came from behind her, but she did not turn around because she felt the presence of a phantom obscured by the vine-covered fence a dozen yards ahead. She swore that she saw him, but he was not there. Leaves rustled, drifting a natural soundtrack in technicolor waves the way that only autumn afternoons can stoke sorrow. Red, orange, yellow: the colors of blood and fire. Blood scabs just like fire hardens. The scent of smoke omnipresent in the fall. Her head lowered toward the earth.

"Son, where have you gone?"

The Beast in the Pines

Chapter Ten

Father rose out of the Atlantic Ocean, same in all of his terrible form save scale, of which his true size was nearly incomprehensible, towering miles into the night sky. Around him rose inky columns etched in ancient runes. Great, dark green webs of stringy sargassum seaweed hung from both the monstrous figure and unknowable structures. Waves of horrible lengths crashed about, as if the very ocean had been lifted and turned upside down and inside out, dropped upon the mantle of the earth's crust by the unimaginable power that infinitely expands the universe itself. Dark energy pulsed through the air, emitting wavelengths immeasurable by human beings. Surely, this was the end of all things.

A faint light. Fetid miasma filling nostrils, evaporated time etching a wordless phantom across a subconscious. When what was done becomes invisible history. There was always this labyrinth. Why a mother cannot be blamed for cursing her soon-to-be-born child. The expectation of pain, pain looming in the dark ready to pounce on you at your most vulnerable. Why a suicide cannot be blamed for desiring death. But he knew now that he wanted to survive. Even if it was too late. He could not yet mourn. It was unfathomable until it was not, until he could fathom a similar fate.

Cody woke in a chamber of the dungeon beneath the mansion. His feet were buried in the sand floor, and he sat in a wooden chair, his hands were shackled behind his back by metal cuffs, which tore into his skin where he felt blood trickling. He stared at his sunken ankles from under the hair hanging over the top of his eyes. His breathing quickened until it became uncontrollable. He could hear his heart pounding spastically. In his desperation, he began to pray aloud, first at a whisper, and then louder, as he was able to regain control over his breath.

"Our father, who art in heaven, hallowed be thy name, thy kingdom come, thy will be done, on earth as it is in heaven. Give us this day our daily bread, and forgive us our trespasses, as we forgive those who trespass against us, and lead us not into temptation, but deliver us from evil."

"Amen!" A cackle in the dark. A steady sound of wood slamming against stone. A voice called out to him, "you're praying to our Father, but I'm not so sure he'll forgive you after that little stunt you tried to pull."

"Who's there?"

"You made a terrible mistake, Cody. You should have never attacked Father like that, especially while Father was feasting. You and your friends were deceitful in your reason for coming here. You didn't come here to buy drugs. You didn't come here to return Father's book about the devil. You didn't come here to tell Father about buried treasure. You came here looking for someone. You didn't find who you were looking for, but he's here."

It was Max talking to him. His voice was not coming from far away, but the sound bounced around the room, so that it was impossible to know where it was coming from exactly. Footsteps paced around him.

"Father is displeased with you, Cody. Father is always right. Father could not stand for the girl to escape, nor could Father tolerate your friend's insolence," every time Max said father he spoke louder. His sunken, scabby face emerged from the darkness. "Father had to punish you by killing your friend. I have seen Father do many great things. I saw Father fix this abandoned dump and return it to its past glory. I saw Father charm and control the local cops and politicians who now turn a blind eye to us, who've even joined us! I saw Father locate and dig up Captain Kidd's lost treasure. I saw Father kill the Jersey Devil with his bare hands. Father caught the beast out of the sky as it lunged toward me out in the Pine Barrens and choked it with his fists. Father may seem old and slow to you, but that's not really the case. Sometimes Father tires and falls into a sleeping state with his eyes open, but once Father awakes, there is a new sense of power. Father consumes what Father wants and that gives Father even more power. Father's power is necessary Cody, you would have come to understand if you joined us. Father was able to defeat the beast. Father becomes what Father consumes and I one day hope to be consumed by Father myself." Max leaned in close and peered into Cody's half-opened eyes. "I love Father, cousin. I really do, and Father loves me. Father loves us all so much that Father must devour all of us. It's something you can't understand. Father will become us all and when we are all consumed by Father then humanity will be saved by its own destruction by being destroyed itself. Father is all powerful, more powerful than you could ever know, and he's hunting your little friend now. She stands no chance against his power."

"I swear to God, if you say Father one more time, I'll save you the trouble and fucking kill myself."

"Your shitty sense of humor isn't going to save you, cousin."

A figure wearing a police uniform appeared before Cody holding a lamp with Max wheeling around to lurk behind him in the shadows. Cody raised his eyes and found that the man was recognizable. He was none other than Mike Ciliberti's father, his childhood bully who harangued him and had attacked Vinny by the pier in Woodville the week before. It felt like a different lifetime and a different world to him.

"Well, well, well, if it isn't this little prick," the cop pulled up Cody's bangs clutching a fistful of hair and tilting his chin with a hairy finger. "You know you're fucked, kid? You were in possession of a stolen firearm. You shot an innocent man while attempting to buy drugs. Your blood-covered jacket has been found. You and your friends murdered another innocent man. I saw you kill him myself. I was there. Then we found your video camera, which contains evidence against you. We found it all in your friend's pickup truck, which also has traces of blood on it. Who knows how many people you scumbags have killed? The child abuse on your video camera must be the tip of the iceberg. Now, we can't see the faces of the men in the video who were committing such a heinous act, but that doesn't matter. You're clearly complicit in that crime as well. Maybe one of the men was your loser father? You're fucked."

"Lies," Cody whispered.

"What the fuck did you just say little boy?"

"You're lying," the officer punched him in the side of the head, and the strike was hard enough that Cody toppled over with the chair. His bloodied face sank into the sand, and he coughed slightly, choking as it half-filled his mouth. He was pulled back upright by his hair and hung like a rag doll while still attached to the chair.

"Why are you and your moron son so obsessed with me?"

Mr. Ciliberti punched Cody in the face again, but this time he wasn't knocked over. The cop lifted the necklace from around Cody's neck and threw it back at his chest, "just because you're wearing a cross around your neck doesn't make you Christian, boy."

"I'm not fucking Christian," the man seemed confused and irritated by Cody's response, so he just struck him again and laughed.

"So who were you praying to if not the big man upstairs? You know what, I don't give a shit. I gotta' get going. You'll be getting more than just a few punches later. Now that it's a reasonable hour I have to go and file these police reports against you. And that little piney whore, she'll get what's coming to her. In the meantime, your cousin here will take care of you."

Cody quietly grimaced. Officer Ciliberti left the cell and strutted into the darkness toward various moans and shouts that Cody only now began to notice. A hatch slammed shut. Max disappeared from view as well, but Cody could still feel his presence adrift among the murmurs of what could be none other than fellow captives in the distance. The cold metal of the handcuffs cut deeper into his forearms as he slid the steel slowly down his thick forearms onto his thinner wrists. The handcuffs would not fit over his left hand, but he was inspired with newfound hope when he realized that his right hand could possibly come loose due to his thumb on the side being softer at the joint. The injury from his failed punch against his captor's son could save him. He popped his thumb out of place and in that moment his hand jerked out of the cuff. His left hand was still attached to the chair by chain so he placed his knee on the seat for leverage and pulled as hard as he could until the wooden slate snapped off the back of the chair. He winced, grinning in a fit of desperate triumph, the crack a din, the wooden rod slapping back at him and cutting him even more in the face, but he did not mind, his wounds numbed by adrenaline. There was a loud thud that came from the other side of the basement. He suddenly stood up, the blood rushing to his head, making him feel dizzy. His bloody chain dangled from his left wrist like an umbilical cord he could not get rid of, but he was free. He snapped his right thumb back into place with a cringe and tried to get his bearings before Max appeared holding a baseball bat wrapped in barbed wire and with nails driven into the wood. The spikes were dulled with use and darkened with stains.

"Now you've done it, cousin. I was going to persuade you to join us. I wanted to convince you to be with Father, to become one with Father, because that was Father's will, but now you've gone and done it. Father was going to grant you mercy for telling us about Blackbeard's buried treasure."

"That shit's not real man, you're fucking nuts."

"Oh that's where you're wrong, cousin. You could have joined us, and Father would have shared with you the spoils. But once you betray Father there is no turning back. You can't reason with Father. Now your eyeballs will be served at Father's next feast."

Max swung the bat at Cody but missed. He lunged with a flurry of strikes against Cody and beat the toothed bat into arm flesh. The metallic smell of both blood and nails mixed together. Max's face contorted, possessed with the pleasure of enacting violence upon his cousin. The bat swung wildly. Cody was quicker and stronger though, and once Max got a nail caught in the chain of the handcuffs, Cody was able to grab onto the end of the cord and pull the weapon free from Max's grasp. The bat changed hands in an instant, and Cody held the bludgeon aloft.

"Hit me! Why don't you hit me back? Beat me like I beat you!"

Cody hesitated, "no, I can't do that to you."

"What? Just do it cousin. Violence will save you. Come on and hit me. It will bring you pleasure. I am begging you to beat me."

"I'm not going to hit you."

"Do it pussy! Why can't you? You're a coward. Fuck you, you little bitch. Fuck you and your fucking dead friend."

"I'm not going to hit you," Cody calmly repeated, self-enlightened by his decision.

The silent standoff after the exchange of words lasted only moments before Max ran off down the hall, sand spraying in his wake. Cody followed the sound through the darkness of his cousin scampering away, picking up speed for fear of Father's return from hunting Sara. He worried that Sara was already caught but tried to focus only forward on his blind chase. Max stomped up wooden stairs and emerged above ground before Cody could get to the bottom stairs. The trapdoor slammed shut and Cody tried to push it up, but it was barred from the top. A glimpse upstairs was visible through iron bars, between which Max's wan face appeared. He spat into Cody's eye and smiled.

Father quietly loomed behind Max and mirrored his smile. Cody froze, wide eyed, as he watched the beast grab his cousin's throat from behind, his meaty hand completely encircling Max's neck. A brief shriek and then the larynx popped as ghastly fingernails pierced skin and flesh. Max struggled, flailing his arms about while gasping for air. His eyes burst from his face, and he exhaled blood. The eyeballs dangled lifelessly in the light. Father raised Max's body limp like a puppet and shoved it face first between the iron bars, each oculus hanging by optic nerves and splashing foul liquid into Cody's open mouth. The eyeballs hung from their sockets, staring blankly at Cody for a long moment. Father cast aside the body, and looked longingly down at his captive, then took a few steps back. Cody could not move until he felt warm liquid pouring over him, washing away the blood, and he coughed and sputtered, gagging until there was silence from above; he tasted ammonia. The man emitted a deep sniffing like a bear on the prowl in the wilderness.

"I shall return little one," Father said. Cody waited, looking down in disbelief with the bat in his hand, and then heard Father stomp away.

The putrid liquids he had swallowed made him heave and he vomited what little was inside of him onto the stairs. He turned around to find an electric torch that had a skeleton key attached to it and was relieved to be able to turn the lamp on and then immediately regretted doing so because of what he saw. Children in advanced states of filth and degradation inhabited the cellar among refuse and bales of straw that they fed upon, with bits of stalk stuck to their mouths. They were all crammed into wooden shelving stacked upon one another like cubby holes, their faces sticking out with limbs hanging all chained together as if they were livestock waiting for the slaughter. Each child held their head up to face the light shining upon them, jaws agape and brows shielding nothing below then downturned with shame the way a punished mendicant appears when shackled to a pillory in a town square. Cody could not see what was lacking in their faces and found the end of their connected chains that was locked to the wall and followed it, then subsequently unlocked each manacle with the key that was attached to the torch, the metal clanging to the floor. The children slowly emerged from their holes, falling onto the floor in pathetic heaps.

There were seven of them. Small creatures garbed in sackcloth. They stared bleary but eyeless at him. Little boys and girls caught in faint light like rats. Hellish cherubs, emaciated and blackened by dirt as if they were 19th century child coal miners. Some cried out, some garbled incoherent noises, but they all approached him stumbling without being able to say a word. He remembered the boy in the Supercenter held aloft by the beast and could not believe that he recognized one of them as that very same child. There was something wrong with his face, something absent. He had the same unmistakably long, curly hair, but something was off. Overridden with guilt, yet still pulsing with the strength of action caused by pain, Cody pretended to ignore the abused victims while he searched the basement for any other possible exit.

The light of the torch showed him a cavity in the stone wall above where he had been chained to the chair. In the recess there was plywood nailed to what looked like a window frame. A commotion upstairs. All sorts of yelling and pounding. Cody suspected that Father had returned from his hunt and was horrified to think that that beast had captured Sara. His arm felt like it was on fire, but he knew what he had to do and began to work on his task. He set the electric torch down facing the stairwell so that he could watch out for the enemy and went over to the chair and dragged it to what he thought must be a boarded-up window. The back of the chair was broken off, and he was just tall enough to be able to reach the hole while standing on top of it.

He swung the baseball bat at the sides of the plywood, trying to use leverage to catch the edges with the exposed nails in order to rip the barricade off. Every time he smacked the bat against the side of the plank, he dug a nail between the cracks to pry at the wood. Sulfur fumes filled the air but was hard to decipher with all of the other smells that permeated the cellar. The children surrounded him moaning as he did this and he kept looking back in terror behind them, expecting Father to appear. They were moving their mouths, but if they said any words, he could not hear them, his ears ringing inexplicably, and he kept imagining the beast barreling toward them from the stairwell as he tried to focus on breaking out. Instead when he turned his head again what he saw through the light of the lamp was somehow worse. A wall of dark smoke came from up the stairs through the iron bars of the trapdoor.

"The house is on fire," Cody yelled. The children gravitated closer to him in earnest.

He could finally hear the children screaming tiny words of lament. One jumped up and down while repeatedly wailing the word help. Was this it? The end seemed close. How eager human beings are to survive even at their lowest state.

"Cover your mouths," he commanded them gently, and they obeyed.

He went back to work, resisting the urge to stop even though he thought his arm was going to fall off of his body, the handcuff still attached to his wrist constantly smacking against him as he swung the baseball bat over and over chopping at the wood until he caught a snag and got stuck then leaned hard against the hilt using all of his weight to pull at the board, and to his amazement it broke off. He hacked at the wood again and again. Swinging the bat every which way like an axe until he could use the bat as a crowbar. Smoke filled the entirety of the basement, and the children were coughing and crying but otherwise patient as Cody fashioned a hole that gave a glimpse of the outside world. The sun pierced through, and Cody smashed the glass with the end of the bat then gasped at fresh air, but the smoke started to enter from that way too, so he dropped his bat and turned to the children with his hands outstretched in a sign to be calm. He coughed and had to return to covering his mouth and nose with his sleeve. His eyes burned with smoke, and he could barely see.

He picked up the children one by one, burrowing his face into his shoulder and shoving their emaciated bodies through the gap as they crawled out and ran towards the woods. The last child was sent through to escape and he panted into his sleeve wheezing from smoke inhalation. He finally climbed himself up the wall, struggling and kicking the chair over in the process, almost falling, hanging against cement in a purgatory between the outer world and hell. He could not see through the smoke at all anymore and screamed in agony thinking that he was being pulled from behind by the beast until he realized in spite of inertia that he was being dragged forward, having been freed from the gaping maw of captivity.

The mansion was ablaze, and the heat burned his body as he was dragged through the sand and grass and finally he got the smoke out of his eyes to see the welcoming faces of Sara and Erica. They carried him across the front lawn into the trees where the children stood in utter wretchedness as birds chirped while the brightness of day and the inferno pulsed together in lucid awe. It was only then that he came to understand that the children had no eyes. In place of eyeballs were indents filled with burned skin. The blind children all faced the burning house as if they were watching anyway. He turned his head to see a body prostrated towards the pines with a bullet hole in the back of the head. It was the corpse of Officer Ciliberti, his police uniform sticky with dark blood.

"I shot him," Erica said, proudly, like it was a deer they'd been stalking for mere hours and the scene before them was a tranquil afternoon in the beauty of nature and not the blaze of a collapsing house. The structure split in the middle as it gradually fell apart and Cody feared the fire approaching them, but the sand that surrounded the house appeared to stop the blaze from spreading.

"We barred them inside and lit the flame. We knew that piece of shit cousin of yours and that disgusting thing they called Father were in there, but we didn't know… I'm so sorry, Cody. I thought they killed y'all when I ran away because I heard screaming. I didn't know you were still alive, and that…" for lack of words she gestured towards the pitiful eyeless children who were all facing the fire while standing around empty jugs of gasoline.

"It's okay," Cody whispered.

"Holy shit," Sara moaned, as she noticed the children's faces. Erica covered her mouth and approached them, then backed away in horror while shielding her eyes.

"These kids…"

"Yeah, Father ate their eyes," Cody said in shock.

"Vinny, is he, what did they do, did he actually?" Sara already knew the answer to her question but did not know what else to say.

"Yeah, Father killed him," Cody began to breathe normally.

"We have Vinny's truck. Let's get the fuck out of here, Erica, help me throw some of this shit out of the back of it so we can fit these kids in," Cody could not move, and felt catharsis laying there in a bed of grass surrounded by sand and pine needles. He pulled his necklace off and cast it beside the corpse. Officer Ciliberti's lifeless body reached beyond him. The crucifix sank into the sand as the sisters picked him up and placed him on the bench in the cab of the truck.

"Erica, help me bring the body as close to the house as possible."

They dragged the corpse as close as they could get while holding it from either end, swung the body back and forth for momentum, and tossed it towards the flames, then with the same dirtied hands, they helped each other bring the children onto the back of the pickup.

"Where are we going to take them?" Erica asked Sara.

"To the hospital."

Sara hopped in the driver's seat and reached under the steering wheel and sparked the ignition wires and then shifted the vehicle into gear to speed down the dirt path as Cody watched the house implode while engulfed in flames through the rearview mirror, the heads of the blinded children swaying with the bumps in the road as they sat huddled together holding each other.

Chapter Eleven

They took back roads, hardly passing another soul, the few cars they did pass driving too fast to recognize their bizarre cargo. Sara drove past tall pines and through a sparse dwarf forest and finally through fields of dandelions and nameless weeds that looked like they survived through millions of years from the Cretaceous period before pulling into the rural hospital parking lot trailing a cloud of dust. Squalid refugees lounged patiently in a metal bed; their brains not yet having dredged back up the pushed down memories in order to continue operating.

Cody kept looking back at the blinded children, fearing one would fall out of the vehicle or even purposely fling themselves onto the asphalt in order to erase the reality of what had happened to them. Instead they held on to each other and to the rails of the truck, skinny shoulders exposed with bony spider leg arms in silent communal survival. Red and yellow leaves half-covered some of the trees surrounding the hospital. Many of the trees were already completely bare. They had escaped the eternal green of the pine forest.

"How are we gonna explain this shit to the hospital staff?"

"I don't know, Sara, this was your idea. Not saying it's a bad idea, I mean where else would we take them? Definitely not a police station," Erica pondered as they parked on the outskirts of the lot. Cody remained silent.

"Hey bud," Sara turned to him, "you look like you need a fixin' up in there yourself. You're bleeding all over the place. Just, don't say nothin' to them about what happened. Or you know what? We can drop them off here and then take you to the hospital in Atlantic City and say like, you got in a fight or somethin'. God, you smell awful. I'm sorry, but never mind, let's just let you out here. I've been wantin' to throw up this whole time."

"Where are we at now?" Cody found the willpower to turn his head and look at her but could only keep his eyes on her lips.

"We're in Voorhees, close to Cherry Hill. This hospital is brand new. You'll be fine here; I think we're far enough away from the fire and it won't be suspicious."

"Where's my stuff?"

"I don't know. When I escaped there was nothin' inside the truck. Someone must of took it. Maybe it was the creepy dude Virgil who led us there?"

He did not answer, not caring about Sara's indecisiveness about where to drop him off, or who took what or why, and just stared ahead at the hospital building thinking about how trivial it was that he regretted his possessions becoming lost, especially the video camera stolen from the Supercenter, the gun taken from the man Sara killed, and the book about the Jersey Devil. The Jersey Devil.

He remembered the sewn together mixture of decayed body parts. A crazed jester's fever hallucination of an infant demon. Was it all a dream? No. This was reality, and it could be explained. Or could it? Cody thought at first that the corpse of the Jersey Devil was a madman's reproduction, but he was not so sure. Deep inside he believed that was the Jersey Devil. Maybe it was real. He had forgotten for a time about the whole reason why they got into this mess. It was all his fault, he thought. The guilt became overwhelming, and then he remembered what happened to Sara and Erica's little brother.

"Where's Steve?"

"Joanna been watchin' him," Sara said.

"Who?"

"Joanna, she's my… you met her. She was the bartender at the Mud Hole Inn."

"Oh yeah, does she know what happened to Steve?"

"She knows enough. Now, what exactly are we gonna' tell these hospital folk? I say we just drop them kids off and be on our way."

"We could explain…" his words drifted away.

"Explain, how? Let's just let the kids go through first and then you go after them, Cody, and pretend like you don't know them," Sara's tone was stern.

"How the fuck are they gonna' get in the hospital without our help? They don't have fucking eyeballs, for Christ's sake," Cody yelled.

"Geez, okay, I'll take care of it," Sara said.

"How about we stop worrying about ourselves and get these kids to safety?" Erica raised her voice angrily when she asked the question. She had enough with their bickering and turned back to look through the window with wide eyes at the children and their downcast heads.

"Erica's right," Cody said, "let's get this over with…"

"Okay, but first let me get that handcuff off your wrist," Sara pulled a hair pin from her bun and straightened the frail metal into a rudimentary lock pick then worked at the hole in the cuff until she was able to press the tiny button inside and pop it off. She looked up and smiled weakly at him, then got out and picked up the children one by one, whispering in their ears while forming them in a single file, guiding them to the hospital entrance and running back to the truck before anyone could see her.

The children entered through the automatic hospital doors, shuffling into the emergency room lobby covered in ash, excrement, blood, and wearing tattered rags. A woman at the front desk raised her head from her paperwork and switched between her two glasses with her mouth open witnessing these tattered children enter her otherwise mundane day. She dropped her glasses and picked up the telephone and muttered some words into it and a group of nurses and doctors rushed into the room to take the coughing children beyond the doors into the inner workings of the hospital. Cody walked in as soon as they were gone and stood until he was able to get her attention. He turned to see that Erica and Sara had never entered with him even though he thought they were right behind him. Through the window he could see the pickup truck drive away back east towards the Pine Barrens.

He said he had been in a car accident and was handed some paperwork and asked to have a seat in one of the thin cloth waiting room chairs. The woman was crying silently behind her desk. Enervated finally by everything that had happened, he collapsed onto the linoleum floor, mumbling repeatedly that he was okay. A gurney was brought out for him and he climbed exhausted onto the lowered bed and fell face first into the cushion that smelled sterile and felt stiff but soft. Someone tossed him on his side and asked him questions and he moaned yes or no until he was brought into a room where they took a needle connected to a bag and hooked him up to fluids through his good arm. He had no identification, no possessions, just his ragged clothes and his injuries. Kind faces hovered above him. Mouths with reassuring smiles and eyes glazed over yet still somehow communicating concern. He fell into a deep sleep.

A body made vermiculite. Torches fluttering in a deep abyss until the tiny fires merge to fill a furnace. In the organic vessel lie countless seeds. Flies inhabiting flesh. Porous sand shifting. An explosion in a faraway desert. Camouflaged soldiers escaping the hatch of a burning tank. Gunshots crackling in sunlight. Bullets pinging off metal. Men yelling in Arabic about God and men yelling in English about hell. A blinding flash washed off the darkness.

He woke up alone to oblique patterns of light warmly caressing his skin. He felt sore but good, refreshed, brighter and cheerier than he could ever imagine. He half expected to see his friends approach him, Vinny in particular, and hug him and tell him it was all right, that it was just a bad dream and he had gotten too drunk and high, but that nothing terrible had happened besides an intoxicated accident. His bandages were clean, and he must have been changed by someone because he wore a hospital gown. His IV was empty and he could hear authoritative voices in the hall.

An ache remained where the handcuffs had been and he felt a sudden panic that the hospital had mistaken him for a runaway fugitive even though Sara took off the handcuffs because you could still see the marks it left, so he pulled the tube out of his arm and covered the blood with some leftover bandage he found next to him before rising and creeping to the door to peek down the hall and see police officers speaking with doctors and nurses. He exited the room and snuck in the opposite direction, his bare behind exposed, and ducked into the nearest opening to find a row of lockers with no locks on them. With deft silence, he shut the door and unrobed himself and looked at what little of his enfeebled state he could see, then rifled through the lockers to find clothing that suited him. He found some jeans that were only a few inches too long for him and a shirt and hooded jacket that were a bit oversized too but worked in a pinch. He looked like a child trying on adult clothes, so he cuffed everything and was relieved to find change and a few crumpled dollar bills in his new pockets, enough for bus fare and then some, and so in his hurry he left behind everything else to climb out of the first floor window, falling into some bushes and crawling across the lawn until he could duck behind a car and check to make sure he was not being followed. Then he gathered himself to sprint across the parking lot toward the woods he had so recently escaped.

Hunger enveloped him. He followed a path in the fields until he saw a highway that he followed for a few hours to an intersection by a suburban development. Stomach pangs haunted him. A suburban development filled with houses that all looked the same. White tiled wooden structures prefabricated to hold fabrications. Gray clouds stretched in the blue abyss beyond. A lone black metal bench planted on the corner by a sign for New Jersey Transit that depicted a bus along with numbers that meant nothing to him. The bus arrived and he smiled at the bored driver while placing coins into the slot and sat down, careful to seem nonchalant. He gazed through the dirty window until he began to recognize the Pine Barrens in the light of day.

A bearded vagabond sat across from him and asked if he could have the newspaper on the bench close-by. Cody said yes and handed it to him. The headline on the front page read, "CALIFORNIA CEDAR FIRE KILLS 15, DESTROYS

2,000 HOMES AND QUARTER MILLION ACRES," and below it, "FLORIDA UPSETS NEW YORK IN WORLD SERIES," he regretted missing watching the World Series, an activity he would share with his father every fall. He thought about how there was a forest fire at the same time in California as there was in New Jersey, and wondered whether fires were always burning, destroying something somewhere in the world. He began to hate the color red and noticed it everywhere. He saw red mailboxes, red flowers, red cars, red leaves, and red lights.

It was not long before the bus passed a building that seemed familiar to him. He noticed then that the Mud Hole Inn was home to an old-fashioned, rusting, paint chipped red fire truck parked at the forefront of its gravel parking lot. He had second thoughts about stopping there, but his hunger overtook his reasoning. He pulled the rope to be let off and had to walk back about ten minutes to the Mud Hole Inn. A pillar of smoke drifted in the distance. The scarecrow stood naked in the field across the street, no longer wearing a firefighter's jacket; why it was removed he could not comprehend. He felt like he was starving so he walked into the bar without hesitation and sat on a stool and wondered whether the attractive bartender would remember him. He forgot her name for a moment while walking towards the barstool, then was relieved when he saw her face and remembered that it was Joanna, and that there was something peculiar about her. Her red hair shined under fluorescent lights. While fingering the quarters in his jeans he looked at the people around him: pineys, retirees, some young construction workers in their neon yellow vests on lunch break. No one regarded him with more suspicion than usual, and he felt secure. The bartender approached him with indifference until she got close.

"I know you," she said, and his stomach churned even though nothing was inside save liquid.

"Yeah, let me explain," he whispered.

"No need honey, you look a little worse for wear, but you're a friend of Sara's, so you're a friend of mine. What can I get you?"

After the bus fare there was less than five dollars on him, but it was enough for french fries and a glass of light beer. He ordered and tried to slowly savor the beer even though it was more refreshing than any glass of water he had ever drank before and he ate the fries dipped in ketchup with delight until he was struck by a flashing memory of the beast with his penis dragging through ketchup and destroying chinaware. Disgusted, he pushed the half-filled basket away even though he was still hungry. The ketchup was a darker red than what he thought it should be, a crimson mound. When she saw that he was finished, she asked if he wanted another beer. He said he could not afford it, but she handed him a pint and winked at him.

"Don't worry about it, sweetheart."

He was comfortable in his new clothes and sauntered to the bathroom to urinate and wash his hands and face. The bathroom smelled of bleach. He barely recognized himself in the mirror. When he returned to his bar stool the man sitting next to him was bragging to a construction worker about how he lied to the cops after hitting his girlfriend and that they believed him. Cody felt déjà vu and side eyed him, and then noticed that the bartender was looking at him and shaking her head as if to say do not say anything. He heeded her unspoken instructions.

"Joanna, right?"

"Yes honey, what's up?"

"Can you do me a favor and call Sara's house to see if she's home? I forgot her phone number."

"Her house doesn't have a phone, but I can try to reach her on her cell," she said suspiciously.

"Please?"

"What's the matter, um, remind me your name again?"

"It's Cody."

"Got it. Why do you need to speak with her?"

"Please, it's urgent and I can't really talk about it."

"Well, we'll see what she has to say about that."

While she spoke on the phone, he overheard two old folks across the bar talking about how they saw that there was a big fire not far away and that three different township's fire departments were called out to stop it from becoming a massive forest fire. He wondered whether the fire was strong enough to burn the corpses to a crisp and make them unidentifiable, but then remembered from shows he would watch on TV with his dad that there was new DNA technology that could identify even the most destroyed of bodies, was it the teeth that they used? He was not sure, but worried about being thought of as guilty and his mind began to race because previously, he had thought himself in the clear, having escaped questioning from the police at the hospital that morning. Joanna was speaking with Sara on the phone for what seemed like a long time while intermittently looking back at Cody. She hung up and walked over to him. Her demeanor had changed from suspicion to empathy.

"She's on her way over, honey."

"Great, thanks so much."

The television played cable news over a backdrop of a Washington D.C. skyline. The corner of the TV screen said it was 3:16 PM ET, October 29th. One of the old men across the bar who was watching intently with his head tilted up at the TV wore a t-shirt depicting Jesus hanging from the cross with an American flag draped around his shoulders. The blood from his crown of thorns missed dripping onto the flag, the symbol unblemished. Cody had seen a rack of those shirts on display when he worked at the Supercenter. The closed captioning on the TV was tiny, but he could make out some words: "Two GIs killed in Iraq. M1 Abrams Tank disabled by roadside bomb. Crew attacked by unidentified gunmen. First American tank to be destroyed since the end of major combat in May. A recent wave of attacks by insurgents…" Cody had forgotten about the war. The pundits argued whether more American soldiers were needed to be sent to Iraq.

When Sara arrived, she gave Joanna a hug and a kiss and had a shot of whiskey and a beer and Cody felt like things were back to normal. He considered criticizing Sara for abandoning him twice, and then decided against it for fear of her doing so a third time. He did not know who else to turn to, where else to go. She acted like nothing had happened. She smiled at him briefly, her elbow leaning against the polished pine bar.

Joanna spoke with Sara while Cody stared at the TV screen and wondered what it would be like if he was able to enlist and be deployed to Iraq, if it would have been any worse than the horrors he had experienced in New Jersey. Sara paid their tab and kissed Joanna again, longer this time, on the mouth, while touching her cheek tenderly; a few older patrons glared at her as she ushered Cody out to the parking lot where Vinny's old pickup truck sat newly painted red instead of blue with a fixed bumper and side view mirror and a different license plate.

"Wow, how did you do that so quick?"

"My dad used to be a mechanic. We've got a bunch of parts and stuff at the house. You'll see once we get there."

"That's impressive. Uh, are you and Joanna… uh?"

"A thing? Yes."

"That's cool, but isn't she?"

"A bit older? Yeah, but not that much, she's only thirty, and she's smokin' hot."

"Yeah, dude, she is, uh, hey, you mind if I call my folks real quick? I just want to let them know I'm okay."

"Sure, just be careful what you say."

Cody fit some change in the slot then picked up the pay phone and dialed the number for his parent's house, one of only three he had memorized. The other ones were Vinny's house, where he did not dare think of calling, and his sister Emma's cell phone, which he considered dialing, but then realized he would feel compelled to tell her everything because of how close he used to be to her, so he decided against it; he did not want to get her involved in any trouble. An incessant bell ringing. He tapped the rusty bottom of the pay phone box, and a sigh materialized on the other end.

"Hello, who's this?"

"Dad, it's me."

"Cody, your mother is worried sick about you. What's going on?"

"Nothing dad, I just went camping and fishing with Vinny like I told you we would, and it's gone on a bit longer than I thought because I lost my phone in the woods and we were looking for it," he tried to think of a better lie but could not and so he just trailed off to silence on the line. "Dad?"

"Yeah, I'm here son. Your mom is at work. I'll let her know you're okay. How's Vinny doing?"

"Fine."

"Catch anything big?"

"Yeah, we uh, we caught a real big one," tears began streaming down his cheeks. Sara glanced at him sympathetically then looked down at the gravel she stood on and lazily kicked rocks around.

"When are you coming back home?"

"Tell mom that I love her," and at that he hung up the phone, the plastic clanging on the metal receiver, and leaned his forehead against the cold payphone booth. He cried silently for a little until he felt her hand on his shoulder.

"Come on, let's go."

"Where are we going?"

"Home."

They drove south, away from the smoke, multiple fire trucks flying by them in the opposite direction. It was a full on forest fire. The smell drifted for miles. He looked back, listening to the blaring sirens. The bed of the pickup truck was clean and empty. The sky was dirty with both clouds and smoke. The black smoke pillar had expanded. The image made Cody recall where he was when 9/11 happened two years before, how he was sitting in history class in high school and the principal made an announcement over the intercom that there had been an incident in New York. The teacher rolled a television into the classroom and turned on the news for everyone to watch the billowing black columns of smoke hovering over the city. How the room full of teenagers just sat there in silence, watching. Sara turned off the highway onto a dirt road and they rocked in the truck as if adrift deep in the stormy Atlantic. The pine trees had thin trunks and were lined up orderly in this part of the woods. They could no longer see any smoke but could smell a faint trace of it in the air as they exited the truck. Cody followed Sara up the path to her house.

"Hey Sara, why does that sign on that tree say Ong's Hat?"

"That's the name of this town."

"I don't see a town."

"That's because it's a ghost town, Cody."

"So it used to be a town? When? And who or what is an Ong?"

Sara stopped Cody, placing her hand on his shoulder. "A few hundred years ago there was this guy named Ong. Ong was a fine lookin' fella for the time and the place. There was lots of rumors about what he was, a highwayman robber, a disinherited nobleman, even a castaway pirate. He certainly wasn't no local piney, that's for sure, and his mustache was shinier and longer than any other man's in the county, which the ladies liked. He also had this black silk hat that he was real proud of, you know, the big kind with the long brim that them three musketeers used to wear. It was out of fashion even for then, which was the 1700's, before the revolution, and no one knows for sure where he found that hat, some say he stole it off a man he done robbed and killed in the pines, but he fancied it and felt like the damned hat gave him some sort of divine right to flirt with every pretty woman he ever done saw. One day he came to this tavern nearby to where we're standing here right now. There was a dance that night, all the folks from the surrounding farms came together to drink moonshine and swing around to the sound of fiddles and hand drums. Ong saw this one pretty lady who seemed to be alone at the time; she wore one of them corsets that pushed her tits up and had long curly locks. He offered out his hand to hers and asked her to dance. She smiled and blushed and before she could answer he took her by the waist and began spinning her around with him. That moment her young husband came out from pissing behind a tree, saw his new wife being groped by the most notorious fancy man in all of the land, and punched Ong in the back of the head. Ong's hat fell off; the woman's husband took it from the ground and threw it up in the air. The hat landed high up on the end of the branch of a big pine tree. Yes, that one yonder there. Ong wasn't too happy about that. He got up out of the mud, pulled out a big blade and stabbed the man in the heart. The woman screamed and ran away, but the rest of the crowd grabbed Ong and tied him up with ropes while they debated on what to do with him. Most of the people wanted to take him to the sheriff to be tried and hanged legally, but the brothers of the man Ong murdered were also there that night, and they overpowered the others, drew him up and lynched him right on that same branch where his hat hung. The next day the same woman he was flirting with cut Ong down and buried him in a shallow grave nearby, but the story is that his hat hung there on that branch along with the rope for many months, if not years afterwards. That's why they call this place Ong's Hat."

"Jesus."

"Yep. Them's were my ancestors."

"Who? Ong, or the guys that killed him?"

"The guys that killed him." Sara gave Cody a wink. He was stunned into silence by the story.

They walked under the branch where the rope that killed Ong once hung centuries before. Her house was an unpainted wooden building in a clearing in the middle of the woods with a medley of rusted-out and broken-down cars strewn about. Aluminum rooftops dressed in the white waste of birds. The cars were in various states of disrepair. Some cars seemed to be in almost working condition and others were simply metal frames resting interminably on cinder blocks. She guided him into the screened concrete and wood porch and into the small vestibule of her home. What looked like a rustic cabin on the outside belied the inside, which was much larger than he thought it would be, with multiple rooms and an L shaped staircase leading to the second floor.

His eyes adjusted to the darkness until he could identify what looked like a living room with torn antique sofas and an array of curiosities: trinkets, dolls, an ancient manual sewing machine, old lamps, dusty books, a large RCA radio, and a phonograph. There was no TV and the electricity seemed weak, the lighting dim and few electronics. Cody assumed the house operated off of a generator. The kitchen was filled with a complete mess of cookware, but only because Erica was in the middle of baking. She was covered in flour, and stopped to smile and say hello to Cody then went back to work. Steve sat on the couch in the living room reading a comic book. The boy looked up briefly from what he was studying and then lowered his eyes, and they remained fixated at a point on the page. Cody turned to Sara.

"Is your dad home? What should I say to him?"

"Yes, he's upstairs. I wouldn't worry about saying nothin' to him. He ain't gonna' answer."

"What do you mean? I don't want him to be upset that a stranger is here."

"He won't be upset. He can't really understand what's goin' on anyway."

"What, why?"

"He's bedridden. Can't talk."

"He's sick?"

"Sure is, been like that for the last year. Thought he'd be gone sooner."

"I'm so sorry," Cody whispered.

"Well, he's actually pretty much dead; we keep him around for the disability checks," Sara laughed at her own joke, and her morbid sarcasm went over Cody's head as he gave her a concerned frown.

"What about your mom?"

"Oh, she died years ago."

"I'm sorry."

"Don't worry about it and quit sayin' sorry. It was a long time ago. Do you want to see for yourself?"

"Your dead mom?"

"No, yah' goofball, my dad. You can come say hi to him, since you seem so interested."

"Uh, okay."

He followed her up the creaky stairs onto the small second floor. There were two bedrooms and one bathroom. She guided him through the darkness into one of the rooms and then lit a lamp that was sitting on a table within, until then his heartbeat so hard he thought he was going to go into cardiac arrest. This was the first time he had been in a dark, confined space since the incident. He took deep breaths of the musty air. Faint light illuminated the room, at the center was an old bed covered with mounds of tattered blankets and quilts. Sara walked over to it and uncovered the body of a man whose eyes were open, and he was still. He looked like a skeleton with yellow skin still clinging to it. Whatever remnants of wispy, brown hair left on his head stood up from static. Cody stayed at the threshold.

"It's okay, you can come in…"

Cody stepped a few feet closer. "Uh, hello."

"Dad, this is Cody. He's a friend of ours that needs to stay the night and is gonna' sleep on the couch downstairs," Sara stated. The man moaned and wheezed a fit of weak coughs.

Cody was surprised that he had made a sound at all and was convinced before that moment that their dad was actually a corpse, and that Sara was crazy and really did keep a dead body around for disability checks. She took a sponge that was bedside and placed it in a bowl of water, then dabbed the man's mouth. The daughter fixed some pillows and pulled the blankets back over her father then ushered Cody out of the room and back downstairs.

"What's wrong with him?" Cody whispered as they walked down the stairs.

"He has lung cancer," Sara said.

"Oh, I'm sorry."

"Thanks."

"How's Steve?"

"He's doing the best he can, why don't you go hangout with him in the living room while I talk to Erica?"

"Okay."

He went to sit next to the boy on the floral-patterned couch and the child shifted away from him but looked up and said hello.

"Hi," Cody said, "what're you reading?"

"Comic book," said the boy.

"Is that the mutant series? The one where the big guy defeats the alien robots from the alternate dimension?"

"Yeah," Steve's eyes lit up a little.

"That's one of my all-time favorite comics. He can be the strongest being in the universe, but only when he gets real upset about something."

"I know. That's why he's my favorite superhero."

Cody's heart sank in his chest as he remembered what happened to Steve. Sara came back into the room with her hands on her hips. She looked at the two of them on the couch and smiled and then told Cody that he could stay the night until he figured out what he was going to do. He thanked her and then returned to talking about mutant superheroes with Steve and went over his comic book collection with him while dinner was being prepared. The smell was delightful and as night fell Cody helped build a fire in the fireplace. Erica brought dinner out to the living room on paper plates, and they sat around the coffee table drinking juice that came from powdered mix and dug into their food.

"What is this, like shepherd's pie or something?" Cody asked Erica, "no, it's venison meat pie."

"It's good!"

"Thanks, just be careful to look out for bullet fragments."

"Really?"

"She's kidding," Steve said, and chuckled.

After dinner, Cody laid on the couch while everyone else went upstairs. He slept a dreamless sleep that night and woke after nothingness to shafts of light infiltrating the cabin in a dazzling array like a laser show. Sara came downstairs in the morning and told him to get dressed.

"We're going into town to get some stuff."

"Okay."

They drove to a convenience store on the outskirts of Hammonton. While Sara was getting gas Cody walked into the store and looked at a man who dropped a freshly printed bundle onto the rack. He approached with caution. It was the local newspaper. The headline read, "FIRE IN THE PINE BARRENS, BODIES FOUND," Cody dropped the paper to the ground as Sara came inside. She saw it but did not say anything nor did she interrupt her looking around the small store as if she was searching for something in particular. He picked up the paper and put it back on the rack, not daring to read the article. Then he went outside to smoke his last cigarette. It burned far too fast. Sara came back out carrying a plastic bag holding cigarettes and a burner cell phone and looked toward the White Horse Pike. He watched the drivers and passengers in the cars pass by and covered his face. A hand on his shoulder.

"Maybe it's best we part ways, Cody."

"Yeah, I guess."

"I'll give you a few bucks. Lay low, head to Atlantic City, Philly, or New York. Or go back to your folks. Do whatever you want."

"I can't decide."

"You'll figure it out, kid."

"I'm sorry about your brother. And your dad."

"I'm sorry too: about him, my dad, and your friend Vinny. The world is fucked up, man. The only thing you got is to stick with family."

"Not me."

"Oh come on, y'all's relationship can't be that bad."

"I don't know."

"Listen to me. Just give it a try, what's the worst that could happen? No one's going to think you killed anyone. Tell them you got mixed up with the wrong crowd. A drug deal went bad and you ran away, but you can't just keep running from everything. Go back home. I'll drop you off at the bus stop and give you a few bucks."

"Okay."

"Just do me a favor and don't tell no one about me or my family. I don't want anyone to come lookin' for us. You promise?"

"I swear I won't tell anyone. I don't want to get in trouble either."

She looked at him for a moment, like she was convincing herself that he would not betray her. He offered her his pinky and they interlocked fingers. They got into the truck and drove down the street wordlessly. She slowed to a halt in front of a bus stop and waved him goodbye as he got out, leaving him under a simple shelter as the sun reached its apex in the blank slate above.

Chapter Twelve

"Mom."

She realized it was not her dead son calling to her but her living daughter. The revenant outcast watched Bianca approach her mother from behind the vine covered fence. He had observed the whole burial from behind that cover and cried in silence so as not to alert anyone of his presence. All that was left of the bereaved were the mother and sister. The graveyard workers milled about smoking cigarettes in the background by a tractor. Cars regularly sped down the highway in the distance, its constant drone negating any peace that might have been otherwise found in that place. He could not hear what the daughter was saying to her mother as she held her but felt it. They embraced for a long time. Cody wanted nothing more than to speak with his ex-girlfriend and dead best friend's sister.

The mother walked away to the parking lot while her daughter stayed behind and stared at the grave without a headstone. He eyed her with a mixture of sadness and longing. She wore a black lace dress that came down to just above her knees and her bare brown legs in the cold were covered in goosebumps. He looked her up and down and she was unblemished all about the skin except for two dried rivers of inky mascara in delicate lines along her high cheeks. Her hair half up and half resting in curled waves ruffling with the wind. He worked up the courage to call out to her.

"Hey, Bianca."

She looked toward him with her cunning brown eyes and immediately stepped in his direction, her heels piercing the grass. He wanted her to kiss him but thought for a second that she was going to attack him because of the intensity of her stare. She stopped for a second and then moved gracefully closer toward him.

"Cody, what happened?" She asked in a hurried whisper. They stood face to face with the fence in between them. She was crying silently.

"It's a long story, but you have to believe me. "

"Where exactly have you been?"

"Just please listen to me."

"What do you think I'm doing?"

"We were camping, you know, Vin and me, you know, just hanging out, you know, getting high and drunk, fishing and shooting the shit. Joking around about looking for the Jersey Devil. Then we wanted to buy some drugs and followed this weird guy we met at a bar to this wild abandoned mansion, and then that's when shit went crazy."

"And by shit went crazy you mean my fucking brother died and you disappeared?"

"Listen, please, I know it sounds nuts, but just hear me out."

"Okay," she breathed heavily.

"Thank you, Bee, well my cousin Max was there dealing drugs and he was following the orders of this insane cult leader dude who like, kidnapped children and shit and then this police officer was there, fucking Mike Ciliberti's fucking dad; he was in on it with the cult leader guy, Father, who murdered Vin, then I got trapped in this dungeon with all the missing children,"

"Wait, wait, wait, so you're saying your father killed Vinny?"

"No! Oh my God no, I mean, that was what they called the insane cult leader dude, Father, I mean he wasn't anyone's father, he wasn't even a man, he was a fucking beast. I mean he was a man. He was just fucking crazy. He claimed to be like a founding father or something. And he dug up buried treasure and caught the Jersey Devil. He attacked Vinny and me and then Max handcuffed me, and I was chained up in the basement and they were going to have their way with me or whatever but then the house caught fire and I thought that killed the bad guys and I was able to escape and help the children free…"

"Cody, Cody, calm down, this sounds crazy."

"I know," Cody was panting, almost hyperventilating. He considered telling Bianca about Sara and Erica, and then decided to keep his promise to them and not tell anyone about their existence. An uncomfortable silence ensued.

Bianca had backed up a few paces while Cody was frantically telling her what had happened. She looked back to make sure no one had wandered back into the graveyard and noticed she was speaking to him. "Do you want to know what they're saying?"

"Who?" Cody gripped the chain links of the fence.

"Everyone, it's on the local news."

"What?"

"That the fire was set on purpose."

"What?"

"That someone is wanted on suspicion for the deaths of my brother, your cousin, and Mr. Ciliberti. They didn't say your name, but…"

"That's, that's not what happened. What about Father, I mean, the beast?"

"Cody, they didn't say nothing about no cult leader. They only mentioned how they found bodies in the burned house." Bianca began to cry harder and wiped her face with some crumpled tissues she had taken out of her purse. "Like I said, they found Vinny, Max, and the cop. There coulda' been more people there but I don't know. They think that there was a drug deal gone bad. Then I found out you went missing. You called your dad and hung up. Your parents called hospitals looking for you. A hospital reported that someone matching your description was a patient there and that you left without permission. That was a couple days ago. Where have you been?"

"Surviving. I've been wandering around taking buses. Sleeping when I can. A few pineys helped me out with food and a place to stay."

"Do you realize how weird that sounds?"

"Yeah, but, what about the kids? They can vouch for me. I saved them."

"Who?"

"The children, what about the missing children? They were blind. I brought them to the hospital."

"Blind?"

"Blinded. They were fucking, the fucking cult guy ate their eyes," Cody's voice was shaking.

"What the hell? No. No one said nothing about that."

"Fuck," he dropped to his knees. Bianca walked closer to Cody, leaned against the fence, and looked down at him hunched over in supplication to the earth, grasping the grass and quivering.

The tone of her voice changed, "Cody, I'm not saying that anyone is out to get you, I'm just pointing out that it's weird you disappeared, and now you're saying all that crazy shit happened. Go back home. Your parents are worried about you."

"I can't. It looks like I did it. It looks like I'm guilty."

"No, I didn't mean it like that. Look, maybe they're not saying anything about the kids for a good reason. To protect their privacy or something."

"No, that must mean that Father took them."

"How? I thought you said that he died in the fire?"

"I thought so, but you just said that the news is saying they only found three bodies, and not mentioning the children, and that must mean… it must mean that he escaped, and that when the children went into the hospital that he found them and took them."

"Cody, how would that happen if you said you brought the children to the hospital? That means they're safe."

"No, it doesn't. One of the men that was hurting them was a police officer. It was fucking Mr. Ciliberti. I saw the beast, or Father, or whatever, kidnap a child in broad daylight at the Supercenter when I worked there. Oh, and I forgot, he was also the guy who made a scene at my mom's job and left behind the book about the Jersey Devil, and then after that is when he kidnapped that kid at the Supercenter. It was a few weeks ago." Head bowed and on his knees, Cody shook the chain links as he rapidly spoke.

"Wait, hold on, you've seen him before? Why didn't you say anything then?"

"Because I didn't know it was happening for real while it was happening. I guess I didn't have the courage and I made an excuse to myself thinking that the guy was just a weirdo and maybe it was his kid even though things didn't seem right. I thought that he was Amish because he spoke like he was from old times."

"Cody, it sounds like this guy is in your imagination."

"He's fucking not. There's a bunch of people who've seen him and shit," Cody clutched the grass beneath him.

"Okay, okay. I get it. I'm sure the kids are okay though. That cop is dead and the crazy guy you're talking about is probably dead too, maybe he got burnt up to a crisp and they couldn't find his body because of that, and if he's not he's got to be on the run somewhere and he'll get caught. This is nuts."

"It is nuts, but you gotta' believe me. You know I wouldn't ever do anything to hurt Vinny. He was my best friend," Cody started sobbing.

"I don't know why, but I believe you. I know you wouldn't do anything like that…"

"Really?" Cody looked up at her.

"I shouldn't, but I do. Look, I got to get going. My mother is beside herself and I'm worried about her. I can barely hold on myself. I've been able to keep it together enough just to be there for my mom."

"I'm sorry Bee…"

"Your parents were at the funeral. They didn't come to the burial. Like I said, they're worried about you. Why don't you go back home and tell them the truth?"

"I said I can't, they won't believe me."

"I do."

"But that's because you get me. My parents don't."

"Cody, that's not true. You're just acting all fucking crazy because you clearly seen some crazy shit. And people don't understand you, but that doesn't mean that in the end things won't be made right."

"I feel like I'm going crazy. I mean, you think that I made up the Father dude, but I swear to fucking God he was real. It sounds unbelievable. That's why people won't believe me, and my parents will be pissed at me. I don't feel like myself anymore. Something's changed in me. I don't know how to live with myself. I don't know. Can you just…"

Cody got to his feet. He wiped his hands off onto his dirty jeans and brushed his hair away from his eyes. Bianca's mother was calling her name from far away. She peeked behind her and then motioned with her hand for him to hurry, "What, Cody?"

"I feel bad asking, but can you give me a few bucks just to get by for the next day or so while I figure out what to say when I come out of hiding?"

"Normally I wouldn't help your broke ass, but here, this is all I got on me right now," she handed him a folded twenty.

"Thanks Bee."

"Now don't tell no one that I helped you. Get your fuckin' shit together and then go home to your parents. Figure it out. I shouldn't be doing this…"

"I won't tell anyone, and I'll figure it out soon, I promise. Bianca," he turned away and then slowly looked back, "I love you."

"No, don't say that, you don't love me like you think you do. Get the hell out of here," and at that she turned and walked away, her dress lifting a little with the wind and Cody feeling simultaneous lust and guilt only yards from her brother's burned and head cloven corpse entrapped within a casket and buried beneath dirt.

Chapter Thirteen

Cody's bus ride away from the graveyard was filled with trepidation. He spent the day thinking about what to do with the twenty-dollar bill Bianca had given him. The bus drivers would generally let him ride for free and doze off as long as he kept to himself. Sometimes he would drop a single dime in, and the driver would ignore it. At other times he would score big by finding quarters rolling across the floor. He slept in the Atlantic City bus station terminal with other homeless people. His wariness grew as police officers would sometimes look at him for a little too long, but he did not resemble the young man he was before. He hobbled from his injuries after his assault and captivity, not to mention being unbathed and patchily unshaven, which did not amount to a full beard and furthered his disheveled look. His hair had turned from dirty blond to a much darker shade.

He woke up the next morning on the floor of the terminal and took the next bus down south towards his hometown, looking out of the window as he tried to count the trees. In his peripheral vision Cody noticed an old man across the aisle muttering to himself. He glanced at him with a side eye, then stared straight ahead to make it seem like he was ignoring him while actually trying to listen. The bus driver looked back contemptuously at both of them and continued to drive. Cody leaned toward the old man, resting his elbow on his knee and his hand on his temple, realizing that the man's eyes were rolled almost all the way back, pointing upwards, bloodshot veins like tributaries of an infernal river. His long gray beard was filled with twigs and other debris, and he was bald except for patches at the sides that overlapped with his beard. He wore a large trench coat slightly open to reveal a bare, skeletal, fuzzy sternum, above which hung a six-pointed star on a silver necklace. All he wore underneath was a mule skin loincloth.

After getting a better look at the old man, Cody experienced a swift succession of strange phenomena: first a wave of sorrow washed over him, and he lamented all that he had witnessed in the past week, then he felt severe heartburn like a fire suddenly burning inside his chest, then he became certain that death was imminent, and finally he forgot who he was, drifting into a state of temporary amnesia. Mystified, he turned toward the old man, now openly listening to what at first seemed to be random ramblings until he was able to focus more closely on them.

"You cannot permanently run away from anything, ever. Whatever you are running from will always catch up with you. I understand that makes me seem like a hypocrite, but there's a difference between running and wandering. You wander because you're lost. You wander in order to find something, at first thinking that it's something external that you're looking for, and then realizing that it's internal. So why should you wander the world if what you're looking for is inside of yourself? The answer is that you can only find what's inside of yourself once you've traveled long enough. I have been tasked with journeying to every corner of the Earth. That is my purpose, in and of itself."

Cody looked to his left and right. Before he would have been too afraid to engage with the old man, thinking that he was a crazy homeless person, but now with his gift of forgetfulness, Cody was able to overcome such trivialities. He decided to play along, asking, "I don't know what I'm doing here. I mean, clearly, I'm on a bus that's driving through the woods, but I don't know why. Do I know you?"

"Yes, yes, yes, yet you only know a quarter of me. I've been wandering for a long time as well, much longer than you, though. I've been wandering my entire life. You wonder why? It's because I insulted a man who wasn't a man. He called himself the son of man, but his friends claimed that he wasn't the son of any man. There are many that call it a curse that's befallen me. I have come to learn that is not the case. I have attempted what you will attempt, and it will not work. The rope will break. I know the plan your subconscious has concocted, and I am here to tell you that it will fail, not because you are a failure, quite the opposite; you will survive, and you deserve to, even if it's solely for the sake of living in and of itself. You will live, yes, but first you must wander."

"Why should I wander?"

"You should wander for a time in order to reflect. You will not come to understand, but you will come to understand enough. You suffer for a reason. Your suffering has meaning. Your purpose is to help those who cannot help themselves. You have done that already. You have the choice now to keep doing that, or to succumb to the dread that what you have done isn't enough, and that what you do will never be enough. I'm telling you now that is foolhardy, with that mindset you will never be happy. Be satisfied."

The old man pulled at the rope above him, even though the road was desolate, with pine trees lining the highway. A loud screech of the brakes snapped Cody back from his amnestic trance as the wanderer walked up the aisle, down the stairs out of the bus, across the grass, and into a patch of purple spiderwort flowers and through the woods. The bus driver scoffed.

"Don't listen to that crazy old man, kid. You're too young to be homeless. Stop doing drugs, get a job, and contribute to society, and eventually good things will come your way," and at this the bus driver turned his eyes back to the road and put his foot on the gas. Cody did not answer him but stared off at the passing trees.

He got off the bus in a town he did not know the name of on the edge of the Pine Barrens. His presence had been becoming too noticeable by the driver and passengers who had gotten on, and he was paranoid that someone would question him. Too many eyeballs passed over his pitiful state for his liking. There were no sidewalks to be had in this town. The place was not meant for walking. Cars sped by him as he negotiated his way through dead leaves and trash. A red street sign stated that he was on Tuckahoe Road. There was a church a few blocks from where he had disembarked. The building's modest steeple towered over every other house in town, a sparse collection of ranchers. The trees were taller than the church.

He tilted his chin upwards as he stumbled toward the house of God. A sign stood on the front lawn, "CHURCH OF THE RESURRECTION, CONFESSION 5PM, VIGIL 6PM, MASS SUN 9AM, 11AM." The brackish scent of the Great Egg Harbor Bay drifted through the air, so he knew he was somewhere off Route 9 that was close to the ocean. He tripped over a crack in the street and scraped the palms of his hands on the pavement to stop himself. While wiping the blood repeatedly off onto his jeans, he walked up to the wide church stairs. The door was open.

Inside the darkness of the church, he could see a figure standing by the altar. It was a modern church, and lacked the grandeur of any old cathedral, except for the exquisite stained-glass windows, emitting bluish light, that lined the walls. As he placed his hand into the metal bowl by the door, tar and blood spread throughout the cold holy water. His palm stung as if his hand was pierced by an icicle, and he sucked on his broken skin to try to relieve the pain, the salt drying his mouth. The socks that he wore were wet with warm blood. Blisters had formed on his feet from constant walking. He stared at a stained-glass window that depicted a woman in a blue robe on her knees with her hands covering her face in lamentation. He sat down in the nearest pew and clasped his palms together until the stinging abated, rubbing a splinter in the wooden bench with his pink knuckles until it broke off and fell onto the dark tiles below. His head was lowered, and he pretended to pray, but could not find the words.

"Hello, son."

"Uh, hi father."

"Are you here for confession?"

"Sure."

There was nowhere else to confess. It was not like the movies. Cody expected the priest to usher him into a booth where there was a screen between them, but there was no privacy here. All of the figures in the stained glass stared at him. He was sitting on the wooden pew. There was nowhere else to go. He panicked, breathing becoming heavier. The priest patiently gave him a reproachful look. A young man, early thirties, wearing glasses, combed over hair, and an earnestness that could not be eroded. There was nowhere else.

"Go on…."

"Where are we going?"

"Nowhere. You can make the act of reconciliation right here. Have you gone to confession before?"

"Uh, yeah. Okay, well, um… forgive me father, for I have sinned. It has been…"

"It's okay if you don't know. Just make the sign of the cross and you may begin, I'll help you along."

"Okay. I don't know where to begin."

"Do you feel guilty about having done anything?"

Cody paused, he could not bear to confess his guilt of having failed to prevent his friend from getting killed or mentioning anything that had happened in the last few weeks, "I cheated on my girlfriend," he said.

"Then you must tell her and ask for her forgiveness."

"She found out and broke up with me."

"I'm sorry to hear that, but you're young. Infidelity is one of the most common sins, and so is sex before marriage. You must avoid it at all costs because it will only tear you apart on the inside and stray you further away from the Lord. It's a serious sin, but not a mortal sin. God will forgive you, and you must forgive yourself. Anything else?"

Cody was silent, and he could not decipher a coherent thought. He began to choke up and resisted the urge to cry. It was impossible.

"I threw away a necklace that my sister gave me," Cody was sobbing. "It was a crucifix. I took it off and threw it on the ground, and now it's lost."

"It's okay, son. Were you upset with her?"

"No, I haven't seen her in a long time."

"So you miss her. I see. Do not worry, that gift will stay with you, even if it's lost physically. She will come to understand."

"Okay," his breathing slowed down.

"Now, I have to prepare for the vigil. You're welcome to stay. In the meantime, say three Hail Mary's, and three Our Father's. I'll help you with the Act of Contrition. Repeat after me: oh my God, I am heartily sorry for having offended Thee, and I detest all my sins because of thy just punishments, but most of all because they offend Thee, my God, who art all good and deserving of all my love. I firmly resolve with the help of Thy grace to sin no more and to avoid the near occasion of sin. Amen," Cody repeated all of the words of the prayer after every few seconds when the priest would pause and beckon him to speak. When they were finished Cody stood up and moved to rush out of the church as parishioners began to enter.

Mr. Johnston, his former boss at the pharmacy, walked through the door, arm interlocked with his wife's. His wife wore a white dress imprinted with sunflower patterns and a yellow hat with veil mesh shading her eyes. Cody immediately stopped and turned his face so that he could not be recognized. His heart started beating quickly and in an odd rhythm. They were far enough away that Cody could slip out of the other door without them noticing him. He covered his eyes from the glare of the sun and ran back to the bus stop to wait for the next one out of town. The bus arrived and to his relief it was empty this time. He dozed off while watching the pine trees pass.

He got off the bus and bought a gas station ham and cheese sandwich wrapped in plastic and a pint of Irish whiskey along with a pack of Turkish cigarettes from a highway liquor store. The inside smelled pungent, as if goats used the store as a barn overnight, and the clerk up-charged him for being underage. There was still some money left over. He fingered the cold change in his jean pockets, flipping quarters back and forth between his thumb and index. Sometimes his thumb would still crack and pop, but the pain had faded. There were scabs on his hands. The blisters on his feet kept breaking. He wandered through woods and strip mall parking lots and avoided suburban developments and cul-de-sacs so as not to get picked up by the cops. He always kept his hood up and he forgot what day it was.

He briefly took another bus north, considering trying to return to Steve, Erica, and Sara, but suddenly decided against it, afraid of being caught. He thought returning to their house, The Mudhole Inn, or the campsite would mean his doom because he worried that by now police must be staking out for him. He got off the bus after a few miles and waited on a desolate highway corner to head back south. His days of indecisive wandering built up his anxiety and grew to the point that he had to make a choice, even if that choice filled him with fear. The whiskey he sipped dulled his anxiety. He decided to return home to his parents and tell them everything in the hope that they would believe him as Bianca had said. He disembarked the bus at the foot of Leeds Hill.

As he walked into town, he saw groups of children wandering sidewalks in packs dressed up like ghosts, monsters, witches, princesses, and superheroes in generic plastic costumes, hauling their candy loot in pillowcases and baskets. He had forgotten that Halloween existed. The absurdity of the holiday dawned on him for the first time. He stared at the small beasts and beauties running across the front lawns covered in plastic decorations. Some houses set up phantasmagoric displays that gave Cody an uncanny feeling, but he did not associate it with any specific memory.

There were families walking around holding hands. Moms and dads laughing with or chastising their children. Human beings connected with each other, whether positively or negatively. Cody could not imagine being able to have that kind of connection with someone else again.

It was nighttime when he arrived home and saw the light coming from the living room window. There was a half empty bowl of candy left out on the front step. Cody took a stride forward, but then shook his head and walked away. He stopped, turned back around, heading for the front door. He knocked.

"Oh my God, Jesus, David, it's Cody," his mother grabbed her own face, then his, as she took the Lord's name in vain. She hugged him, crying.

"What, Anna?"

"David, Cody's back home," his father hobbled up to them, no longer with a cast on his foot. Cody was ushered inside his old home.

"Son, what happened?"

"There was a cult. They killed Vinny."

"No, Cody, he died in a fire. That's what the authorities say. Your mother and I were at the funeral."

"You were doing drugs, weren't you?"

"I was only smoking weed, mom."

"Weed is a drug. And you say your friend was murdered by a cult? The police said nothing about a cult. There are no cults in New Jersey. This isn't California! You must have been hallucinating from the drugs," his mother was practically yelling at him.

"I'm telling the truth."

His mom frowned as she grabbed his shoulders, "and you ran off to do drugs with your cousin Max didn't you? The police are saying that Mr. Ciliberti was killed in a shootout with drug addicts, and then the crack house burned down. Were you there when it happened?"

"I was. I escaped the fire," Cody cried.

He had no other words. His mother fussed over him. She insisted that he take a shower while she made dinner. He walked upstairs and turned the shower on, watching the water wash down the drain. Feeling empty and afraid to undress, he did not get in the tub. Instead, he went to his bedroom and looked out of the window into the darkness. Crawling into bed, he passed out covered in filth.

"Wake up, Cody."

He saw his mother standing over him, dressed in her waitress uniform. She had her hands on her hips and was tapping her shoe on the carpet.

"I was going to wake you up last night, but figured you needed the rest. Now I'll insist that you take a shower and eat breakfast. You have a long day ahead of you."

"What, why?"

"I called Johnny and got you a job down at the diner. You need to get back to work. Work brings dignity. And then after work you have to go down to the police station and answer some questions about what happened. Don't worry, you're not in trouble. They just need more information about the incident."

Cody turned over and rolled his eyes. He stared at the wall in silence, waiting for his mother to leave the room.

"I'm not asking you; I'm telling you. It's time for you to turn your life around. Get up!"

He sighed. His knee began to uncontrollably shake. "Fine," he blurted out, and got up to shower.

He went to take a shower for the first time in many days. The dirt washed off of him in black streams across the porcelain floor and into the drain. After breakfast, he and his mother walked downtown to the diner. It was close to 7am and Woodville was covered in a cloak of grayness. He kept his distance from her, following her a few feet behind. She kept looking back and slowed down.

"Tomorrow is All Souls Day you know, maybe after work we can make it to church and say a prayer for your friend." He stared forward and did not respond to her.

His mom kept trying to ask him questions about his time away, but he could not pay attention to her, and kept demurring that he would tell her later. He dreaded that he was going to be questioned by the police. They walked into the diner through the kitchen back door. Johnny the cook was staring at his watch as they came in, his meaty wrist bulging around it, the silver band standing out wrapped around his fur covered arm.

The cook threw a white apron at Cody, saying "the sonovabitch dishwasher walked out on his shift last night. All that shit's leftover from then. Get to work."

There were mountains of dirty dishes already piled in, on, and around the three sinks. Grease covered pots, pans, knives, spatulas, baking sheets, and every other form of cookware imaginable with all sorts of grime caked on them, hardened onto the surfaces, almost becoming one with them. He started pulling everything out of the sinks and placing them on the floor for the time being. His mom showed him how to fill the sinks properly: hot water and dish soap in the leftmost sink, lukewarm water in the second, and finally placing blue sanitation tablets into the cold water in the rightmost sink until the liquid became an unnatural cobalt color.

He got to work. It almost felt good eventually, hours passed by, and the numbness of his fingers spread to his mind, so that he did not have to think any more about the past. The memories were wiped away clean. He scrubbed and scrubbed and thought he could get used to this work.

"Look at all this shit. I gotta' pick up the slack bussing tables for your lousy mother."

Cody was in a trance washing dishes when Johnny the cook shoved a pile of plates covered in ketchup into his shoulder. He turned to look as a dish dropped to the floor breaking in half, a streak of ketchup marking his dirtied apron and getting onto his skin. The coldness of the ketchup consumed him. He looked up at the cook and saw Father smiling down at him. Screaming, he fled the kitchen through the back door, trying to wipe the ketchup from his scarred arm, taking off the apron and curling up by the dumpster.

He could hear the cook yelling at his mother from the open back door, "I shoulda' never listened to you Anna. That's the last favor I do for you, hiring your dumbass son as a dishwasher. What is he, a fuckin' retard or somethin'?"

"That's it Johnny. That's the final straw. It's one thing for you to treat me rotten, but my son, who's been through a lot lately, like I told you, is too much for me to bear. Goodbye."

"What're you gonna' do? Quit? Fine! Go home to your deadbeat husband and get the fuck out of my diner! I'm the one who does all the work around here anyway. Go on."

"That's right, I quit!"

She came outside, crossed the pavement, and placed her hand on Cody's shoulder. He looked up at her, said, "I'm sorry, mom."

"It's okay honey, let's go home."

They walked home in silence. On their way they passed by the Woodville water tower. Cody looked up at the rusting metal beams and remembered how as a child he would think the water tower looked like a rocket ship left abandoned by aliens in an otherwise boring environment. He thought of Vinny, who once climbed halfway up the ladder of the water tower on Cody's dare, then shimmied back down when the wind was blowing too hard. Tears welled up in his eyes and he looked in the opposite direction of his mother so that she could not see his face. When they arrived at the house, his father was asleep on the couch with a book on his belly. Cody climbed upstairs to his bedroom and closed the door.

His mother would be coming in soon to take him to the police station for questioning. He dreaded having to speak to them. He felt something screaming inside him. Darkness spread. He looked around his room and paced back and forth with his chin pointing down at the carpet where he had prepared with push ups and sit ups for months in order to enlist in the military only to be rejected and he stopped and breathed in and out deeply and he pulled at his hair until clumps came out between his fingers and then he climbed out of the window, stepping onto the roof and then slid down the tree trunk. The birch bark was smooth, and he almost fell.

His feet, in oversized shoes, his blistered heels caking blood into his socks, guided him thoughtlessly until he stopped in front of the pharmacy where he used to work. He went around back and opened the door by prying off the thin, rotting plywood on the same window he had previously broken, reaching inside to unlock and turn the doorknob.

The store was now completely empty. He stood there for a while, then went to the door that led to the abandoned apartment upstairs. He looked around his old workplace without remembering anything specifically, only feeling consumed by darkness, and walked up unhindered by thoughts. He opened the door to the abandoned second floor apartment. Streetlights were on and faintly shone through the window. The moon was low in the sky. Police sirens briefly blared and red and blue lights sailed across the wall. Cody stood rigid and listened for a while but heard nothing else. A mouse scurried across the floor, stopping in the middle of the room and turning to look at him, then scampered into a hole. He shuffled over to where he had hidden the bag of weed weeks before and peeled open the floorboard, expecting emptiness and finding just that, then he took off his coat and laid it upon the floor and tried to fall asleep even though it was early in the evening. The rodent had crawled into the wall and kept making scratching sounds. He kept his eyes closed and pulled the coat over him while shivering and then flattened out on his stomach and laid completely still until he could picture behind his eyelids how he saw the Atlantic Ocean once from a nameless memory when it was calm and he was a boy on the beach.

Darkness passed over him and his eyes opened but he could not move. In the corner of the vacant room he saw Father aloft with his terrible smile. He was prone and felt like he was flopping like a fish out of water, but he was frozen. There was nothing that could be done so he stayed where he was and wondered if what was happening was real. The beast was wearing a luminous diadem engraved with symbols that he could not understand, etchings that looked like they were in some ancient language. He could see the terrible mouth of the beast open wide with its impossible teeth, "ye sleepeth til' ye shan't awaken ever again, son of David," screeched the phantom. His voice boomed inside of Cody's mind and caused an unbearable ringing in his ears. The beast found him and had his way with him. He stood over his body. A bloodied sledgehammer swung at his face.

When he woke there was no beast, only a small bird perched on the windowsill staring at him. It was dawn. His jaw hurt. He put his hand to his cheek and rubbed his face in pain. The sparrow chirped, cocked its head to its side as if asking a question, then began to peck repeatedly at the window, little bonk sounds on the glass. He thought about opening it but did not have the energy to get up and instead lay there for a long time. The bird finally flew away. He rolled over onto his back and squinted his eyes. The brightness of morning was an aching reminder that he was alive. The wind wailed, undulating from low to high pitches in a complex language, and the glass of the windowpane responded, flexing, gyrating, in and out: the fragility of the man-made against primal nature.

His stomach churned and he imagined the bile inside of him shifting, his intestines inflamed from the combination of stress and poor diet. He no longer even cared if he soiled himself, and because he did not care if it would happen or not of course it did not happen. That thought gave him a momentary sense of relief but then faded. If he went back into the world that would mean he would care about himself again and if he cared again then the human waste would strike from the inside and his bowels would be his own internal enemy once again. His heart would flutter and prevent him from doing what he wanted, a murmur squelching movement. He did not want anything to happen, least of all experience it.

He looked over his skin and saw it yellowing in the light. He lightly traced his fingers along his arm hair, tickling himself in order to feel something, anything good. He could not tell whether the discoloration was from bruising or early onset jaundice. Red bumpy scars on his arms formed wavy lines like rivers where he was attacked by his cousin with a spiked bat. He smelled and then saw black mold on the ceiling above him. Liquid dripped from it into his mouth. He spit a heavily coagulated loogie into the air, the green phlegm landing on his outstretched arm. He wiped it off with his right hand and his thumb cracked in the process. He could taste what seemed like sour ketchup. He kept coughing, hacking up nothing but gasps of air. He considered that there might be something like a twig stuck in his throat. His mouth became so dry that he thought that his saliva had solidified completely. He imagined he was levitating above the floor and could not tell dream from reality.

Eventually snapping out of his daze, Cody rose from his makeshift bed and went downstairs and rummaged around in the closet until he found a frayed rope. It was long and still thick around the middle. He picked it up and tied a noose. He tossed the other end over a ceiling rafter and then climbed onto the counter and tied that side together and then fitted the loop around his neck. He stood on the counter for a moment breathing heavily. He tightened the rope to his throat and jumped.

Chapter Fourteen

He dragged the soles of his feet back and forth across the gray tiled floor, his green grippy socks rubbing against the linoleum, causing soft squeaks in regular intervals. A steady pattern echoed in his chest. Two beats in a row without a stutter. The hospital gown he wore bunched up between him and his seat like a dress. His name was being repeated through the ringing in his ears. Her mouth opened and closed as if in slow motion. It was just cold enough in the nearly empty room to be uncomfortable, although not enough to shiver. A vague smell of bleach permeated the air. Fluorescent lights beamed unnaturally.

"Cody. Are you paying attention to me?"

"Yeah, sorry, I'm just still getting used to the medicine."

"That's understandable. You will adjust to it with time."

"Okay."

Her name was Vanessa. She had been speaking to Cody three times a day, every day for twelve days now. Vanessa had long red hair that was up in a ponytail, wore a maroon blazer, and a cream-colored blouse. Her glasses fit tight around her face, shielding her inquisitive blue eyes.

"I haven't asked you this question yet, because it's a difficult one."

"Go ahead. I'm fine."

"Why did you do it?" She had a genuine expression of empathy when she asked, her head tilting slightly.

"Do what?"

"Attempt suicide."

"What do you mean, why?"

"What triggered it? You had no past attempts. No self-harm. No history of depression."

"I was sad my best friend died."

"And how did your best friend die?"

"In a fire."

"Is there something you're not telling me? You told me a different story before."

"No, you said I had delusions, we worked them out. You helped me. I can separate reality from what's in my mind now."

"Are you just repeating back to me what we've gone over in previous sessions?"

"I'm just saying what I've learned, and I believe it. I feel better."

"Well, that's good. We've made tremendous progress these last two weeks, Cody."

"Thanks, I appreciate it."

"You can go off to the common room now."

Cody left the office and drifted down the hallway to a room lit with actual sunshine from barred windows. Oblong shafts of yellow light yawned across the carpet while cloaked patients passed through them as if they were ghosts. The television hung from the top of the wall, so that the people who were watching had to tilt their chins upwards and stare wide eyed like they were waiting for an asteroid to crash through the ceiling.

The game show where contestants pretended to buy commodities ended and the noon hour of local news began playing on the television. The anchor asked the viewers if they were worried that their child was in danger, that if not, they should be, because there were reports of a serial abductor on the loose. He was described as older, heavy, and tall, in his fifties or sixties, around two hundred seventy pounds, between six foot six and six foot nine.

The screen showed an artist's sketch of the suspect: a bald head the shape of a tombstone, wild, block-like eyes, a large mouth with sharp teeth, the face perfectly symmetrical, peculiarly inhuman. The girl across from Cody screamed when she saw the crude drawing on the television, to the point where orderlies in blue scrubs rushed in to subdue and medicate her, then return her to her room. Her screams slowly faded until there was silence. It was snowing outside. Cody stood up and looked out of the window, beyond the frosty iron bars, and into the copse of white covered young pine trees wavering in the distance. He decided he was going to put an end to the beast. The trick was to pretend like it did not exist. At least until he got out.

"You're not getting out of this place any time soon, the way you keep lying to Vanessa like that, young man," said the patient across from him. A woman in her fifties, sitting straight and still like a statue. "I'm Sandra," she stated, with a warm, knowing look through her bifocal glasses. She had unkempt short, black hair with silver streaks. Cody turned around and approached her, sitting in a chair across from her.

"Hi, I'm Cody. How do you know about that? Did Vanessa tell you?"

"Boy, they don't tell you nothin' in here. You just know."

Cody stared at where her knees would be. He saw only an indent of her gown, "but how do you know?"

"I could die today and would have lived a full life. Not you, in spite of what you seen. Your brief sojourn in hell was silver lined with a certain kind of beauty. Remember that's what you desired to begin with: violence, death. The thrill you sought; the rush felt. A violent waterfall's power overwhelmed you. You witnessed the hanging gardens of Babylon in your exile. That's your problem: exile, although self-imposed. My problem is that I stopped creating and started destroying. Self-destruction, I've succumbed to it. It's too late to experiment with creating for me. As I get older, I only become more comfortable and familiar with destruction. So have you, except at too young an age. I could see it around your neck when you walked up in here, the bruises," Cody placed his fingers on his Adam's apple. He could still feel the coarse rope against his skin.

"So what? Everyone's in here for that, or something like that."

"I can tell you're lying about the why, though. Not everyone in here has seen what you've seen, well, maybe a few, like that girl who just screamed at that bad man on the TV. I knew one day I was going to end up seeing his face again. It's been so many years."

Cody's pulse quickened as he remembered blurry flashes of the 19th century drug den mansion, of his best friend's head being torn asunder by a gargantuan wielding a sledgehammer, "you know about Father?"

"That's what he goes by now? Certainly not your father. Nor anyone's for that matter. That man cannot reproduce. Nothing is made in his image. He is unique in that way." Cody rocked his knee up and down. He did not want to make eye contact with her, so he stared at the blank wall beyond her. She sighed in response to Cody's silence, "Father, how typical. Shouldn't be surprised. I seen the way you looked at the TV when they was talkin' about that man. He is only a man, remember that," Sandra nodded her head as she said this to be reassuring.

"How do you know him?"

"I used to belong to an art collective in West Philly back in the 80's. Right on Baltimore Ave, an anarchist group. He joined and tried to turn the commune into a cult. It was a tumultuous time; the city was divided, there were protests on both sides over Mumia Abu-Jamal, and then the MOVE bombing happened just a few blocks from our house. You know about all that?"

"No…"

"No, you wouldn't. They don't teach stuff like that in schools. After a standoff, the cops dropped C-4 out of a helicopter on a row home where a black liberation group called MOVE was living. Eleven were killed, some of them children, and a lot of people made homeless."

"That's crazy."

"It is crazy. The man you call Father showed up in the neighborhood right after that happened. Tried to take advantage of people's fears. Some of my friends thought he was an undercover agent sent to infiltrate left wing organizations. I don't know about that, but I do know he's a dangerous man. Remember though, he's just a man. The ones who followed him thought otherwise."

"Like what?"

"Like he was some kind of messiah," Sandra smiled and shook her head.

"Yeah, that makes sense. His followers in the drug den, old mansion, whatever it was, seemed completely brainwashed by him. My cousin was one of them. I never thought that I'd find myself running into a cult, and no one believed me about it afterwards. That's why I ended up here. He did a lot of bad things, he kidnapped children, and he killed my friend, and I couldn't take the guilt anymore." Cody cast his head towards the floor.

"Child, that is not why you ended up here. You ended up here long before you ever actually came here." The woman had a cold stare.

"Okay, but he killed my friend. That changed everything. I tried my best to help him, but I couldn't. That man imprisoned me, but I escaped, and even freed the kids he captured. Now no one believes me. Everyone thinks I'm crazy, so I feel like I have a pretty good excuse to be upset."

"I'm sorry that happened. No matter what occurred, you have to learn to live with it. Everyone has an excuse, some more than others, but no matter how big the excuse is, it's still an excuse," after she said this, Cody was silent for a few minutes.

He looked out of the window, in spite of the disturbing news on the television and the uncomfortable setting of the psych ward common room, he was able to appreciate the sight of snow for the first time that he could recall since being a little boy. In the last few years he was indifferent to winter and did not care if it was snowing. Now he was making a conscious effort to notice the beautiful subtleties of life, something that his new therapist had taught him. After a long time of confinement in the psych ward, he held a new fondness for silence, and the snow blanketing the outside brought him a fresh comfort of visual quietude. At that moment he realized for the first time that the psychiatric medicine was having an effect on him. He turned back to look at her and was surprised that she smiled at him with warmth. He considered what to say next.

"All right then, maybe I have to learn acceptance or whatever, so then why are you still in here if you're so wise? What's your excuse?"

Sandra laughed, "I ran into the same trouble as you: disbelief. No one believed me that that man either stole or destroyed everything I had and made it his own. I was the only one who stood up to him face to face after he tried to take control of the collective and told him to leave. He had the fanatics on his side that left with him."

Cody placed his hands on his legs and gripped his thighs. "That's wild. I'm sorry that happened to you. What did you do at the art collective thing?"

"I worked the whole printing operation at the commune, publishing artwork and books. I wrote a novel under a pseudonym and self-published it in beautifully bound black leather with gold inlaid lettering. The night I finished printing the first run that man broke into the shop with his cronies and wrecked everything. The collective fell apart after that, and I became despondent. That's why I'm here. I've come to terms with it, but they still won't let me out."

"I'm sorry, that sucks. What was the book about?"

"It was called The Jersey Devil."

"You wrote The Jersey Devil?"

"Indeed I did, young man. You say that as if you read it. Did you see a copy of it in that man's cult?"

Cody's jaw dropped, "no, it wasn't at the cult. Father left a copy at my mom's job. It somehow led me to him."

"Did you mean to join his cult?"

"No, I wanted to try to make a documentary about the Jersey Devil with my friend. Why, do I look like someone who would join a cult?"

"Did your cousin look like someone who would join a cult? Do not be too quick to judge people who feel the compulsion to join a cause. I wasn't trying to accuse you of anything, I just know that that man's extremely persuasive to certain kinds of other men, men who are impressionable for whatever reason in a certain period of their lives. What did you think of the book, by the way?"

"It was pretty good, uh, I mean it inspired me to go to the Pine Barrens and look for evidence of the Jersey Devil."

"You didn't finish reading the book, did you?"

"No," he felt ashamed admitting this, but knew he could not lie to the author herself about not finishing her book. He often could not finish reading books, instead skimming through them because he had trouble paying enough attention. He especially regretted not finishing The Jersey Devil, because now he knew that he would never be able to find another copy. "I'm sorry I didn't finish it. I got caught up with Father just when it was getting good. I lost the book when I was captured by the cult. It went missing from my friend Vinny's car. It must have been destroyed in the fire that burned down the drug den."

"Sounds like you've had quite an adventure. That was probably the last copy left in existence. If you had finished it, then you would know that it wasn't actually about the Jersey Devil; you would have learned a great deal about the founding of America, and how this country is based on lies. Long story short: Benjamin Franklin invented the Jersey

Devil in order to steal money from another man, a rival printer named Titan Leeds. In doing so he slandered that man's wife, Jane Leeds. Ben Franklin claimed that Jane gave birth to the Jersey Devil and that it proceeded to kill Titan Leeds. In Poor Richard's Almanack, Ben Franklin wrote that Titan Leeds was publishing his own almanac as a ghost after having been killed by the demon. That's where the whole myth about the Jersey Devil began. I wanted to turn the myth on its head, reveal the truth, the oppression behind it." Sandra shifted in her chair while wincing in pain and holding onto her lower back.

"Okay, so Father stole it from you and said that he wrote it. Then why would he use it for his cult?"

She leaned forward while rubbing her back and straining to look at Cody. "Ironic, isn't it? Not that it mattered why he did what he did; there were not nearly enough copies for him to make anything out of it. Meaning was meaningless to him. It was all about power. The joy that he felt in exerting his arbitrary authority over others. Stealing the very essence of people, their motivations. He used the novel I wrote as a mystical text for his followers. It would be one thing if he were simply a plagiarist, but he wasn't. He's a different kind of thief. A stealer of souls. That man's a monster. The man's a product of our society amplified to the highest degree. He's a fraud, but that's what people want. That's what Americans want. Someone who can give them easy answers to their problems."

Cody looked sympathetically at Sandra's expressions of pain, although he was caught up in wanting to know more, so he continued, "Father told his followers that he killed the Jersey Devil. He kept what he said was the body of it next to him in his hideout in the Pine Barrens. It was a crazy looking corpse that looked like a demon, like it was a bunch of different kinds of animal parts put together. He also said he found some pirate's buried treasure and poured a bunch of gold coins out of a pouch to prove it."

"That man's a con artist. The gold must have been fake. I also remember he was obsessed with taxidermy when he first joined the art collective. He probably sewed a bunch of animal parts together and passed it off as the Jersey Devil."

"Jesus Christ, that's what Vinny said when I first saw it, but for some reason I still believed that it was real, like Father held some kind of power over me," Cody muttered. Sandra raised an eyebrow and nodded her head.

The snow outside penetrated inside the psych ward through a tiny opening in the window. Little flakes flew through the crack in the windowsill beneath metal bars. Everything was covered by the cold. Everyone Cody had ever loved had fallen away from him, he thought, but he did not care anymore. Those emotions were lost in particles of frozen dust. He looked at a stunted sapling with bare branches on the edge of the parking lot. Christmastime approached, with its own cavernous sorrows and loneliness. A white blanket covered the earth that held roots, rocks, bones, and other remains. Shattered skeletons spread throughout the soil. The empty parking lot extended to where the woods began, a bit beyond that, train tracks cut through the forest. There was a man making noises and rocking himself in a chair close to Cody by the window. The television played a commercial advertising superglue.

A train howled. Cody wondered whether the man who invented the train horn realized that its choo choo call sounded melancholy, and whether he meant for that to be the case. He rose from his seat and moved towards the window without saying anything else to Sandra.

This was the most exciting part of the day. Patients gathered at the window to watch the train chug along in the distance through the glass and the metal bars beyond it. The man standing next to Cody mimicked the train's sound. Patches of snow flung from the train while it sped along. As the crowd of patients surrounded the window, Sandra slipped away. Cody placed his right hand on the chilled windowpane and covered half of his face with his left. He spread his fingers apart so he could see through them. Between his fingers, the glass, and the bars, was the outside world covered in white. From the second-floor vantage point of the common room they could catch glimpses of the train cars hauling freight between snowy pine trees. They did not know what the machine hauled, but they knew it was going somewhere. The train crawled east towards the gray Atlantic Ocean, a cold mechanical beast slicing through the pines to the sea beyond.

The Beast in the Pines

Chapter Fifteen

He sat in the therapist's office, tapping his toe on the floor. Vanessa wrote in a leather-bound journal as he stared at the nothingness in the corner of the room. Cody was never one for small talk, and they had exhausted all talk both big and small in the weeks of therapy he had endured. The day before he had held a conversation on the phone with his mother which led him to believe his release was coming close. It was with that hope that he smiled and in turn Vanessa looked up from her notes to smile back at him.

"So, Cody, we've talked about your parents at length, but I wanted to ask you candidly, how do you feel about your relationship with your father?" She clicked her pen.

"Uh, well, he doesn't talk much."

"Yes, and how does that make you feel?"

"Fine, I guess," he rubbed his grippy socks against the floor.

"You don't wish that he'd open up more?"

"Sure, but I'm not too bothered by it."

"I see. Well, I'm only asking because of the whole incident that happened, what with the terrible tragedy of your friend dying and all that you said about who you thought had done it; when we originally went over that story, you said there was a man you called Father who killed him?"

"Yeah, but you know, like you said, that didn't really happen. It was the fire that killed Vinny."

"Is that what you believe now?"

"Uh, yeah. The fire was an accident that I escaped from, and it killed everyone else. I thought I would get in trouble for being there buying drugs, and so I made everything else up." He thought about Sara and her family and wondered what they were doing. Whether or not Steve was okay. His leg shook as he tried to forget about them, and he made sure never to mention that part of the story to Vanessa.

She wrote some words down in her notebook. "That makes sense. Don't worry. You're not going to get in trouble. You didn't hurt anyone. The cops found the perpetrator who killed the police officer and burned the house down."

Cody's spine seized. He worried that they had caught Sara and her sister. His breathing quickened, but he tried to remain calm as he asked, "who was it?"

Vanessa tilted her head, "a man named Virgil, I believe. Do you know him?"

Cody breathed deeply with relief. It was the guy who led them to the drug den. "No, I don't know who that is," Cody said as quickly and convincingly as he could.

"Okay. Back to what I was getting at, this man called Father that you made up, did he resemble your father at all?"

Cody closed his eyes and rubbed his eyelids with his fingers. "No, he was the complete opposite."

Vanessa tilted her head again. "How so?"

"My dad's small and quiet. This guy was big and loud."

"I see, and he was the leader of a cult?"

"Look, I'm okay now. I realize these were delusions brought on by the mental breakdown."

"Were you taking drugs?"

"I smoked a lot of weed."

"Cody," she took off her glasses and placed them on the desk, "I want you to be honest with me. That place was a notorious house. They sold hard drugs there."

"I am being honest with you; it was just weed. I'm not a drug addict and I'm doing better now. I like the medicine you give me. It sucked at first, but it's starting to make me feel normal. I understand that I have to be more responsible and get a job that makes me happy or study and go off to school."

"Yes, I think you're quite bright. College would be good for you. You can move out of your parent's house, which I think is an important step."

"Yeah, well, that's why I wanted to join the Army in the first place."

"In order to get away from home?"

"Yes."

Vanessa leaned forward, "was there any abuse going on at home?"

Cody sighed, "I've told you before. No, there wasn't any abuse. I'm not lying to you."

"There's no reason to get testy. I'm trying to help you."

"I know, and I appreciate it, it's just that I feel like you already made up your mind about how I think and feel and what happened to me, and that when I tell you the truth you think that I'm lying to you."

"I understand, Cody. That must be frustrating. I'm just concerned that you might still think that this Father character is real." Vanessa bit the end of her pen. It was the first time Cody had seen her do such a thing.

"You think that I made up Father in order to cover up something my actual dad did?"

"It's not far-fetched."

"Not as far-fetched as Father actually being real and killing Vinny?"

"In the police report it said that your friend died in a fire in an abandoned house that was being used by drug dealers and addicts. It didn't say anything about a cult. Father is not real, Cody; he can't hurt you."

Vanessa suddenly pulled her chair out as the fire alarm started to blare in the hallway outside. They could hear loud banging sounds out in the lobby. Cody jumped up.

"It's okay, Cody, the alarm probably went off by accident. Follow me calmly and quietly."

They walked down the hallway into the common room where patients were hiding behind chairs. The man in a hospital gown who liked to mimic train sounds was trying to pry open the window when he fell into a bloody heap on the floor. Cody covered his ears as pops and booms echoed throughout the common room. A giant figure in a long trench coat turned the corner that led to the only exit. He wore a black cowboy hat and held a shotgun that was strapped to his chest. Vanessa put her arms up to shield her face as Father lowered his shotgun with his left hand and raised a pistol with his right hand to her forehead and then pulled the trigger. Her blood spattered onto the white wall and her body crumpled over. Cody froze and met eyes with Father as he pointed his gun away from him and shot three other patients in succession as they tried to run past him. People screamed and moaned and then were silent while Father unloaded the semiautomatic handgun clip into crawling victims.

Out of the corner of his eye, Cody could see Sandra hiding behind a chair. She had shimmied underneath a dead body as some of the other patients tried to make their escape and stared at Cody before lifting a finger to her mouth in a signal for him to be quiet. He nodded his head without looking at her. Father was sweating profusely and wiped his face with his sleeve before glaring at Cody. The man's skin was covered in burn scars. Another patient in the corner of the room moved and Father shot him and then tossed the empty pistol onto the floor. He raised his shotgun while checking the corners of the room to make sure there were no other survivors. Sandra wheezed underneath the body that was on top of her as blood spilled out onto the floor around her. Her hiding could not last long. Cody coughed to distract Father. He looked again at Cody, who stood shaking while liquid leaked from under his gown.

"Cody, mine child, thou hast soiled thyself," Father approached him casually while holding the shotgun aloft, pointing upwards as if to intend no harm.

"What do you want from me?" Cody yelped.

"Thy knowledge, of course. Methinks thou wouldst comprehend this, and I must admit, I am disappointed in thine cowardice," Father turned his gaze from Cody over to the television that hung from the ceiling close to Sandra, then walked over and stood right next to her. The TV could not be heard over the fire alarm, so Father read the closed captions aloud to Cody. "Saddam Hussein captured today. The war in Iraq is over." Father chuckled for a few moments, then frowned as he sniffed the air and looked around the room at the carnage. "War is never over," he said.

Cody gulped, "my knowledge?" He asked, while still side eyeing Sandra, who was shuddering underneath the corpse.

"Ah, yes. Thou art the only person who knows the whereabouts of Blackbeard's treasure. I attempted to glean the information out of thy father, although he was of no help, perhaps out of the folly of pride, or perchance he refused to tell me the location out of some other ignorance. No matter, he divulged your whereabouts easily enough, and then I found it necessary to dispose of him."

Cody's heart, which had been ramming against his chest, suddenly felt like it had stopped. He looked around the room, as if something could save him.

"Oh, and thy mother. She did very much love to squeal at my fingertips. And she especially squirmed from my largest appendage."

"You can't get away with this, you… you must be lying. You lie about everything!" Cody balled his hands into fists. Father laughed as he stepped closer to Cody and then placed the twin shotgun nozzles to his face. The metal was hot against his cheek, and he could feel Vanessa's blood on his skin. He spread his hands out and slowly raised his palms up towards Father in surrender.

"Come, child, I shalt forget that thou hast scornfully insulted me and show thee mercy yet, if ye deliver to me the quarry that is rightfully mine by providence."

Father motioned with the shotgun for Cody to move. Cody's socks dampened as he trudged through the red slop toward the exit doors. He tried not to look at the bodies. Cody turned his head back to see Sandra staring at them. Father stopped and looked around the room. There was a moment Cody thought she would be caught until he distracted Father again by coughing. The fire alarm kept ringing and Father nudged Cody with his gun to move faster out of the unlocked doors and into the lobby where the security guard basked wide eyed upwards in a pool of blood. Exploded brains scattered on the floor. Father walked over to a coat rack where he took a puffy jacket and handed it to Cody then ushered him out into the parking lot. The sunlight blinded Cody for a moment until his eyes adjusted to see a Woodville police cruiser parked in front of the psych ward. The forest was a dull mass in the background.

Father hid his shotgun inside his long coat and opened the door of the car to shove Cody into the back seat. Cody sat on the hard plastic and recoiled when he saw the desiccated chimera corpse resting beside him. The Jersey Devil mummy was blackened even more so than the last time he saw it as it was half burnt. Sirens were getting louder, and Father hurried into the driver's seat to peel out of the parking lot and speed off down the highway. A fire truck and an ambulance passed them as Father drove south. Two cop cars followed, and Father took a turn down a side road before they could get too close and see him in the stolen police cruiser. The Jersey Devil corpse slid over and fell into Cody and the putrid smell of the thing made him gag as he pushed it to the other side of the back bench. Father turned on the police transponder. Static hissed in between the words.

"How about that 10-82? Any word on the fire reported at South Jersey Psychiatric Hospital?"

"Negative, dispatch. No 10-82 here. I don't know the code for it. It appears we have a uh, mass casualty incident."

"No 10-82? You sure? Am I hearing you right? I need to know what level of alarm the fire is, do we have to get more fire departments involved?"

"Uh, no. Repeat, no 10-82. No fire here. We got um, a 10-67. Looks like we got a uh, Columbine type situation on our hands."

"10-4. What's the status? 10-0. Active shooter?"

"Negative. We got, uh, one survivor here, female, a patient by the name Sandra, she's giving a description of the suspect. Said the shooter fled with an apparent hostage. That the perp is the guy who's wanted for kidnapping? I don't know. She's fucking crazy and covered in blood. She was hiding under a body. One of the workers must have pulled the fire alarm while the shooting was happening."

"What? How can we be sure she wasn't just hallucinating? Are you messing with me again? You sure it's not just another fight between the psychos locked up in there?"

"Yeah, that's a negative dispatch, it's awful messy in here. Blood and bodies. 10-67. I repeat, 10-67. Got, uh, several bodies. Lots of bullet casings and an empty pistol left behind."

"Lord almighty."

Father turned down the police radio and looked back at Cody, "you hear that, child? Even the centurions hath recognized the work of the lord."

"Is that what you think? Do you think you're God?" Cody asked as he stared at Father through the rearview mirror.

"What you call God, what you think is an omnipotent deity, tis' solely a forsaken, limited creature crafted by the pathetic spirit of man. He doth exist, and yet only within the confines of thine own, puny mind."

Cody looked at the pine trees rolling along out of the window as the car jostled over the dirt road. "Is this Officer Ciliberti's car?"

"Aye, child, a loyal servant he was, until that girl laid waste to his body. Thine friend ruined our feast in me own hall. I'll find her yet and smite her feeble vessel."

Cody stayed silent while stuck in a daze. They drove south for a long time, and he could smell the brackish water of the marshes leading up to the Delaware Bay, even with the stink of blood, his soiled self, and the sewn together medley of body parts sitting beside him. Father pulled the police cruiser into a gravel parking lot by a dock. A small wooden building stood at the foot of a long fishing pier. He exited the vehicle and looked around. There was no one in sight. A few anchored boats wobbled in the water. Father opened the back door and pulled Cody out.

"Take thy brother with thee."

"What?"

"Do not leave him behind!" Father yelled while pointing at the Jersey Devil. Cody picked up the thing and its skin flaked off onto his hands. He held it like it was a child and coughed at its stench. Father opened the trunk of the car and produced a shovel. "Walk in front," Father commanded.

They entered the dock office to see an old, bearded man sleeping at a desk. Father approached him and slammed his fist on the wood next to the old man's ear. He bounced and howled, then fumed. "What the hell did you have to go and do that for, what the, what's that boy got in his hands?"

"Silence thy decrepit tongue! Thou shalt provide me with a vessel for sailing."

"Well excuse you. What are yah, one of them Amish folk? It's the offseason. I ain't got no boats to rent."

Father leaned the shovel against the wall and pulled the shotgun out from under his trench coat and pointed it in the man's face. "On second thought, you can use mine. Here, here's the keys. I don't want no trouble."

"Thou shall ferry us there."

The old man clenched his jaw, then complied. Father grabbed the shovel then urged the old man along and out of the door while Cody followed listlessly, the stones from the parking lot stabbing at his shoeless feet. His hospital grippy socks were covered in blood and dirt. He held the Jersey Devil tightly against the oversized puffy jacket that he wore and could feel a cold draft coming up between his legs because he was not wearing pants. His thighs were sticky from blood and urine. When they climbed aboard the small fishing boat, Cody almost slipped and fell into the bay but was caught by the old man who was already on board. Father pushed the old man toward the ship's wheel.

"Cody, boy, aid the captain with navigation."

The old man turned to look at Cody, "where in God's name are we going?"

Father stared at Cody, who stuttered at first, "No, no, no, not far, we're going to one of those islands in the bay. The one that's right across from where the Maurice River starts, by that abandoned factory in Woodville." The old sailor nodded and started the engine.

A cold wind picked up as they sailed away from the shoreline. Father watched the old man work the controls of the boat while holding his shotgun. Cody felt queasy as waves rocked the boat and he set the Jersey Devil down on the deck so that he could grip onto the railing. There was a dead horseshoe crab floating upside down in the water. Its slimy belly covered in seaweed. The ancient looking animal disappeared into darkness in the wake of the boat. Cody threw up green bile into the bay. He threw up for a long time. When there was no liquid left he kept heaving air, the salt pulsing in and out of him. He felt a hard slap on his back and looked behind at Father, whose cowboy hat covered his eyes.

"Steel thyself young acolyte, do we draw near?"

Cody coughed and then wiped his mouth with his sleeve while looking around, "yeah, it's that island. The one in the middle."

There were three islets that all held rusty shipping containers. As they approached it, Cody pointed out to the old man which island to sail towards. They docked at a crumbling jetty, the wood aged and rotten. The old man threw a rope around one of its pillars. Father grabbed the old man by his collar and shoved him to the bayside of the deck. He lifted his shotgun and pulled the trigger. The top half of the old man's head blew off, the bottom half of the jaw exposed, the body falling overboard into the water. Cody covered his ears. Father reloaded the shotgun.

"Take thy brother and set him down on the dock, disembark, and tie the rope."

Cody picked up the Jersey Devil and carefully placed it over the railing and onto the wood. He climbed up the railing and jumped onto the jetty, slipping and falling into the Jersey Devil. Its wing broke underneath him. Father stood over them and nudged Cody with the butt of the shotgun.

"Arise and be mindful. Now, show me the place where we shall dig."

Cody held the Jersey Devil by its broken wing so that Father would not notice and then walked off of the jetty towards the nearest shipping container. He looked around and pretended to find the spot of the buried treasure. There was a patch of sand by a red shipping container that looked easy to dig. He placed the Jersey Devil up against the metal wall and pointed at the ground.

"It's here, right in the middle. At least that's what my dad told me."

"Excellent. Thou shalt be rewarded with thy life if that is the truth."

"If not?"

"Then I shall presume thou art lying and I will defile thee."

Father tossed Cody the shovel and he began to dig. He shivered and wiped his face often as he worked. Clouds covered the sun, and it began to grow dark with the overcast. Father stood over Cody while holding his shotgun without speaking and focused on the digging. His stare was endless. After digging a few feet deep, the sand became hard and wet and it was more difficult to dig, so Cody widened the hole to find an easier spot.

Dusk arrived and Cody was overwhelmed with coldness. He continued to dig and dug until blisters formed on his palms. He stopped for a moment, panting, and looked up at Father. The man stared right through him, holding his shotgun, and then lifted it to point it at Cody.

"Wait, I just needed to take a breath. I'm sure it's here."

"Mine patience is faltering."

"Give me a minute, please."

"Art thou certain this is the place?"

"Yeah, I'm sure."

"Then proceed with haste."

Cody bent over and applied all of his strength to digging deeper. A puddle of water had formed in the hole and his socks were stuck. He kept digging, tossing sand over his head until the hole was as deep as his height. Just when he thought he could not bear it any longer he hit something hard. The metal of the shovel clanged against something.

"You hear that? I think I've found it!"

"I cannot behold the sight. Tis' a chest?"

"It's gotta be, hold on, let me dig around it some more."

"Do not dare to damage it!"

Cody dug some more and saw and felt what it was, a rock. His heart, which felt like it was about to give out, sank.

He knew at the beginning he was not going to find any buried treasure here; that it was all a fairy tale, but he had, in his delirium while digging, tricked himself into believing he had a way out of dying. A thought occurred to him. He began to cover the rock with sand while acting like he was digging around it. There was just enough of it poking out to look like it could be something else. Cody threw the shovel out of the hole and then climbed out and stood facing Father.

"Well, what dost thou see?" Father asked, while peering into the hole.

"It's definitely a chest. Go down and see for yourself. I just stopped shoveling because I didn't want to break it, like you said."

Father jumped into the hole and placed the shotgun close at hand inside of it. He kicked some sand around with his boots and grunted, then looked up at Cody, who swung the shovel at his face. The blade cut his eye and he stumbled backwards. Cody gathered his strength to swing again and cut the other side of Father's face. Father screamed and reached for his shotgun. Cody was faster and pulled the gun out of the hole. Father blindly grabbed at Cody, yanking his leg and he slipped and fell into the pit while still holding onto the shovel. Cody was on his back as Father reached to strangle him, blood coming out of his eyes. Mud caked Cody's body as he held the shovel over his head then swung again, this time at Father's groin. Father toppled over and Cody scrambled out of the hole, using the shovel for leverage. Cody dropped the shovel and picked up the shotgun. He had seen how Father had used it and mimicked him, pumping it and pointing it at Father's torso as he yelled and rushed towards him. Father slipped and fell into a heap after Cody pulled the trigger to a deafening roar. Blood darkened the water in the hole. Cody felt a sharp pain in his shoulder as he was knocked down backwards by the blast.

He gasped for air as he stood up and felt the wind knocked out of him. While gathering his breath, hands on his knees, wheezing, he looked at the Jersey Devil leaning against the shipping container. He walked over to it and picked it up and threw it into the pit. The wings fell to his feet as Cody chucked the body. It dropped on top of Father as he lay in the hole. He gathered the broken wings and tossed them in as well. His heart beat slower and slower until he could not feel it anymore. A crescent new moon appeared between the clouds. He looked up and breathed deeply, placed his palm on his chest, stumbled back to the boat, and climbed aboard. He untied the rope and started the engine. The boat moved through the water. Cody took one last look back at the island and saw a form rising from the hole in the moonlight. He whispered to himself that he was just seeing things. Or was he? A screech in the night. Darkness spread, but the wind died down, and as he set sail through the fog, he no longer felt nauseous.

The boat rocked back and forth. Cody tried to make out where the mainland was but could not see. He shivered and slipped on the deck as he steered the boat. He needed to know that Father was lying. He needed to know that his parents were still alive.

A rumble and then a lurch. Cody fell on his bare ass, the coldness and the wetness shocking him out of his daze. His hospital gown was a tattered mess. The puffy jacket Father gave him was soaking wet. He struggled as he lifted himself up and clambered onto the rail.

There was a light coming from a plane in the sky and a faint glow from Woodville in the distance. The boat had moored onto the beach of the bay by the docks where he and Vinny would smoke weed growing up. He remembered how just weeks before they sat on the pier and smoked a joint rolled from a page of the bible and got in a fight with Officer

Ciliberti's son, how he shoved Vinny into the freezing water and Vinny pretended to drown. His friend's face was a blur in his mind. He had already forgotten the sound of his voice. Officer Ciliberti's head had been blown off by the piney sisters. Vinny's head caved in two by Father's sledgehammer. Cody balled his fists.

He could not think anymore as he waded through the shallow, icy water until he was able to climb the embankment and find the steel of the railroad tracks with his bloody feet and he walked along them until through shifting phases of visibility he was able to convince himself that he could make it all of the way home.

Splinters stuck into the soles of his wet-socked feet. He kept on until he saw the scattered lights of houses. Cody stood for a few minutes shaking in the frigid air then trudged on and eventually he saw his home. There was a strange darkness emanating from the living room windows. The door was unlocked. He walked into the living room, holding onto the doorway, then the furniture. It was silent. Eyes wandering, feeling his way like a blind man, Cody scoured the house up and down for any sign of his parents. He finally flipped a light switch. They were not home.

Cody went back downstairs, breathing heavily, holding his chest, wondering what happened. He turned his head toward the open door that taunted him with the outside world that he could no longer return to, and in the periphery of his vision he saw the book sitting on the coffee table. It was The Jersey Devil. He could not believe what he was seeing. Trembling with fear, he sat down on the stiff couch and opened the book. He could feel a sharp pain in his sternum. The book felt like it was on fire. How could this be? Was Father here? Where were his parents? Breathing became heavier and then near impossible. The world spun until he passed out on the floor. The book beside him. He looked like a murder victim washed ashore in his hospital gown stained with blood, the weapon left behind next to him, his entire body caked with mud and dirt from digging for fantasized buried treasure.

Wind gusts blew into the house, shaking curtains, animating all inanimate objects. He breathed easier, eyes closed. A car pulled into the driveway, the high beams shined into the living room. The thud of metal shutting. A man and a woman got out of the car and rushed towards the open door. He opened his eyes and found that he could finally control his breath as the wind blew into his face.